"T... ...ble
wh... ...dly
Daggers is a delightful mystery." —*Midwest Book Review*

"Will keep you entertained from the first duel to the last surprise . . . If you like fun reads that will let you leave this world for a time, this series is for you."
—*The Romance Readers Connection*

"Never a dull moment! Filled with interesting characters, a fast-paced story, and plenty of humor, this series never lets its readers down . . . You're bound to feel an overwhelming craving for a giant turkey leg and the urge to toast to the king's health with a big mug of ale as you enjoy this thematic cozy mystery!" —*Fresh Fiction*

Ghastly Glass

"A unique look at a renaissance faire. This is a colorful, exciting amateur sleuth mystery filled with quirky characters who endear themselves to the reader as Joyce and Jim Lavene write a delightful whodunit." —*Midwest Book Review*

Wicked Weaves

"Offers a vibrant background for the mysterious goings-on and the colorful cast of characters."
—Kaye Morgan, author of *Ghost Sudoku*

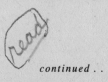

continued . . .

"This jolly series debut . . . serves up medieval murder and mayhem."
—*Publishers Weekly*

"Fast-paced, clever, delightful."
—John J. Lamb, author of *The Treacherous Teddy*

"A creative, fascinating whodunit, transporting readers to a world of make-believe that entertains and educates."
—*Fresh Fiction*

"[A] new exciting . . . series . . . Part of the fun of this solid whodunit is the vivid description of the Renaissance Village; anyone who has not been to one will want to go . . . [C]leverly developed."
—*Midwest Book Review*

"[A] terrific mystery series . . . A feast for the reader . . . Character development in this new series is energetic and eloquent; Jessie is charming and intelligent, with . . . saucy strength."
—*MyShelf.com*

"I cannot imagine a cozier setting than Renaissance Faire Village, a closed community of rather eccentric—and very interesting—characters, [with] lots of potential . . . A great start to a new series by a veteran duo of mystery authors."
—*Cozy Library*

Praise for the Peggy Lee Garden Mysteries

Poisoned Petals

"A delightful botany mystery."
—*The Best Reviews*

"A top-notch, over-the-fence mystery read with beloved characters, a fast-paced story line, and a wallop of an ending."
—*Midwest Book Review*

Berkley Prime Crime titles by Joyce and Jim Lavene

Peggy Lee Garden Mysteries

PRETTY POISON
FRUIT OF THE POISONED TREE
POISONED PETALS
PERFECT POISON
A CORPSE FOR YEW

Renaissance Faire Mysteries

WICKED WEAVES
GHASTLY GLASS
DEADLY DAGGERS
HARROWING HATS

Missing Pieces Mysteries

A TIMELY VISION
A TOUCH OF GOLD

HARROWING HATS

Joyce and Jim Lavene

BERKLEY PRIME CRIME, NEW YORK

THE BERKLEY PUBLISHING GROUP
Published by the Penguin Group
Penguin Group (USA) Inc.
375 Hudson Street, New York, New York 10014, USA
Penguin Group (Canada), 90 Eglinton Avenue East, Suite 700, Toronto, Ontario M4P 2Y3, Canada
(a division of Pearson Penguin Canada Inc.)
Penguin Books Ltd., 80 Strand, London WC2R 0RL, England
Penguin Group Ireland, 25 St. Stephen's Green, Dublin 2, Ireland (a division of Penguin Books Ltd.)
Penguin Group (Australia), 250 Camberwell Road, Camberwell, Victoria 3124, Australia
(a division of Pearson Australia Group Pty. Ltd.)
Penguin Books India Pvt. Ltd., 11 Community Centre, Panchsheel Park, New Delhi—110 017, India
Penguin Group (NZ), 67 Apollo Drive, Rosedale, North Shore 0632, New Zealand
(a division of Pearson New Zealand Ltd.)
Penguin Books (South Africa) (Pty.) Ltd., 24 Sturdee Avenue, Rosebank, Johannesburg 2196,
South Africa

Penguin Books Ltd., Registered Offices: 80 Strand, London WC2R 0RL, England

This is a work of fiction. Names, characters, places, and incidents either are the product of the author's imagination or are used fictitiously, and any resemblance to actual persons, living or dead, business establishments, events, or locales is entirely coincidental. The publisher does not have any control over and does not assume any responsibility for author or third-party websites or their content.

PUBLISHER'S NOTE: The recipes contained in this book are to be followed exactly as written. The publisher is not responsible for your specific health or allergy needs that may require medical supervision. The publisher is not responsible for any adverse reactions to the recipes contained in this book.

HARROWING HATS

A Berkley Prime Crime Book / published by arrangement with the authors

PRINTING HISTORY
Berkley Prime Crime mass-market edition / August 2011

Copyright © 2011 by Joyce Lavene and Jim Lavene.
Cover design by Lesley Worrell.
Cover illustration by Ben Perini.
Interior text design by Laura K. Corless.

ISBN: 978-0-425-24277-3

BERKLEY® PRIME CRIME
Berkley Prime Crime Books are published by The Berkley Publishing Group,
a division of Penguin Group (USA) Inc.,
375 Hudson Street, New York, New York 10014.
BERKLEY® PRIME CRIME and the PRIME CRIME logo are trademarks of Penguin Group (USA) Inc.

PRINTED IN THE UNITED STATES OF AMERICA

10   9   8   7   6   5   4   3   2   1

One

"How many frogs do I get for a dollar?" The boy asking was about ten years old. He had a buzz cut that almost made his blond hair invisible in the sun. His attitude was exactly what one might expect from a young male of noble blood.

I plastered a smile on my face and shifted my corset under my low-cut blouse for the hundredth time in the last hour. Whoever thought it would be a good idea to make all the women in Renaissance Faire Village and Market Place look like floozy tavern wenches needed to be out here doing it instead of me.

"You get five frogs for five dollars, young sir." I managed to keep my tone civil. It wasn't easy.

"That's not many frogs for a lot of money," he said.

"I do not make the rules. I only take the money and give you the frogs to put on the catapult. Dost thou wish to throw frogs or not?"

He looked at the targets that could net him some of the

prizes above them. There were swords, of course, shields, a lance or two, and for the girls, fairy wings and flower head-dresses. "I guess that'll be okay."

He handed me the money and I went to the water trough below the targets where the frogs ended up whether they hit their mark or not. The water was cold—the only good thing about this job. It was July fourth and at least a hundred degrees in Myrtle Beach, South Carolina. If nothing else, as new people lined up at the frog-catapult game, I got to put my hands in cold water and flick some up at my face and showy bosom. Amazing what a push-up bra can do.

So I got the five frogs, lingering an extra second or two to splash cold water on my face. I took the frogs back to the lit-tle Viking and handed him the first one to load on the cata-pult.

He looked at the frog in his hand and squinted up at me. "It's not real."

"Pardon me, sir?"

"The frog. It's not real. I thought the frogs were *real*."

I laughed a little and gripped the four, slimy rubber frogs that were left a little tighter. That was to keep from injuring my obnoxious customer. "Of course the frogs aren't real, sir. That wouldn't be allowed. But they are wet and will connect with yon target if your aim is good. And there are plentiful rewards for a young master like yourself who can do so."

He looked at the frog again and shrugged. "Okay."

The first frog almost went out of the booth where the frog catapult was set. The second fared not much better. The third made it to the water trough. The fourth and fifth frogs fell to the ground before reaching the water.

"Well done, young sir!" I fetched the consolation prize—a Pan's pipe—and gave it to him with a flourish. "No doubt you shall someday be a great catapulter!"

"That wasn't fair," he complained, not reaching for the pipe. "I was prepared for real frogs, not those fake ones. I needed the real frog weight to reach the prizes. You tricked me. I want my money back."

My smile felt like it was cutting into my face. "Good sir, I am only allowed to abide by the rules of the game. I cannot refund your money because you lost."

"I didn't lose. You cheated. Where are the real frogs?"

"Yes." Our resident wizard, Merlin, joined the fray. "Where are the real frogs, Lady Jessie? Why haven't you brought out the best for this fine young man?"

It was bad enough that I was here, helping people at the Renaissance Faire catapult frogs. I should've been studying a craft for my dissertation—"The Proliferation of Medieval Crafts in Modern Times."

I had put in for my apprenticeship at Pope's Pots and Kellie's Kites months before it was necessary. Pope's decided not to have an apprentice this summer and Kellie was taking a three-month sabbatical. By the time I found out, no other apprenticeships were available.

That left me a choice of waiting tables at the Pleasant Pheasant or doing the frog catapult. Not much of a choice. It was better than *not* working at Renaissance Faire Village over my vacation from the University of South Carolina at Columbia, where I'm an assistant history professor in my everyday life. But not by much.

"Merlin, perhaps you can explain to this good gentleman that there are no real frogs."

The wizard looked at me like I'd lost my mind. His purple robe with gold stars matched the crooked pointed hat on his head. His white hair and straggly white beard helped him look the part even more. "What do you mean, there are no real frogs? Find a swamp and bring some here, wench! We must keep the customers happy."

And that was truly the motto at the Village this year. Times were tight. Customers had thinned out, at least according to management. Though the cobblestone streets

looked to me as full as ever of laughing tourists wearing
Ren Faire finery and brandishing weaponry.

Adventure Land, the parent company of Renaissance
Faire Village, was pulling out all the stops to bring in more
paying customers. I certainly wouldn't have been wearing
this blouse otherwise. The new posters advertising the Village used the word *more* at least twice in every sentence.

But even though I loved the Village, there was only so
much I was willing to do. I'd been a kitchen wench, cleaned
the stables, sat with sick elephants, and cleaned out dirty
fountains in my time. But I had to draw the line somewhere.

Digging up frogs to throw across the booth wasn't one of
the things I was willing to do. It didn't even sound like one
of the things I *should* do. Wasn't there some law against killing frogs? "Perhaps you should use your magic, Sir Wizard,
and compel frogs to come here and leap upon yon catapult."

The little boy turned his gaze from me to Merlin. "Yeah.
That makes sense."

"Of course! I should have thought of that myself!" Merlin made a face and threw out some magic powder that spar-
kled in the sunlight. "I command all frogs to come forth and
display themselves for our young friend."

By this time, as was always the case in the Village, a small
crowd had gathered to see what was going on. At any time
during the day, visitors could see one of Robin Hood's Merry
Men captured by the Sheriff of Nottingham, listen to Shakespeare reciting his odes, or watch knights joust on the battle-
field. You never knew where to look for the next amusement.

"Well?" the boy asked after a moment. "Where are the
frogs?"

"Is something wrong, Kenny?" A large, male version of the
young boy joined us. "Is someone giving you a hard time?"

Kenny at once launched into his horrific tale of being
cheated because I only had fake frogs. His father seemed to
understand completely and turned to me. "I think that makes
sense. Give my son his money back."

I glanced at Merlin. Not many residents who lived in the Village knew that he was the CEO of Adventure Land. I wasn't totally sure, but if he wanted to put real frogs into the game, that was his prerogative. And he could definitely decide if the boy (and his ogrelike father) should get their money back.

But he distanced himself, performing magic tricks for the crowd around us. That meant I had to handle it. I adjusted my bosom again and addressed Kenny's father. "We do not use real frogs here, sir. I cannot refund the money your son paid. I did offer him a consolation prize." I held out the Pan's pipe again.

"That's for girls!" Kenny's father proclaimed. "Are you saying my son is a sissy? I want to talk to someone in charge! There must be a *man* around here who knows what's going on."

I glanced at Merlin again. He was playing with the gold cord braided at his waist. Clearly he was not going to be in charge of this incident.

"Is there a problem?" Village Bailiff (and my main man) Chase Manhattan entered the fray. He's like the police chief and circuit court judge rolled into one very attractive package.

Seeing him there had to make Kenny and his father quake in their fake boots. Chase was six foot eight and two hundred fifty pounds of former jousting star—not to mention a college football hero. He wore his long brown hair in a braid that was carelessly tossed over one shoulder to reveal a gold earring. His tight black leather vest molded itself to his broad, muscled chest. He looked tough and determined.

Kenny began running through his list of complaints. His father seemed a little less willing to back his son up now that he was facing Chase. "Maybe live frogs are a little too much to expect, son."

"No matter. We shall gladly refund your money, young sir." Chase swept the boy a gallant bow. "Mayhap you can find another game to your liking."

"But—" I started to complain. What would stop everyone from playing any game in the Village and asking for their money back when they were done? Truly, Chase wasn't considering the consequences.

Delicious brown eyes, like Dove dark chocolates, gazed serenely back at me while he addressed our visitors. "Thank you for visiting Renaissance Faire Village and Market Place, good sirs. Enjoy a wonderful afternoon!"

The crowd, sensing the moment was over, started to move away, looking for other excitement. I gave Kenny and his father their money, adjusted my bosom, and went to pick up the frogs that had missed their mark.

"Well done, my boy!" Merlin commended Chase. "Really, I had no idea what to do. It was such a quandary. Lady Jessie seemed intent on cheating the poor lad. I'm wondering if some time in the stocks might do her some good."

"All you had to do was tell me to give him his money back," I said to Merlin. I was still holding a slimy, non-real frog, considering if I should hit the wizard squarely in the face, when Chase stayed my hand.

"I have some good news," he said.

Merlin wandered away, the breeze whipping at the ends of his long robe—not an inspiring sight, since the wizard had a habit of flashing residents from time to time.

"Does it involve any kind of live animal or children?"

"Probably not. I think I may have found you an apprenticeship for the summer. Interested?"

I hugged him tightly. "Desperately so. I don't care what it is, as long as I'm not out here on the front lines."

"I don't know." His dark eyes crinkled at the corners when he smiled. "You look good in that blouse, wench."

"Thanks." I adjusted the bosom again (just for him). "Now where is yon apprenticeship?" I gratefully put up the Closed sign on the Frog Catapult.

I didn't want to sound ungrateful so I refrained from asking if it would fit in with the craft plan for my dissertation.

Most of the crafts here would, but there were a few that were questionable. The Village maintained the air of the sixteenth century, for the most part. Weaving baskets at Wicked Weaves, making glass ornaments at the Glass Gryphon, or throwing pottery at Pope's Pots could all be useful to me and my research.

On the other hand, Totally Toad Footstools or Lady Cathy's Crochet might not be. I wasn't sure about crochet. I'd have to check into it.

But on this clear, hot day, I wasn't going to be particular. If it got me away from the frog catapult, it was a blessing. "Are you keeping it a secret?" I asked him as we crossed the cobblestones past the King's Tarts Pie Shop and Brewster's Tavern.

Chase swept a gallant bow to a group of female visitors in brightly colored gowns wearing matching hats, gloves, and boots. The ladies giggled and nodded back, mindful of their positions. "I know this might be something you wouldn't normally consider, Jessie. I don't want you to prejudge the position until you take a look."

His reticence was starting to make me wonder how bad this was. We crossed the crowded Village Square and the Green where jugglers and fire eaters performed for the crowd. The visitors were a mesh of sunburned shoulders, shorts, and flip-flops rubbing elbows with knights in armor, magicians, and ladies dressed like queens. If there was a scarcity of visitors this summer, I sure couldn't tell. The place was packed, as usual. Adventure Land execs were probably just worried over nothing.

We walked past Fractured Fairy Tales, where the actors were getting plenty of laughs as they performed their weird version of *Cinderella*. "Where did you say this was?" I asked again.

"You know, there were lots of crafts going on during the Renaissance, including making clothes," Chase lectured me on my specialty.

Then it hit me. "Oh no! You aren't saying Portia wants me at the costume shop, are you? You know it's a trap. She hates me, Chase. They wouldn't offer me an apprenticeship unless they had something nefarious in mind. Besides, I don't think I can sew. I have to throw things out when they get holes in them."

"I knew you were going to be this way. That's why I didn't tell you. But you said anything was better than the frog catapult, right? You've repeated that since you got here last week. Working with Andre Hariot will be fun."

"Who?" I thought I knew all the craft people in the Village. The name wasn't familiar.

"Harriet's Hat House," he explained. "They did the name wrong on the shop and it was never corrected. Andre makes hats. That's a Ren craft, right?"

Hat making. I had never really considered it. I was relieved it wasn't clothes making, but my mind was blank. Obviously they made hats during the Renaissance. This could work for me. "How did you hear about it?"

"Andre lost his apprentice this week. Her parents needed her at home for the summer. Andre makes all the hats for the whole village. He always needs someone, and I thought it might as well be you."

"Hat making could be fun. I don't know anything about it. Usually I research before I apprentice. But it could be fine. What's he like?"

"Andre? He's a nice guy. A little strange. But so is everyone else around here." He shrugged as we passed the three brick houses that made up Squires' Lane. "Andre got his start in Hollywood. He knows everything about every movie ever made. You'll see. You'll like him."

The fact that he had to reassure me made me nervous. I could see Harriet's Hat House from here. There was a sign shaped like a fancy hat outside the tiny shop with the upstairs living quarters—like all the other shops in the Village.

I had probably passed the Hat House a thousand times

since I'd started coming here the year I left college. I just never paid it much attention. I never considered hat making as a craft, but I supposed it was. And Chase was right. It probably would be interesting, though not necessarily my kind of thing.

I wanted to throw pottery, make swords, shoot arrows—that kind of thing. But hats were good. I could include them in my dissertation. I adjusted my bodice again and put a smile on my face. Hats were *great*! I was the luckiest woman in the world!

Chase ducked his head to get into the hat shop. I followed him in time to see a small, well-dressed man with graying brown hair tossing yards of material into the air. He wore an orange and brown tunic with the matching short pants and hose. His little goatee curled up at the end.

Hats of all sizes, shapes, and colors were strewn about in careless abandon. Several young college or high school students were clustered around Andre Hariot. All of them looked tense.

"What must I do to have you make quality? You must think about the customer. How will he or she look wearing one of our hats? You all sicken me with your incompetence. Go away! I don't want to see any of you again until tomorrow."

I looked at Chase, who smiled back at me and grabbed my hand as though he was worried that I might leave. "Andre, I brought Jessie to meet you. Lady Jessie Morton, meet Andre Hariot, hatmaker to the stars."

The dapper little man (probably just five feet tall, at least a foot shorter than me) sat down heavily on a fabric-covered chair. He looked to be in his early fifties but was dressed very youthfully. "Not today, Chase. I can't face another failure today. Maybe tomorrow. I know I need a new apprentice, but these youngsters are not qualified."

I felt like this was my thing now. Chase got me here—got me interested. Now that I was facing the hat-making promised land, it was up to me to find my place. "I'm Jessie Morton." I moved toward him and held out my hand. "I'd love to be your apprentice and make hats this summer."

Andre looked straight up from his vantage point until he reached my face. To his credit, his eyes didn't linger *too* long on my bosom. I liked him, but I'm impulsive that way.

"My, you're a tall one, aren't you? Did you know most of Hollywood's leading men were very short? They stood on stools to kiss their leading ladies in many cases. Can you name any of them?"

"James Cagney was one of them, right?"

"That's right!" He smiled a little. "You like the movies?"

"I do. How did those short leading men jump on horses if they had to stand on stools to kiss the girls?"

Andre laughed in a quiet, elegant manner and smoothed his hand across his already flat hair. "It's funny you should ask that, Jessie. Many of them had to be helped into the saddle from the side the camera couldn't see. Of course there were always stunt men to fill in."

And just like that, Andre Hariot and I were friends. Chase waved as he backed out of the shop, and I smiled in return. I could tell this was going to be a good summer at the Village.

But you know how you should never say things are too good? There's some kind of ancient Chinese curse about that. I had doomed myself.

Two

Not that the rest of the day at Hariot's wasn't awesome. Working with him was so different than making swords or any of the other things I'd done at the Village. He was demanding, fastidious, detailed, and focused. But he also made me laugh with his Hollywood stories from his heyday in the 1980s. I never realized how important hat making was to movies and TV.

It was my first day, so I didn't get to do much actual hat making. But it was amazing looking at all the colors, fabric textures, and styles of hats that Andre had made for Village residents and visitors. Unlike most of the items in other shops, Andre's hats were usually special orders. Customers didn't wander in off the cobblestones as much and flip out Lady Visa. There wasn't that feeling of being a slave to the cash register.

"You might want to consider a change of costume to work as my apprentice," Andre remarked as I was getting ready to leave for the day. "Bosomy wenches are wonderful out there. In here, perhaps something a little more tasteful. See you tomorrow, Jessie."

I knew that meant tackling Portia for a new outfit. Not something I was looking forward to. The costume mistress didn't like costume changes by residents. Once you were assigned a costume, you were supposed to keep it—at least that style—for the entire time you were working.

Portia was responsible for costumes that were worn by Village actors as well as visitors. There was always a long line of people waiting to see her. I saw her pale, tired face and black hair as she leaned on the counter at the costume shop. Good old Portia. She never changed.

"What now?" she demanded when she saw me.

"I started working as an apprentice at Hariot's today. He said I need something tasteful. I'm not sure what that would be, something different than this, obviously. I'd appreciate whatever you can dig up for me that's appropriate."

I braced myself for her usual rant about expecting too much from her. No matter that we'd known each other for years and I'd even helped her with her love life once (matchmaking is a sideline of mine), Portia always complained. We never got through a summer (or any other time) without clashing.

To my surprise, she put a pale green gown on the counter. It would be considered a day dress or work gown for a lady of leisure. It was modest and looked pretty good. When she added a pair of matching green slippers, I felt ready to drop on the sandy ground in amazement.

"These are great!" I raved, hoping that would encourage her in the future. "Thanks!"

"Anything for Andre." She sighed as she so often does. "You know Beth has had a thing for him for years. He can't see her though. I guess we're all doomed to be alone and unhappy our whole lives. Enjoy the dress while you can."

Well, the doom and gloom aspect was Portia's natural demeanor, kind of like gossip. There was always a heaping helping of both from her. I smiled, thanked her again, and made a quick retreat. I had what I wanted.

Beth and Andre seemed like a good match to me—both in fashion, close to the same age and character. I might have to follow up on that. I was probably the best matchmaker in the Village, at one time or another. Too bad that wasn't a craft.

I hummed a little as I passed the Main Gate, which was closing for the day. Visitors leaving the Village were serenaded by musicians while jugglers juggled and ladies waved tearful good-byes. A few crones gave out candy to the children, inviting them to return for more.

The entrance to Sherwood Forest was close by. It was unusually quiet. There was normally something going on in or around the five acres of woods that made up Robin Hood's kingdom. Maybe the sultry day with a hint of rain was keeping them in their tree houses.

One of the new carriage rides went past me on the cobblestones, headed for the Main Gate. The carriages were open and very pretty with their blue and gold design—fit for Cinderella. There was barely enough room to pass on the road, however, and I stepped to the side on the grass.

One of the Village minions followed behind the horses, picking up what they had left behind. It wouldn't do for an expensive costume to drag through animal poop. Goats, sheep, a few pigs, and some chickens kept by Village characters also had to be cleaned up after. I wouldn't want that job.

I was surprised to find Chase already finished for the day and waiting at the Dungeon when I got back. Because he's the bailiff for the Village, he lives in an apartment above the dungeon area, where displays of prisoners in fake cells draw in visitors each day. The stocks, where vegetable justice is done, are right outside. For a fee, good friends can hit each other with squishy vegetables. On a slow day, Village folk are recruited to take their places in the stocks. It's a favorite attraction for visitors.

The apartment is nice, especially compared to standard

Village housing. It's cozy—two big rooms and a bathroom—and the shower always has hot water. It has plenty of space for the two of us.

"Greetings, fair lady." Chase bowed gallantly before me at the door. "I have been anxiously awaiting your arrival. Would you deign to sup with me this eve?"

I curtsied (not so worried about my peasant blouse showing a little too much in this case) and smiled at him. "I would happily sup with you, good sir. Allow me to go upstairs and take a shower, as you have already done."

He kissed me lightly. "Hurry, wench. I'm hungry."

That was either the *worst* protocol I've ever heard or a very quick fall from grace. "I beg thee to recall, sir, that the king himself named me *Lady* Jessie for my deeds. Just because I'm dressed like a wench, doesn't make me one."

"My apologies, lady. I am ready when you are ready."

I laughed, not really caring what he called me. Whenever Chase was around, everything was good. "Thanks for linking me up with Andre. I wouldn't have looked in that direction for a craft experience. But I think this is going to be great!"

On that note, I went upstairs and changed into more modern clothes—shorts and a tank top. It was the only way to compete with the cute, disgusting fairies flitting around the Village showing off a lot more than some cleavage. I have legs, too!

Once the visitors went home and the Village closed down for the day, it was like a big, weird neighborhood filled with storybook creatures—and actors with big egos. The taverns and restaurants offered whatever food was left over from the day free to employees. Even the places that took your money took less of it when the Village was closed.

Chase and I had a nice dinner at the Pleasant Pheasant right across the cobblestones from the Dungeon. We indulged in some ale, too, and left the pub feeling good. There was music coming from the dancing girls who were rehearsing at the Stage Caravan next door. From across the way, elephants bellowed, waiting for their dinner, while Bo Peep's sheep *baaed* in time to the music. The sights and sounds of life in the Village were heavenly to me.

Chase and I retired for the night, grateful for another Dungeon indulgence—air-conditioning. Life was good. Portia might like to find fault with all of this, but it was what kept me going when I was away most of the year in Columbia at the university. I wished I could let myself go and trust that everything would always be this good. I could take up Chase's invitation to live here full-time with him.

But a tiny voice in the back of my head reminded me that I needed more. Someday I might not be here. Chase might not be here. I needed that PhD to make enough money to buy a place of my own. This was make-believe. Wonderful and seductive—but still make-believe.

A little after two A.M., Chase's radio—one of the few modern-day devices allowed in the Village while visitors were there, went off. They needed him at one of the shops.

"What is it?" I whispered as he got dressed.

"I'm not sure. Security found something strange over at the Three Chocolatiers Shoppe."

"I want to come." I got up, too, and searched in the dark for my hastily tossed shorts and sandals. "I've heard they make their chocolate early in the morning. Maybe they made too much and need to give some away."

"It might be better if you stay here. It could be anything. A few weeks ago, one of the goats got into Fabulous Funnels. It was a mess."

"Like I said—chocolate all over the place. How bad can it be?"

Chase gave in gracefully. We walked across the dark, still Village. Most people were asleep, dreaming about what lunacy they would get into tomorrow. The lamps glowed softly, showing us the way. As though we were at one with the sleeping houses, we were quiet, too.

Two security guards were waiting outside the chocolate shop. The front door was open beneath three crossed swords symbolizing the Chocolatiers' coat of arms. There was a faint light coming from inside.

I nudged Chase with my elbow. "See? What did I tell you? Plenty of chocolate to be had."

He didn't respond, turning to the security men instead. "What's up? It better be more than an open door."

"You have to see it," one of them, a man I didn't recognize, blurted out.

"The door was open, like Fabulous Funnels." The other security guard shrugged as though that statement explained it all. "We just walked inside. We didn't know what was going on. We didn't touch anything."

I noticed they stayed outside as Chase and I went in. I wasn't sure if that was because what happened wasn't serious enough to call Chase and they were scared to come in or because they'd already seen whatever it was and didn't want to see it again.

Chocolate was, indeed, everywhere. Not really edible, though, unless you like licking it off the floors, walls, and windows. There have been days when I would've done that for a chocolate fix, but the wasted deliciousness wasn't the worst thing about this scene.

The Chocolatiers blended their own chocolate mixture (a dark secret) in a huge, stainless steel vat behind the main counter. In the dim light, I could see someone bending over the vat—a large, red, plumed hat covering him.

"It's Cesar," Chase said. "I guess he had a little too much to drink before he came to make chocolate."

"What a waste!" It was all I could think of—until Chase tried to wake the eldest chocolatier. Cesar fell backward out of the vat, splashing up another few gallons of liquid chocolate across us and the rest of the shop. He was wearing red shorts and a white apron with red hearts beneath his extravagant, plumed hat. Like the rest of the kitchen—he was covered in chocolate.

"I don't think he's drunk after all," Chase said in a subdued voice after checking Cesar's pulse. "I think he's dead."

The security guard coming in behind me sighed. "Poor Cesar. I guess this is what they mean when they say death by chocolate."

Three

It only took the Myrtle Beach Police Department a few minutes to invade the Village with their lights and sirens. By that time, all the lanterns and candles in the Village were lit and residents had begun making their way toward the center of the disturbance.

Chase shook hands with Detective Donald Almond. Detective Almond was assigned to the Village as a contact for the more serious offenses that happened—not the petty thefts or even simple assaults. Chase and the regular security force took care of those things. Of course, all the offenders ended up in the Myrtle Beach jail anyway.

"This better be good, Manhattan," Detective Almond said. His gray shirt and too-tight black pants looked even more wrinkled than usual. Obviously, he'd searched around in the dark for clothes, too.

"I don't know about *good* but Cesar Rizzo is dead."

At almost the same instant that Chase said his name, Cesar's brothers—Bernardo and Marco—came running, pushing their way through the crowd to find out what had happened.

"Hold on there, boys." Detective Almond held up his hand. "Where's the fire?"

All three Chocolatiers were tall, buff, good-looking specimens of Renaissance manhood. Cesar had been the oldest, probably in his forties. "We heard our brother is dead," Bernardo said with great angst in his voice. "You tell us what's going on."

"Chase?" Marco asked in a less-demanding voice. He was the youngest and the least obnoxious of the trio. "Did something happen to Cesar?"

"I'm afraid he's dead." Chase put a hand on each one of the younger Rizzo brothers' shoulders. "I'm not sure what happened to him yet. The police will figure it out."

"Let's take a look before we start making rash statements." Detective Almond hitched up his pants and snorted a little in the damp night air. "I give you a lot of credit for keeping everything straight out here, Manhattan. But you better let an expert take a look before you make wild statements. You're not the coroner, you know."

Following his statement, Detective Almond went into the chocolate shop. He came right back out again. "Looks like you might be right. That man is definitely dead."

I started to say, *duh*, but held my tongue. Mary, Mary Quite Contrary stood next to me, trying to see what was happening. "Did Cesar really die making chocolate?" she asked me.

"It looks like it."

"I hope he got to eat some of it."

I didn't answer, since it looked like he might've eaten a little *too* much chocolate. Chase and Detective Almond went back into the shop, leaving Marco and Bernardo sobbing loudly in the street over their brother's demise.

"What's it like in there?" Fred the Red Dragon asked, wearing only the bottom half of his costume.

"Chocolate everywhere," I told him. "It looks kind of like his blender went crazy."

Everyone from Lady Godiva to Galileo and Mother Goose began speculating on what could've killed Cesar. It looked like an unfortunate accident to me. But it was hard to tell what happened with chocolate covering everything. The coroner's van pulled up a few minutes later to add more fuel to Village speculation.

Security men began to urge everyone to go home. Two fairies had taken Bernardo and Marco in hand—as they frequently did. The Three Chocolatiers were probably the most eligible bachelors in the Village.

Merlin came through the thinning crowd, no pointed wizard's hat or robe, just a pair of purple silk pajamas covering his thin frame. "Good heavens! I could hear all of this going on at the other end of the Village. Can you keep it down? There's a lot going on tomorrow. I need my rest."

"There's been a death," Sam Da Vinci told him. "Cesar Rizzo."

"You don't say. What do they think happened to him?" The wizard-CEO stroked his straggly white beard.

"They haven't said yet," Lady Lindsey said. "But I heard Chase say he died in chocolate."

Merlin rocked back on his heels and smiled. "Best way to die—besides sex, of course."

Everyone laughed at that. I figured it was good for them to use humor to alleviate the tension. The Village was a tight-knit community. Aside from a transient population of college and high school drama students who took on the lesser jobs, the shopkeepers and the main characters were mostly people who had been here for years. Cesar's death was bound to affect everyone.

"Well, at least we don't have to compete with him for the ladies anymore," Peter Greenwalt added. He was a chunky man with mutton chops and long hair. He owned Peter's Pub, one of the better taverns in the Village.

Many of the younger (and middle-aged) men around him agreed with that statement. There was a lot of jealousy regarding the Three Chocolatiers. Not only were they physically attractive and single, but they owned a chocolate shop. That's about as good as it gets.

A sound like thunder came from the darkness, headed our way. The small group of residents outside the chocolate shop drew closer together. Even the police officers, charged with holding the line against entry from the cobblestones, looked worried.

"What is that?" I asked just before eight men in black robes brought their horses to an abrupt stop before us.

"I take it you haven't met the new attraction yet," Merlin whispered. "The Knights Templar. They're very popular this summer."

I could see why. The men were wrapped in dark robes and headdresses that allowed only their eyes to show. The horses were huge and extremely well trained. Not one of the animals so much as flicked its tail after the riders stopped.

"Show offs," Peter hissed. "They've taken over the Village. Not even Chase can stop them."

The head police officer stepped forward as the knights moved toward the chocolate shop. "There's no admittance. Best to go home now."

The knight in front nodded. "We have only come to see if we may be of service."

"Why? Run out of things to do in the woods?" I recognized Da Vinci's voice, but he was behind me, apparently not up to yelling that to their faces.

The dark riders looked my way at the same time, and a chill ran down my spine. They were *very* impressive. The monks of the Brotherhood of the Sheaf were a little spooky when you saw them all together. But nothing like this. It was probably the big, black horses. The monks don't ride.

"You question our honorable intentions?" the front rider demanded, still looking right at me.

"I don't," I responded quickly, looking over my shoulder. That coward, Da Vinci, was gone. "It wasn't me. I think you're kind of awesome. And if you say you're here to help, I believe you."

The lead rider dismounted, as did the rest of his men, and walked toward me. I couldn't help but notice the very large scimitar hanging from his side. *Very* impressive. He knelt at my feet and took my hand. "It seems someone hid behind you so they could hurl insults without regard for the consequences. I apologize for your being rudely used, my lady." He kissed my hand.

I've had many people kiss my hand in the Village. Most people don't get that you can't slobber on someone and expect to impress them. This knight knew what he was doing. There was absolutely no slobber.

"That's fine, Sir Knight. I appreciate your concern. No harm, no foul."

"Perhaps a ride on my steed in the night air would be good for you, my lady. You have only to say the word."

"Allow me to say the word," Chase said, interrupting my knightly interlude. "All of you guys go home. Go back to your tents, and let the professionals handle this. And by this, I mean Jessie, too. I hope you get what I'm saying here."

The knight got easily to his feet and gave Chase a curt bow. "We do not mean to trespass, Sir Bailiff. Let us know if you need help maintaining order and stability in the Village. This is our home now, too."

"Thanks," Chase acknowledged him politely. "I think I've got this one."

All of the Knights Templar got on their horses and headed back the way they'd come. Peter joked a little with Chase about needing help from the horsemen. When Chase refused to take the bait, he drifted away with a few of the remaining residents.

"You didn't tell me about them," I said when Chase and I were alone.

"I'm surprised you haven't seen them already. They're the hot ticket this summer. They live in big black tents in the forest. The visitors love them and their horse tricks, but everyone who works here hates them."

"Jealousy."

"Maybe."

"They are kind of awesome."

"You think?"

"Not like you." I backed down from my knight-inspired haze. "But impressive."

We were walking back to the Dungeon, leaving the police and crime scene people to do their jobs. From somewhere in the darkness, a crazed rooster was crowing his heart out, confused by the noise and light into thinking it was morning.

"Did they have any ideas about what happened to Cesar?" The conversation had fallen flat and I felt the urge to talk. Not unusual for me.

"They didn't really say. I think it had something to do with the large hat pin in his eye."

Four

"*Ew!*" I think that summed up my feelings on the subject. My stomach felt a little queasy thinking about it. "I guess he was murdered then. Besides all the jealous men in the Village, who'd want to kill Cesar?"

"You probably just hit the shield with the lance." Chase unlocked the door to the Dungeon. "I'm sure Detective Almond will want to have a word with some of them."

"It was kind of elaborate, wasn't it?" Despite the gross factor, I couldn't keep from thinking—and, therefore, talking—about it. "I mean, why go through all of that staging with the chocolate and covering him with the hat? Why kill him with a hat pin in the eye—which, by the way, is really creepy—and why the rest of the drama? What did the hat pin look like?"

"I don't know, Jessie. I don't like murder in the Village. I can handle the petty thefts and everything else. People being killed here is more than I want to think about. And I think the hat pin had some kind of green stone on it. It was hard to tell with all the chocolate."

He was taking off his shirt and shorts, cleaning off the chocolate, and I was admiring the view. "You handled it very well. Are you starting to regret that you're the bailiff?"

"Not exactly. I didn't think I'd have to deal with something like this when I took the job. I guess when you get a large group of people living together, bad things can happen."

I washed the chocolate off of me, too, and lay down next to him, wrapping my arms around him. "I'm sorry you had to do this. Is there anything I can do to make you feel better?"

He smiled at me and turned off the light. "Let's think about that."

Chase and I were up a few hours later, which was not especially welcome after the tumultuous events of earlier that morning. Every Wednesday morning, Chase hears grievances from the residents of the Village. This is done right outside the Dungeon near the stocks for the occasional bout of vegetable justice that's required to keep everybody happy. Normally this is a small group, since no one gets up early around here, and Adventure Land conveniently allows this time before the gates open for the process.

Chase, as bailiff, hears the grievances, makes judgments on some of them, and takes others to King Harold and Queen Olivia. If that doesn't work, he takes the problem to the Village management team. But mostly, no one wants to involve outsiders, so Chase's word is law.

This particular Wednesday morning, a stream of residents waited outside the Dungeon for Chase to emerge. They seemed unusually angry and hostile to me. Maybe it was just having their sleep interrupted by Cesar's untimely demise.

"We want to know what you're going to do about those Templar Knights," Lord Maximus demanded. He does the "Birds of Prey" program at the Hawk Stage three times a day. "We're tired of putting up with them."

There was a chorus of agreement from the knaves, knights, madmen, and scoundrels behind him. I couldn't help but notice that there wasn't a single woman in the crowd.

"Do you have something in particular that you want to lodge a complaint about?" Chase asked Maximus in particular and the crowd in general.

"You mean besides them showing up during performances, upstaging everyone else, and sneaking around the Village at all hours of the day and night?" Maximus countered.

"And stealing all the women!" a well-dressed woodsman added.

A loud, lusty response followed from the young to middle-aged men. Fists shot into the air to reinforce their unhappiness.

I could see Chase was trying not to smile in the face of this complaint. I knew he took his role very seriously. "Gentlemen, knaves, and varlets—"

"Don't forget madmen!"

"And madmen. I understand your problem with the knights. There's not much I can do about it. My advice is to keep your ladies happy and at home."

"Maybe we should open a chastity belt shop," one of the varlets retorted.

"There has to be something you can do, Chase." My twin brother, Tony, added his voice to the discussion. "I hear they were interested in Jessie last night. She'll end up in the black tents with them before the week is out. Then you'll really understand our problem."

If my brother was having lady problems because of the knights, there must really be an issue. I hadn't seen him since I'd arrived. He lived here year-round like Chase and many of the others. And, usually, women flocked to him like magpies.

Chase held up his hand for silence after allowing a few

minutes of banter regarding Tony's manhood. "I'll talk to the knights. But they aren't kidnapping your girlfriends. If Jessie, or any other lady, decides to go with them, there's not much I can do. But I'll definitely have a word with them about the performances."

No one was very happy with that decision—except for the Tornado Twins, Diego and Lorenzo. They're comedians with a mature audience sticker on all the signs and handouts around the Village.

Diego prostrated himself at Chase's feet. "Take me with you! I want to live in the black tents. I could water their horses or shave their heads. I don't care. I just want to be like them."

His brother, Lorenzo, came up and slipped a leash around his neck. "You're staying home tonight! No more running around the forest with those knights. Maybe these other guys don't know how to keep their partners home, but I know about your secret life of peanut butter and debauchery. Come along!"

A little pig with a tiny pink umbrella fastened to its head went with them, following at their heels like a puppy.

"Anything else?" Chase asked as the male portion of the group began to wander back to their shops and jobs.

Mother Goose, holding Phineas, her live fowl, came forward with one of the Lovely Laundry Ladies. "Yes, Bailiff. We were wondering if you could take us out to help you with the knights. We're both very good at problem solving."

Chase shook his head, his dark braid flipping over his shoulder, the early-morning sunlight glinting on the gold earring he wore. "Ladies, seriously, you know where the tents are. If you want to go out there, do so."

Mother Goose *humphed*. "It's not that easy to get an introduction. I'll bet you take Jessie out there with you."

"Not if he's smart," Tony commented.

"If that's all." Chase tried again to wrap up the justice system in the Village.

"I have a question." Detective Almond seemed to come out of nowhere—still wearing the same clothes he'd been wearing earlier this morning.

"What can I do for you, detective?" Chase asked.

"You can tell me who you think killed your chocolate-making friend. I hate to take you away from all this important stuff, Manhattan. But it looks like you really do have a murder on your hands."

Five

"At least I didn't get out of bed at two A.M. for nothing," Detective Almond joked. "What kind of kangaroo court are you running out here anyway? Those people acted like you're judge and jury."

Chase didn't try to explain. It never went well with someone from the outside anyway. "I guess it was kind of easy for you to tell that Cesar didn't die of natural causes once you found the hat pin in his eye."

"Yep. But that was just some kind of weird symbolism—like the hat, I guess. It's not what killed him."

"What did?" Chase wondered.

"Maybe we should take this inside," Detective Almond suggested, glancing around like someone was listening to him even though it was only the three of us. His gaze finally rested on me. "Police business. You don't mind, do you?"

I realized he was talking to (and about) me. "Of course not. I'm late for work anyway. See you later, Chase."

I wasn't late. The Village wouldn't open for another hour.

I knew Chase would tell me what Detective Almond had to say when we met up later. After all, Chase was the designated protector for the Village, and I was just an apprentice hatmaker. My feelings weren't *really* hurt to be left out of the important discussion.

Tony and I had plenty of time to wander down to the Monastery Bakery and catch up on the last few months. He talked of nothing but the girls he'd dated and his continuing job doing promotion work for Robin Hood. I suppose I was the same about school and Chase.

I could smell coffee and cinnamon rolls on the morning air by the time we'd reached the Dutchman's Stage. A few residents were up already, working on their skits for the day or practicing with their animals. Tom, Tom the Piper's Son, probably had one of the hardest jobs in the Village, since it required him to catch a piglet then let it go and catch it again after the laughter and applause were over.

Lady Godiva, already in her long blond wig and flesh-colored bodysuit, was working with her horse. She had obviously been recently cast, since the animal seemed to have a great distaste for her. I never knew who was going to be the naked lady when I returned to the Village each summer. It was an often-cast part.

I saw the new Green Man practicing on his stilts without his costume. Again, another new addition. Most people only made it through a few weeks with that part, too. They either moved on to something easier than portraying a walking tree, or they left the Village for other, more gainful employment.

I could see the pirate ship, *Queen's Revenge*, under full sail across Mirror Lake. I'd heard they'd added mermaids to the pirate scenario. I hadn't made it to that part of the lake since I arrived, but I was curious about them.

I reminded Tony of when we were kids and our grandmother had taken us to Florida where there were mermaids swimming underwater in glass cases. I thought it was amazing, and I wanted to be a mermaid for a long time after that. Tony didn't remember it at all.

Of course, fairies were flitting here and there on the cobblestones and the grass. Their bright colors and dainty wings were pretty *and* annoying. They wore virtually nothing while the rest of us sweltered (and were completely covered up) in real-life Renaissance clothing. They were a bunch of flirts and troublemakers. I've lost track of how many of them have wasted their time flirting with Chase right in front of me.

By this time, we were at the bakery. There had been some expansion work done in the past season. It looked like the addition of pastries to the regular coffee lineup had been successful for the Brotherhood of the Sheaf. Their breadmaking skills were legendary—which is no doubt what made their cinnamon rolls the best in the world.

"Lady Jessie," Brother Carl greeted me at the door. He smiled and patted my shoulder, an odd gesture, since the black-robed monks were normally very hands off. "It is wonderful to see you again!"

"Thanks. It's good to see you again, too. I'm ready for the biggest mocha you have with a cinnamon roll on the side. Maybe two cinnamon rolls."

Brother Carl smiled wisely. "Man trouble?"

"Yes, but not the kind you think. The police are in the Village. You know what that means."

"Indeed. We heard about the terrible demise of Cesar Rizzo. Are there any suspects?"

"I think everyone here is probably on some suspect list right now." I took my mocha and cinnamon roll from a new, young, handsome monk who was too shy to look me in the eye. "Any ideas?"

Brother Carl shrugged. "One doesn't like to speak ill of the dead, Lady Jessie. But you know Cesar had a penchant for the ladies."

"I know."

"I'm not sure what a penchant is," Tony said with his mouth full of cinnamon roll, "but he slept around a lot, that's for sure."

"There have been many altercations between Cesar and ladies he left behind as well as gentlemen unhappy that his roving gaze fell on their lady. I suppose they have questioned Cesar's brothers?" Brother Carl asked.

"I'm not sure. Are you saying you think one of them could have chocolate-coated him to death?" I sipped my mocha.

"Again, this is only my speculation. But there is a lady who Cesar had been wooing. She had proven difficult for him because she had another suitor. I'm not sure who that lady, or gentleman, is."

"Thanks, Brother Carl. Excellent cinnamon roll, by the way."

"Yeah," Tony agreed. "But let's not worry about Cesar. He's dead. We need to do something about the knights. What about those guys?"

Brother Carl had plenty to say about the knights, too. Of course, the Village was always rife with gossip. When something happened, it was like a juggernaut of speculation and interest. Before Tony and I had left the bakery, at least five other people had stopped in to chat about Cesar's death. Each of them had a different theory.

But because my theory went along with Brother Carl's, I decided he was right and tried to think of ways to proceed. There was nothing wrong with helping Chase and the police. They could probably use it.

Outside the bakery, Tony and I ran into Robin Hood and two of his Merry Men. I'd known Robin and Alex, his right-hand man, for years. I lived in Sherwood Forest during the summers that I dated each man. The tree houses were popular with visitors but not so much once you'd lived there. There was no running water or plumbing—but there was plenty of electricity for toaster ovens and, recently, computers.

"Hail, Lady Jessie." Robin sketched a short bow. All the Merry Men had to be careful or their little green hats fell off. "Have you seen the Bailiff this morning?"

Alex laughed. "Of course she's seen him. They live together!"

Robin gave him a harsh frown. "Indeed. That is common knowledge. I was being polite, something you've obviously forgotten. Prince John and the Sheriff of Nottingham are more polite than you."

"What is this politeness kick you're on, Toby?" Alex demanded.

Robin, aka Toby, grimaced and shushed him. "No wonder we're losing out to the knights. Have you ever heard any of them who weren't polite and well spoken?"

"I don't think that's their appeal," Tony argued. "You need horses, Robin. Big, white horses to compete with them."

"Okay," I said. "I think you guys don't need me for this conversation. See you around."

"No!" Robin stopped me. "We need help, Jessie. Chase won't do what needs to be done with the Templar Knights. Have you seen them? Maid Marion ran off to their encampment yesterday. And they don't think anything of riding into our space in the forest. Something has to be done."

"I heard all the complaints this morning. I have to tell you, except for interrupting performances, Chase wasn't sympathetic."

"Ah, that's where you come in. You could talk to Chase about the problem now that you're here and you've seen it for yourself. You could persuade him to take up arms against the knights." Robin put one arm around my shoulder and leaned in close.

"Yeah. Chase needs to get them off of those horses and kick their butts," Tony agreed in a less quaint style. "I know you can do it, Jessie. He listens to you."

I shrugged. "I'll talk to him about it. But from the way it sounds, the knights are very popular right now. You guys might have to spice up your performances so you get your crowd back. Then Adventure Land would be more likely to listen to complaints about them."

Tony nodded. "Like I said—big, white horses. Chicks love them."

"Thanks, Jessie," Robin added. "We'll see what we can do. Any suggestions?"

I didn't step into that pit of no return. Nothing I could say would really be appreciated by these men who believed wearing green tights and living in the forest was enough for every woman to fall in love with them. Children loved the tree houses, but it sounded like they enjoyed the big black tents, too. Robin and his group of tree dwellers were going to have to find their own way out of this.

I got over to the hat shop at the stroke of nine A.M. The group of assistants were already being dressed down by Andre for their lack of work on recent projects.

"We are short ten hats. Ten! We have only a few days before they're needed at the Stage Caravan. I shouldn't have to tell any of you about this, but it seems I must do it each day. Now go and get busy. If all of you had worked on the movie *Cleopatra*, as my father did, they would still be filming it!"

The assistants ran out of the room, jostling with each other to see who could get out first. I wondered where Andre had found this particular group of young men who seemed more inclined to be squires or jesters than to be working with hats.

"I'm delighted to see that you've returned, Jessie." Andre sat down on a pretty little chair with delicate needlework on the seat. "I hope having you here will make a difference. These boys aren't interested in haberdashery. I don't know why they're here."

A good reason came through the door. Blond hair tousled, blue eyes wide and starlit, the young woman was looking for a green hat to complement her costume. All of the assistants came back from the work area to help her make that choice.

Andre shooed them out of the sales area and personally helped the young woman, who bought a wide-brimmed,
apple green bonnet with pink flowers on it. I played cashier,
amazed at what people were willing to pay for a hat. It was a
very nice hat, to be sure, but it cost more than I made in a
month.

After the lady was gone, Andre seemed preoccupied. He
kept fingering his fashionable yellow and purple scarf that
he wore with his yellow tunic. "I can hardly concentrate for
thinking about the death of Cesar Rizzo," he finally told
me. "Have you heard anything about what happened?"

"I was there this morning. The police have decided it
was a homicide. That's about all I know."

Andre dropped the red hat band he'd been looking at
while I spoke. His face became even paler beneath the
graying brown hair. "That can't be true! Who would want
to kill Cesar? There has to be some mistake."

"Were you friends with Cesar?" I asked him.

"No. Not really. But to think of something like that happening here—it's terrible."

"I know." I tried to divert him, looking around the room
that was crowded with hats of all types, colors, and styles.
"Tell me what I can do to help make hats."

He nodded and pulled himself out of his funk. "Since
we make mostly hats that could be from the Renaissance,
we use a lot of satin, lace, and other older materials. Sometimes velvet and felt. I try to stay realistic."

It was fairly easy to get him talking about his craft. Who
knew how much work went into making hats? I'd never
been much of a hat wearer myself, but I knew hats were
very popular with visitors and residents of the Village.

I tried on a few hats at Andre's insistence. One of them
was very large and made of red satin. It drooped down over
my left eye. Andre adjusted the heavy veil across my face.

"Hats were used in the Renaissance to disguise oneself
when going out shopping or perhaps visiting a paramour.

Madam would adjust the veil so that her face was discreetly hidden. She could go about the town incognito, if she so desired."

I tried on a somewhat smaller purple velvet hat that fit my head tighter. It didn't look too bad—except it made the sides of my hair fluff out in a way that was a little too clown-like for me.

"People even believed that veils could protect them from the plague and other diseases." Andre talked as he fussed over the placement of my hat. "Of course, they may have been onto something, since the masks surgeons wear today aren't any thicker than a good veil."

I was about to try on another hat when a page announced that Queen Olivia was there. The queen was always surrounded by her jesters, musicians, ladies-in-waiting, and the rest of her entourage. She never traveled alone—which made for a huge spectacle whenever she walked through the Village. Livy loved the spotlight and people taking pictures of her better than anyone else I knew.

"Good morning, Sir Hatmaker!" The queen sang the words as she floated into the shop wearing a deep rose-colored bodice and a gray and rose-striped hooped skirt. She wasn't wearing a hat on her bright red hair, but her gold crown was shiny and impressive.

Andre hurried forth to kiss the queen's hand. The two of them chatted quietly for a while. He turned to introduce me to her, but Livy waved away the introduction. "We are very pleased to see the Lady Jessie again this summer's day. We acknowledge her, and her rightful place in the castle, which she has not taken as yet."

"Thank you, Your Majesty." I curtsied to her with a full head bow in deference to her position. It was good practice for when the crowds were around and better suck-up points for getting in trouble later. Livy liked to be recognized correctly. "While I appreciate your offer to allow me to live in the castle, I have chosen to spend the summer at the Dungeon with the bailiff. But I am grateful for your invitation."

It was true. While I was with Chase, nothing could move me out of the Dungeon. But if we weren't together, I'd be all over that invitation. The castle was awesome—large-screen TVs, Internet, and twenty-four/seven meals brought to your room. It was the height of luxury.

Livy had her closest handmaiden remove her crown and place a large, pink, satin hat on her head. She turned this way and that to study her face in a nearby mirror. "We completely understand your decision, Lady Jessie. Forsooth, if the bailiff asked us to live in vulgar Village housing, we would abdicate our position at the castle immediately." She giggled a little. "He is a handsome devil, is he not? We noticed him at once when he first came to our Village. He fought for us as our champion for a few years."

I knew this, of course. Chase had started here as the Black Knight—the bad guy in the jousts. He soon found employment at the castle acting as the Queen's Protector and Champion. Lucky for me that was over when I got here. Not that Chase noticed me right away. It took him awhile, although we were friends for a long time before we were lovers. Let's face it—there are plenty of beautiful ladies in the Village, and I'm not talking about the fairies either.

While we discussed hats and the queen's wardrobe, there was a disturbance outside the hat shop. The queen's entourage tried to stop the two men from entering, but they thrust their way through the door. A commotion followed as jesters, and even one of the queen's champions, continued trying to hold them back. But Bernardo and Marco were excellent swordsmen. No one tried *too* hard in the face of their flashing blades.

"We are here to avenge our brother's death!" Bernardo yelled. "Stand and defend yourself, hatmaker!"

Six

The Three Chocolatiers (two, really, now) were always a sight to behold. They did elaborate shows of swordplay in the Village outside their shop each day. All three brothers were handsome, virile specimens of manhood. Wrap that up in red and gold costumes that featured capes, knee-high boots and large, plumed hats, and you have the best chocolate commercial ever.

The chocolate was really good, too. They formed it into cute little shapes. I think the mainstay was hearts wrapped in red foil, but there were also doves, dragons, and the pièce de résistance was the giant chocolate sword. Five pounds and a month's salary for a Village resident. I'd never had one, but I'd seen plenty of them around the Village, usually devoured by some large Viking or knight.

I wasn't sure what the brothers would do without the third Chocolatier. Everything was based on the three brothers. Bernardo and Marco looked a little lame without Cesar. And

I certainly didn't understand why they had chosen Andre for vengeance.

But there they stood with their swords pointed at Andre's chest. Without warning, Andre fell to the cloth-covered floor in a dead faint. A few of his assistants hurried to his side, disregarding the swords still held in his general direction.

I wasn't sure what would happen next. Fortunately, Livy chose to exert her royal presence with the men. "What do you think you are doing? How dare you threaten our hatmaker and confidant? Have you taken leave of your senses? You have raised your swords in our presence. We have a good mind to call our bailiff and have him put you both in the stocks."

Bernardo looked at Marco, then they both dropped to their knees, groveling to their queen. "It is the sorrow and grief we feel for our brother who was murdered most violently whilst making chocolate this morning, your majesty," Bernardo explained.

"And when we learned that the hatmaker was to blame, we, of course, came to avenge our brother's death," Marco added. "We beg leave to skewer the culprit, your majesty. We demand justice for Cesar."

Livy tapped her chin with her bright red fingernail. "You have a grievance, gentlemen. We understand and appreciate your position. But this is neither the time nor the place. My new hats are not as yet ready. Killing Andre would be very bad for my wardrobe. I forbid it."

Bernardo and Marco argued with Queen Olivia, but the verdict was set. They were welcome to get revenge after the King's Feast in two weeks when her hats would be ready, but not before. Such are the ways of the Village.

A moment later, Chase was there to sort through what was happening. He had a quick smile for me and a kiss for the queen's hand, but then he was all business.

Andre had revived but was still sitting on the floor. His suck-up assistants were gathered around him, rubbing his head and handing him a glass of water. I didn't bother to intrude, but the Two Chocolatiers' accusation about him was intriguing.

"What's this all about?" Chase demanded.

"It matters not, my fine bailiff," the queen told him. "I have forbidden Andre's death until after the King's Feast in a fortnight."

"I beg your pardon, my queen." Chase put one hand on his heart and bent his head. "But it might be a good idea to clear this up now. It is not only a matter for your majesty to deal with but also for the police."

Bernardo and Marco took their opportunity. "Andre killed Cesar," Bernardo claimed, one side of his large hat sliding down his face in his unaccustomed outrage. "We found out there was a hat pin involved. Who else would use a hat pin as a murder weapon?"

"I know a hat pin was found on the body—" Chase began.

"*In* the body," Marco corrected. "In my brother!"

Livy had her handmaiden start waving her fan to cool her face. "We may not be prepared to hear such delicate information."

"My apologies, Queen Olivia," Marco said. "But it is true. One of Andre's hat pins was found in my brother's eye." He broke down in tears and large gulping sobs. "This man has done the most terrible curse known to man. He has stuck a needle in my brother's eye."

Livy copied Andre and slipped to the floor unconscious.

Seven

There was a great deal more fuss about Livy fainting. The small hat shop filled with her personal entourage. They called for Wanda LeFay, the Village nurse, and pulled out smelling salts, waving fans and hats to revive her. Chase, Bernardo, and Marco lifted her to one of the hastily cleared tables—more lace, silk, and netting wafting to the floor around us. As usual, a scene always followed Livy around the Village.

But I assumed that's why they'd made her queen. At some point, she'd just been plain old Olivia Martin, superstar sales person for Adventure Land along with her husband, Harold. They were able to parlay that status into being the permanent king and queen of Renaissance Village. A sweet job if you liked people bowing to your every command and fulfilling your every whim. They were still Adventure Land employees but with pizzazz.

Queen Olivia was moaning, starting to come around, when Wanda LeFay arrived. She might be the only real

English resident here. She and I always had problems. I don't know if it was her cold, blue fish eyes or the fact that she frequently seemed intent on maiming or killing me.

She smiled at me in an evil manner, making me glad there were several worktables and half the room between us. She opened her medical bag as she approached Livy, the queen's attendants parting before her like Swiss cheese on the cutting block.

I shivered. Better Livy than me.

"What's the problem here?" Wanda asked as she reached the side of the table Livy was laid out on. "You look dreadful, dear. You might need to go to hospital. I think you might need a bit of strengthening. Have you been eating those snails as I suggested?"

I put my hand over my mouth to keep from vomiting.

"I tried." Livy's voice was weak. "I couldn't get them down. Especially in the morning after eating the fried eels you pre-scribed. They're terrible. Especially with everything going on and everyone depending on me."

"Well, don't you fret." Wanda patted her hand. "I might need someone to run back to the first-aid station with me." She looked around the room. "Jessie! Why don't you be a love and come with me?"

There was no way I was going anywhere with that woman. Why did she always pick on me? I didn't understand. I dropped to my knees. "I can't leave Andre," I told her. "He needs me."

Unfortunately, that brought the whole episode back around to where Bernardo and Marco had entered the Hat House, swords at the ready. Both Chocolatiers turned around, ready to kill Andre again.

Chase saw the movement and put himself between Andre and the Rizzo brothers. "We need to have a talk, boys. This isn't what you think. There's no proof that Andre killed your brother."

"How fascinating!" Wanda licked her very red lips. "I

didn't realize there was drama going on here. Don't let me stop you. I always like a good fight, especially when there's a little blood."

"What about me?" Livy moaned, upset because the spotlight had moved away from her.

"I suggest you go get some iron pills and a pregnancy test," Wanda said. "I think the royal family may be increasing."

"What?" Livy sat up without a touch of dizziness. "What are you talking about? I'm too old to have a baby."

Wanda cast her baleful eye at the queen. "Are you absolutely *certain* about that, your majesty?"

Livy looked up and muttered something unintelligible, then she burst out crying.

"Go on." Wanda turned back to Chase and the Rizzo brothers. "I'm waiting for the spectacle."

Andre scooted closer to me. The brothers leered menacingly. I wondered what Chase would do. I didn't see any other security guards. I knew Livy's attendants and Andre's assistants wouldn't be any help.

"You need to leave peacefully right now." Chase used his bailiff voice on them, his dark eyes steely as he focused on the brothers. "Let's go outside and find someplace quiet to talk about this. I'll tell you everything I know so far. You tell me your grievance. If not, those swords will be kept peace-tied in my dungeon for the next ninety days. Or worse."

As threats went, it was clear and real. Chase had the authority to do what he had threatened. The loss of their swords would be really bad for the brothers, especially after losing Cesar. Every eye in the room swung to Marco and Bernardo.

Marco was the first to lower his blade. "It's not fair, Chase. He gets away with killing Cesar, and we can't even run him through a few times."

Bernardo followed his lead. "It wasn't like we were going to kill him—although we had a right."

Wanda made a grunting sound and closed her medical

bag. "Bloody hell! You people can't even fight the right way. I need a drink."

When she left, Chase went outside with Bernardo and Marco. Andre took a deep breath and relaxed against the wall behind him. Seeing that he was okay, I raced outside to hear whatever Chase had to say to the brothers. I knew Livy's people would get everything straightened up inside.

I saw Chase, Bernardo, and Marco disappear into one of the cooling tents set up beside the hat shop. It was a place visitors could sit inside and cool off from the heat. It was probably empty—a good place to talk.

I didn't want to barge in, so I stood outside the entrance and listened as the brothers put forth their case against Andre.

Chase listened to their theories, only one really—the hat pin—that made them think Andre had killed their brother. Then it was his turn. "The police told me this morning that the hat pin didn't kill Cesar."

Bernardo moaned. "But it was in his eye, Chase. How could it *not* kill him?"

"We didn't really look at it." Marco shrugged. "Maybe it wasn't in that deep."

"What are you saying?" Bernardo demanded. "You think that hat pin didn't *hurt* him?"

"Guys, let's calm down," Chase suggested. "The hat pin was put in after Cesar was already dead. I'm sorry to have to tell you this way. It looks like Cesar was mixing the chocolate when someone hit him in the head from behind and he fell into the vat. He actually drowned in the chocolate. I don't know why anyone would want to put the hat pin in his eye *after* he was dead, but it's possible whoever did it wanted us to think Andre was responsible. Can you think of any reason someone would want to do that?"

Both brothers were silent while they contemplated Chase's words and stared at each other (although I could hear the gears in their heads turning even outside the tent).

Marco finally turned aside. "I wish Cesar was here. He'd know what to do."

"That's why we're here, idiot." Bernardo slapped his brother lightly on the head.

"I know," Marco agreed. "A lot of people didn't like Cesar. They didn't know him or they would've loved him like we did."

"Yeah," Bernardo said. "Except when he stole our girlfriends. And I'm not talking once in a while like when you accidentally look at a girl your brother is dating. I mean *all* the time. He went out of his way to get every girl we ever wanted."

"And let's not forget all those other men in the Village who he took girls away from," Marco continued. "Not to mention the girls he dumped when he was through with them."

Chase frowned as he listened to them. Not like it was a secret. We all knew how Cesar was. "Has Detective Almond talked to you two yet?"

"Yeah. That's why we're here." Bernardo fingered his sword like he was still contemplating running Andre through. "He accused us of killing our own brother. He didn't realize how much we loved him."

Marco sniffed. "He was like family to us."

I had to put my hand over my mouth not to laugh. Cesar had also been the brains of the Three Chocolatiers. I wasn't sure what Bernardo and Marco would do without him— although they might be able to find and keep smart girlfriends who could tell them what to do.

"I take it both of you had alibis for the time they think Cesar was killed." Chase managed to keep a straight face, too.

"That's right. He accused us but both of us were with other people when Cesar died. Cesar always started the chocolate mixing, and then we finished it up," Bernardo explained.

"Not like we'd hurt Cesar anyway," Marco said. "Maybe

the hatmaker killed Cesar, then stuck the hat pin in his eye so everyone would know he did it."

"That doesn't make any sense!" Bernardo complained. "But I know he did it! If we don't kill him, he'll go to prison, right, Chase?"

"Yes. Well, maybe," Chase answered. "But I think most people try *not* to get caught."

"It might be a signature thing," Marco continued. "Like signing a painting or a sculpture. Maybe he did it before. Maybe he's a serial killer."

"I don't think so," Chase disagreed. "But thanks for the suggestion. I'll let you know if I hear anything else."

"What about our brother's body?" Bernardo asked. "We need to bury him."

"I'll talk to Detective Almond, but they probably won't release him until they know what happened."

Bernardo shook his head. "I don't like to think about it. I can't believe Andre, the scrawny little hatmaker, killed Cesar. I hope we can keep from killing him back."

Chase didn't get into that conversation. When the brothers had left the tent, he leaned against the entrance and smiled at me. "What do you think?"

"I think we're going to need a new chocolate shop. Bernardo and Marco will never be able to figure it out without Cesar."

It was lunchtime, and since Livy was still in the hat shop, I decided to take a break and eat with Chase at Peter's Pub. It was early and wouldn't be crowded yet. Visitors tended to wait until it got really hot outside to eat.

Bo Peep was out on the cobblestones with her crook, looking for her sheep with a group of children. They tried calling the sheep like dogs—whistling and clapping their hands—which only made the sheep run away across the Village Green.

Jugglers and sword-swallowers (in their colorful, obscenely tight new outfits) were performing alongside fire eaters near the Main Gate. They joined musicians and wenches hand-ing out brochures to welcome visitors streaming into the Village.

We went inside Peter's and sat down at a dark corner table. It was cool and smelled like frying food—a wonder-ful combination. Peter's tavern wench (his sister, Maude) was waiting tables that summer while she took a break from East Tennessee University. She brought us ale in two pew-ter mugs, not caring that we had mugs at our sides for free drinks all day. Peter's was always resident friendly.

"So Detective Almond thought the Rizzo brothers were guilty, huh? That was his big secret this morning?" I started after we ordered.

"It makes sense." Chase took a big gulp of ale. "The three of them always fought over women. Maybe one of them got fed up. I should remind you that just because they say they didn't do it, doesn't mean they didn't."

"And they have alibis, right? What do you think?"

"Possibly not great alibis. But I don't think either one of them killed him. It might seem logical from a police stand-point, but I don't believe it."

"Who then?"

He shrugged. "I don't know. I thought Andre looked a little nervous."

"He had two big men with swords facing him," I defended the hatmaker. "Anyone *normal* would seem a little nervous."

"Maybe. But what about the hat pin, Jessie? It had to be there for a reason, even if it wasn't the murder weapon. I like Andre, but the hat pins are kind of his signature, like Marco said."

"He just doesn't seem the type to me. I haven't known him that long, but he can't even intimidate his assistants. Can you imagine him doing something like killing a person?"

Our sandwiches and fries arrived on pewter platters. A hand that wasn't mine reached for one of my fries before I could and a hip slid next to mine on the wooden bench.

"On the other hand, even the most gentle person in the world can work themselves up to kill someone for the right motive," a voice next to me said.

I looked at one of the pirates from the *Queen's Revenge*. He had started out here as an undercover officer, helping Chase. Then Tom Grigg went native, as sometimes happens, and he ended up as a full-time pirate—eye patch, greasy hair, and all.

"Are you saying Andre had a motive for killing Cesar?" I asked him, strategically moving my fries away from him.

"You should talk to the King's Tarts. Eloise in particular. There's been something going on there between Andre, Eloise, and Cesar." Grigg snatched another fry and took a quick gulp of my ale.

"If you know something," Chase said, "you should tell your old boss."

Grigg frowned. "Nah. He always thinks I'm coming back when I talk to him. Besides, no one else will say anything. But they'll talk to *you*, Bailiff. Ask around. You might get some surprising answers."

He reached for my tankard again, but I quickly moved it out of reach. "Get your own! You guys make more money than me."

"We used to—until the Knights Templar decided that what we do doesn't meet with their code of conduct. They've had Crystal over there for the last three days. We can't get near their tents."

Crystal was the pirate queen. All the men worked for her, even babysitting her child, though they were all employees of Adventure Land. "What happened to her bodyguards?" Chase asked.

"No match for the boys on the horses. They've been in the hold since they lost her."

"That's a long time in the hold," Chase remarked. "Get them out of there and I'll talk to the knights again. Be prepared in case Crystal just decided to go over."

"I don't care." Grigg shrugged. "It'll give me a chance to fight Rafe to be king. But if she's gone for good, she needs to come and get her baby."

He gave us both a quick grin to show off his new gold tooth replacements. When he was gone, I asked for a new tankard. "Okay, Crystal is kind of weird but I don't think she'd leave her baby on purpose with the pirates."

"I agree with you. The knights have shows all afternoon, but this evening, I'll pay them a visit."

I was a little surprised by him putting it off again. I watched him, the love of my life, drinking his ale with gusto. Was he afraid of the knights? I've never known Chase to back off any problem—except this one. I wanted to ask him what was wrong, but I didn't want him to think I was accusing him of cowardice. I had to wait for the right moment.

"What's up with those guys anyway?" I asked, hoping to coax it out of him.

"I don't know. It doesn't help that they're so popular. Adventure Land is acting like people are only coming to see them."

Maybe that was the problem. Maybe Adventure Land wasn't backing him up. Maybe he wasn't afraid.

"What are you thinking about?" he asked. "You haven't even touched your food."

"Did you see the hand that stole my fries? *Eww!*"

He laughed. "Want some new ones?"

"No. That's okay. Do you think Grigg is onto something about Andre, Cesar, and Eloise?"

"I guess I'll find out. I'll talk to Eloise first."

I thought about that. The King's Tarts—Eloise, Belle, and Angela—were basically the female counterparts of the Chocolatiers. Large, heaving bosoms, low-cut gowns, beautiful faces—it was pretty easy for them to sell every male at least one slice of pie.

"Why don't you let me do that," I suggested. "Eloise might be more willing to talk to a woman, you know?" Not

that I believed *that* for a second. She'd be crying and slob-
bering all over Chase in a heartbeat. I admit to being worried that Chase could succumb to their wiles in his weakened
state. They might take advantage of him.

"Jessie, I appreciate the offer, but you know I don't like
you to get involved in these things."

"But I've been a big help before, right? Let me do this,
Chase. I can help. You talk to Andre. I still have to work
with him, and he might not like me asking him questions
when I just met him."

He thought it over. "All right. But no conclusions and no
follow-up to whatever Eloise tells you. You come straight
back to me with it."

"You got it."

We (Chase) finished eating, and we kissed at the door as
we were leaving. A large group of Japanese visitors applauded
and took a dozen pictures before they politely asked us to take
pictures with each of them.

When that was over, I scooted past the Romeo and Juliet
pavilion, where that couple was talking to a good-sized
crowd. I went past the Hands of Time clock shop, thinking
that might make an interesting apprenticeship. I'd have to
remember to put in for it. No doubt it was somewhere on
my list already.

The Lovely Laundry Ladies were shouting out bawdy
insults to the crowd that passed them, moving slowly across
the King's Highway. They must've already washed a lot of
clothes at the Village well since they were soaked. Probably felt good in the heat.

Pat Snyder, playing William Shakespeare, was quoting
odes to the pretty girls who went past his pavilion behind
the Glass Gryphon and Sir Latte's Beanery.

It took me almost twenty minutes to reach the King's
Tarts Pie Shop. Maybe Adventure Land was worried about
fewer visitors, but if numbers were down, I couldn't tell.
People in Renaissance garb were crushed in, with visitors

wearing bikini tops and short shorts who rubbed elbows with fairies, trolls, and a goblin or two.

I looked at Brewster's, next to the tart shop, with longing, already sorry I didn't get another tankard of ale after abandoning mine when Grigg's lips touched it. I promised myself a frozen lemonade from one of the traveling carts after talking to Eloise.

The pie shop was busy, large groups of men—all ages, from knaves to knights—trying to get close to one of the women. Apparently, Eloise, Belle, and Angela had also received the Village notice to wear their blouses cut lower. I swear, they left very little to the imagination.

Cherry pie seemed to be the tart of the day. Belle and Angela passed out their wares while Eloise took the money. She looked flushed from the heat but not at all grieving over Cesar's death. If there was something going on between them, she had to be over it already.

I had to wait until the crowd thinned out after King Arthur pulled the sword from the stone. Besides low-cut blouses and pie, the men in the shop seemed to also be drawn to shiny metal objects.

Eloise collapsed into a chair behind the counter while Angela and Belle cleaned up. She was the eldest of the tarts, probably in her midthirties. It was easy to tell who the boss was—she and Cesar would've made a good pair.

"Hi!" I approached her with a smile and a jaunty attitude. "Your visitor numbers don't seem to be down."

"Hi, Jenny." Eloise pulled out a fan and began wafting warm air at her face. "How's Chase?"

"Jessie, actually." I kept smiling. What did I expect? "Chase is fine. He wanted me to pick up some pie. Too bad he hates cherry pie. He wanted blueberry. You know how it is."

"I think he'd like *my* cherry pie, if he'd come himself," Eloise goaded me further. "I guess you don't let him stray too far when you're here. Lucky for him you go back to school in the fall."

I reminded myself that I didn't come here to exchange insults with her. Just the opposite. I gritted my teeth. She was supposed to cry on my shoulder and tell me everything. I had to start over.

"That was a terrible thing that happened to Cesar."

"Yes, it was. He was a lovely man. I've never seen anyone wield a sword the way he could. I miss him already."

"But I thought you were dating Andre." I watched her carefully for any sign of discomfort.

She kept fanning. "Andre?"

"Andre Hariot, at the Hat House. I heard you were seeing him."

"I see a lot of people. Just because I miss Cesar doesn't mean I'm going to hide in a nunnery or something. Even if this was a real Renaissance village, I wouldn't be that kind of girl."

"So you don't know anything about Andre and Cesar fighting over you?"

She leaned forward, her bosom straining her blouse, her long hair falling forward. "*Everyone* fights over me, Jessie. That's who I am. I can't keep them from wanting me. You know how it is. Or maybe you don't."

This conversation seemed to be leading nowhere. There was just one more thing. "What about you, Eloise? Ever get jealous or fight over a man?"

Her face was shuttered as she sat back and put her fan away. "I'm sorry, I can't talk anymore. I have to get back to work. Tell Chase I'll bake him a blueberry pie and bring it over to comfort him—after you leave the Village."

I walked out of the shop with my hands clenched. Too bad someone didn't kill her instead.

Eight

I forgave myself that uncharitable thought as I sat on an elephant-shaped bench drinking a frozen lemonade near a fountain. Talking to Eloise hadn't been what I expected, but I had learned something—it was possible she could have been responsible for Cesar's death.

"I don't think so." Chase didn't agree with my theory when we met up outside the Hat House awhile later. "Even if she wasn't overcome with grief, that doesn't mean she killed him."

"But think about it. She's only a few doors down. She looks strong enough to hit him in the head and hold him in the chocolate. We all know Cesar never took his ladies too seriously. What if she got jealous?"

"I think your conversation with her proves she's not the jealous type. She dates a lot of men. Why suddenly get jealous about Cesar?"

"I don't know. But she looked suspicious when I mentioned it."

"That's not much of a reason."

"How about that she told me she'd bring you blueberry pie after I go back to school? I really don't like her."

He laughed and hugged me. "I don't even like pie. It's too—doughy. I take it she didn't want to have girl talk, huh?"

"Not really. How'd it go with Andre?"

"About the same. He says he barely knew Cesar and would certainly like to be with Eloise. But that goes for most of the men in the Village. Maybe we should trade suspects."

"Okay," I agreed. "But I better not see any cherry pie on you when you get back."

We parted company again until dinner, this time more carefully so that no visitors were watching. Normally I enjoyed living my whole life in the Village like I was on stage. It only bothered me once in a while.

Livy and her groupies were gone when I got back to the Hat House. No doubt everyone in the Village had found out Livy was pregnant while I was questioning Eloise. It was definitely unexpected.

I hoped King Harold was happy with the news. I hoped it was his baby. He and Livy were notorious for their many love affairs. As far as I knew, there had never been any children. This could be a life-changing event for both of them.

I sneaked in and joined the group working on hats like I had been there the whole time. Andre was busy cutting out patterns and kind of looked up but didn't say anything. It wasn't long before I was cutting ribbon with the rest of them.

We were working on thirty hats with wide brims and flowers that would be worn by a group of musicians visiting the Merry Mynstrel's Stage. A flute and harp group would add their music to some of the regulars in the Village. I kind of wondered at their choice of hats. It seemed to me like the brims would be in the way if you were trying to read music and play a flute.

The hats were all natural straw. We were adding ribbon

and flowers, tacking them in place. It was easy work compared to some of my other apprenticeships. I knew I wasn't learning in-depth hat-making skills, but I hoped that would come later.

I looked up when I saw Andre put down his scissors and go sit in a corner by himself. I watched him stare blankly out the window for a few minutes before deciding that this was my chance to speak to him. Maybe I could learn something Chase hadn't.

"I'm sorry I was running a little late from lunch," I began what I hoped would be an informative conversation.

"That's fine." He waved his diminutive hand that was holding a lacy handkerchief. "It doesn't matter. None of it really matters anymore."

"Is something wrong? Is there anything I can do?"

He looked at me and laughed in a melancholy way. "Maybe if you'd made that offer long ago, there might have been something. But that would be saying you had a magic wand and could fix everything in my life."

"Sorry. I don't have that. But I'm a good listener. I was just talking to Eloise—"

The transformation was instantaneous. Andre went from unhappy to alert and smiling. "You were? And how is she? A lovely woman. Did you notice her skin? Like pale, creamy cocoa. And her eyes—like shining brown diamonds. How is she doing today?"

I guess that answered the question about Andre being in love with Eloise. "She seemed fine. I thought she might be upset about Cesar's death. I'd heard they were close. Maybe dating."

He made a spitting sound, but I didn't see any actual saliva. He got to his feet and paced the best he could around hat boxes and yards of satin. "They were *never* dating! Cesar fancied himself such a great lover. But I've had Eloise's heart for a long time. She loves me. Cesar was never her choice."

So what Grigg said was true. Both men were in love—or at least in lust—with Eloise.

"Do you think Eloise could have killed Cesar?" No point in beating around the bush.

He became outraged. "I'm glad I don't have my scissors with me, young woman. Those could be fighting words. It's as ridiculous as asking if *I* killed him."

"Did you?"

"You're only asking because his half-brain brothers think I killed him to gain the hand of the beautiful Eloise. What they don't understand is that she loves me and could never stand Cesar. No need for me to kill him." He seemed to remember who he was speaking to and shrugged. "Not that I would have anyway."

"Of course not." I believed him. Again, common sense seemed in his corner. I couldn't imagine him doing anything remotely violent. He fainted at the sight of Bernardo and Marco's swords. That was in his favor, as far as I was concerned. It was easier (and more fun) for me to imagine Eloise killing Cesar.

There didn't seem to be much more to say. I started to turn away and rejoin the hat-decorating group when Andre stopped me. "I have an errand for you to run, Jessie. I hope you don't mind. I've finished one of Queen Olivia's hats and thought it might cheer her up to take a look at it. Did I ever tell you about when I was on the set of *Xanadu* with Olivia Newton John? Such a wonderful young woman. Such delicate features. It didn't matter what you put on her. It looked good."

While he was telling me his story, he was also putting a large, rose-covered hatbox in my hands. He finished telling me about his run-in with John Travolta, then kind of patted me on the head and sent me on my way to the castle.

It was hotter outside and dark clouds were threatening rain. I hoped the hatbox could protect the hat inside if it got wet. Having a squishy, ruined hat wouldn't make Livy feel any better.

I was surprised to find my very large friend, Bart Van Impe, headed in the same direction. I hadn't seen him since I got to the Village this summer. He'd traded his formal garb as one of the queen's protectors for a simple shopkeeper's outfit. It suited him.

"Hello, fair lady," he greeted me. "I haven't seen you for a while. Did you just get here?"

"I've been here a few days, kind sir. How goes the sword business?"

"Very well." He held up a long, narrow box that looked small in his large hand. "You see? Daisy and I finished a new sword for the king. He's going to love it. Perfect balance!"

"I have a hat for the queen," I told him. "Maybe we should trade. Can I see?"

His heavy features puckered up and he rubbed his chin. "I think you could do that. But don't tell anyone or it could be off with my head."

"I won't tell anyone. Let's duck into one of the alleys between the houses at Squire's Lane and take a look. You can see Livy's hat, if you want."

"Sure. But I'm with you. I'd rather have the sword."

We showed each other what we carried. The sword was amazing. The balance and weight of it was fantastic. It also had little rubies in the hilt. I had definite sword envy.

The hat, on the other hand, was different. It was a very nice white silk hat, lots of red roses and white silk trailing down from it.

Bart and I both shrugged and closed the hatbox again so we could admire the sword together. That got old after a few swishes, too.

"Have you heard the news?" he asked me as we started walking toward the castle again.

This was my chance to share a little gossip. "I heard that Livy got some news today."

"So it's true! The queen is pregnant."

"How did you hear?" I don't know why I bothered asking. The whole Village must know by now.

"I don't remember. I've heard it so many times." He shrugged his massive shoulders and laughed. "It's good news, right? A baby is a good thing."

It was hard to realize, looking at Bart, that he had the soul of a butterfly. He might be a giant in stature but he was like a little boy in his heart.

"A baby is a good thing," I agreed. "I hope Livy thinks so, too."

"I heard there was a murder. One of those chocolate men. I never liked their costumes. Too flashy. I heard one of his brothers might've killed him."

"Really? Which one?"

"I don't know. I can't tell them apart. Daisy says it's because I'm allergic to chocolate or I'd remember them like she does."

I laughed at that. Daisy Reynolds, sword maker, thought all the men in the Village were hot. But at least for now, Bart seemed to be her main man. "Did you hear why one of his brothers supposedly killed him?" I thought I might as well get the scoop from everyone. You never knew where the truth might lie.

"The new fortune-teller next to Wicked Weaves told me Phil from the Sword Spotte told her he saw Cesar and the tart lady arguing by the Swan Swing one night. He told her she had to give back some expensive jewelry she got, and she told him she'd see him dead first. The brothers argued over everything. It makes sense one of them gave her the jewelry."

"Jewelry, huh? And now everyone thinks it was from one of the brothers." I nodded. It made Village sense and probably hit the grapevine like the madmen in the Village hit their spoons on their pots to get attention.

"That's what I heard. But, then again, I heard she got the jewelry from one of the new knights."

Could the Knights Templar be involved in this? If this were one of those crime-solving TV shows, I'd say yes. The knights had been quick to come up and see what was happening after we found Cesar. And murderers always returned to the scene of the crime.

"What makes you say that about the knights?"

He shrugged. "I don't know. Everyone is blaming them for everything else. And they are a little annoying, don't you think? Hey, look! There are the mermaids!"

Nine

The mermaids were in their newly constructed, concrete lagoon. They reminded me of the mermaids in the old Peter Pan movie. The concrete wasn't so noticeable, since it was formed into rocks and shapes around the clear, blue water. It was pretty impressive.

They probably had the best job in the Village, at least during the summer, since they went in and out of the water all day. I wasn't sure if that attraction could hold up to colder breezes in December.

But for now, they basked on the rocks and put flowers in their hair while visitors snapped pictures. They wore shiny bikini tops and had long green and blue fish tails that were probably uncomfortable. I watched them flick their tails a few times for effect, singing pretty little songs that were supposed to lure visitors the way sailors had believed, once upon a time, that mermaids could lure them to their deaths.

The lagoon was carved from a piece of Mirror Lake, where the pirate ship used to dock. It was dammed up from the rest of the water—little, sparkling waterfalls surrounding it.

It was a placid little area of make-believe—like the rest of the Village—until lightning struck too close for comfort, sending all five mermaids screeching into the water. Obviously not the brightest of creatures.

"We'd better hurry," I urged Bart. He was too big to run but he could kind of throw himself headlong in the direction he wanted to go. "Looks like a bad one rolling in for the night."

"And I'm like a human lightning rod with my sword. At least all you have is a hat."

"A hat that will be ruined if it gets wet!" I started running toward the castle. Bart lumbered behind me.

The rain started falling with hard, angry drops as we sprinted (at least I sprinted) past the Hanging Tree and the Lady of the Lake Tavern. Thunder shook the ground as the pirates on the *Queen's Revenge* scurried to take in her sails.

That got me thinking about Crystal, the pirate queen, wondering if she was back yet. I was going to have to figure out some way to urge Chase into the Templar Knights' encampment in case she needed help. Maybe Bart would go, too, in case Chase needed him. They could also ask around to see if any of the knights had given Eloise the jewelry Cesar was so jealous of. My money was still on Eloise as the killer, but I've been known to be wrong.

I'd definitely have to go out with them since I needed to see what was going on in the encampment, too. It was intriguing—so many women lured into the forest. I wasn't worried about the knights' effect on me since I figured I was immune. There couldn't be a knight out there who could match Chase Manhattan.

Breathing hard, Bart and I made it into the castle without too much damage to ourselves or the packages we carried. Master at Arms Gus Fletcher greeted us from his usual spot in the entryway. He was a former professional wrestler (still only half the size of Bart) who liked to pinch ladies' butts as they walked past him. I was careful to maneuver through the doorway keeping Bart between me and Gus.

"Hey, Lady Jessie." Gus grinned and nodded to me. "Where's your fella? If you're looking for someone to keep you company on this rainy day, you know where to find me."

Bart stopped walking and looked down at Gus like he was a small child. "It's not very nice to flirt with other people's ladies. You should be careful that some man doesn't punch you in the nose."

Gus laughed a little, but he also backed away from Bart. That made *me* laugh. Not many people wanted to argue with a giant.

We headed into the castle through the keep, which contained the Great Hall where the King's Feast is held every Sunday evening. The hall was big enough to seat a few hundred visitors above the jousting arena where most of the entertainment took place. I say most of the entertainment because so much went on with the Royal Court at the other end. It was just more subtle, and you had to know the players.

There were fake weapons and coats of arms decorating the stone walls. Imitation wall hangings were bright and colorful for the thousands of visitors who walked through here each day.

But the residential side of the castle was filled with the good stuff. Livy and Harry had brought in hundreds of antiques and other treasures to make their castle fit for the royalty they were. Visitors never entered this part of the castle, unless they were special guests. If they were such nobility, they stayed in luxurious suites with Renaissance flair—and indoor plumbing.

From the moment we passed into the residential quarters, Bart and I could hear the weeping and moaning of Queen Olivia in her royal chambers.

"I don't think we should go in there," he said as we stood outside the closed door to her personal suite. "I think an animal must have got loose in there. Or a ghost. Either way, not good news for mortals like us."

"I don't have much choice. I have to give her this hat and make sure it fits okay." I smiled and patted his shoulder. "Lucky you, all you have to do is find the king."

"What makes you think he isn't in there with her?"

I laughed. "I worked here one summer. The king disappears when the queen goes into her fits."

"But what about her being pregnant? She shouldn't be alone at a time like this."

One bad thing about sneaking around with Bart—he didn't sneak. And he had a loud, booming voice that could be heard across a jousting field when he whispered. The next thing we knew, Queen Olivia had jerked open the door to her chambers and was ready to confront us.

Her eyes were red and puffy. Redheads (even those who used to be redheads and had to frequently visit the royal hairdresser to maintain those titian-esque locks) should never cry. They look even worse than blonds.

"What are you doing sneaking around out here? Are you gossiping about me being pregnant? It's a lie! If I were a real queen, I'd have that evil nurse's head on a pike outside the castle for telling such a falsehood."

I glanced at Bart. He made a hasty retreat down the long, stone hall, muttering about finding the king as he went. I dropped the queen a low, formal curtsy. "I am so sorry to bother you, Your Majesty. But Andre needs to make sure this hat will fit you."

She waved me into her chamber, blowing her nose loudly in a handkerchief. "What does it matter? None of my clothes will fit soon. I'll be a large whale of a queen who no one will want to see. Maybe Andre can make a hat big enough to fit over my whole body."

Olivia isn't exactly a tiny figure of a woman anyway. I didn't say it, but it was possible no one would even notice she was pregnant, especially in the right Renaissance clothes. "Perhaps the evil nurse"—I was certainly willing to agree with her on that point—"has made a mistake."

The queen flounced down on her red velvet sofa. It was then that I noticed all the modern-day pregnancy tests that surrounded her. I wasn't sure what they used in the Renaissance for this purpose, but in this case, all the tests seemed to be positive.

"Whatever will I do, Lady Jessie? The king will no longer love me or want to be with me when he learns I am with child."

I longed, nay, *yearned* to ask the question, *Is the baby Harry's?* But I didn't let the words come out of my mouth. "I'm sure Your Majesty will find the king pleased that he will be a father."

She batted her long eyelashes at me, black smears of mascara running down her pink face. "Do you really think so? We are both a little old to have children. I never even thought about it."

I guessed she was in her forties, probably. Harry, a few years older. It wasn't insane to think they could have a child. But I approached the idea from a different angle. "It would be wonderful for the Village. Imagine the birth of a new prince or princess. Imagine the extra events visitors could attend in conjunction with this blessed event."

Queen Olivia seemed to give that some thought. Before she could speak, however, King Harold himself burst into her chambers, his royal robes flowing around him. "Is it true, Livy? Are you really going to be a mother?"

I glanced toward the open doorway. Bart waved his fingers at me a little with a look on his face that told me how the king had found out about the baby.

"Yes, Harry. It seems I'm going to have a baby." She smiled at him through her tears in such a gentle, loving way. I'd never seen her look like that before.

King Harold stroked his chin and said, "Who's the father, my dear?"

Enraged, Livy got to her feet and began throwing test kits, fruit, and anything else her hand came upon at her husband. "How dare you? I can't believe you'd ask me that at a time like this! You pompous, ignorant, self-righteous man! Get out of here. Don't ever come back."

Harry beat a hasty retreat from the queen's chambers. Despite feeling in charity with Livy, I was glad he asked the question the whole Village would be asking. I wasn't sure if her anger was an answer. In truth, she might not even know who the father was herself.

I couldn't help feeling sorry for her as she stood there crying. She could be a miserable person to get along with since she seemed to really believe she was the queen of Renaissance Village and all that it implied. But right now she was a human being in pain. I went to her and hugged her close.

"He hates me," she sobbed into my bosom since she was too short to reach my shoulder. "He'll never believe it's his baby."

"You'll have to prove it to him," I counseled. "There are tests you can take."

"I won't. Either he believes me or he doesn't. My baby and I will live without him if we have to."

I hated to ask but I really needed her to try on Andre's hat. "If I could trouble Your Majesty to let me measure this hat for you. The hatmaker is waiting for me."

"Of course." She sniffed and raised her chin, wiping her eyes with the back of her hands like a child. "Life goes on, does it not? Let us try on this hat."

Ten

The hat was a perfect fit, and after a few more words of encouragement, I left it with Livy and headed out of the castle. It looked like Bart had left before me. I didn't blame him for going back to Swords and Such—and Daisy. Seeing Livy and Harry arguing over their child made me want to find Chase and hug him.

The king and queen were married and had been for years, but they seemed so unsure of their relationship. It always felt to me like Chase and I were on such solid ground. But would it last through something like this?

The storm was still raging outside. I couldn't hear it inside the castle through all the layers of cement and stone that had covered the old runway tower for the air force base where the Village was built.

I waited for the hard rain and frequent lightning flashes to end, standing in the entryway with a few servant wenches who were flirting with Gus (obviously not everyone minded the pinching).

I wasn't paying much attention until I heard Andre's name mentioned by a buxom blond wench. She'd overheard an argument between Beth Daniels, the Village costume designer, and Andre.

"I've never seen Beth so mad," the blond wench said. "She's usually so laid back, but in a nice way, you know?"

The brunette wench nodded. "I know. I can't believe she has a thing for the hatmaker. He's kind of puny. I don't know. Maybe I just like knights and lords better."

"Someone told me they used to go out. Then the little hatmaker caught Eloise's eye. Beth didn't have a chance after that."

"Who would?" Brunette wench sighed. "There must be more to Andre than we think. If Eloise wanted to date him, he must have something."

Blond wench nudged brunette wench. "Money! I was at Our Lady's Gemstones when he got that necklace. I think Beth heard about it and thought it was for her. Sorry! He gave it to Eloise."

"She probably pawned it."

"Or used it to make somebody else jealous."

They both giggled in a malicious way. "Too bad Cesar is dead. He and Eloise were perfect for each other," blond wench said.

"Yeah. Maybe since he died in chocolate, she'll end up in a pie shell."

The rain had begun to ease up by this time. There was still some thunder, but the lightning had moved away. The wenches made a run for it. Probably meeting a pirate at the Lady of the Lake Tavern. That's where I met my first pirate when I was a castle wench.

I walked a little more sedately down the King's Highway back toward the Hat House with the information from the wenches sizzling in my skull.

This could be the information that would help in the investigation of Cesar's death. Since I knew someone had heard Cesar and Eloise arguing about expensive jewelry she'd received, the wenches' conversation might clear some things up.

I already knew Andre had a thing for Eloise that wasn't necessarily returned—but she wasn't above taking gifts from him. She was obviously involved with Cesar and was flaunting her gift at him, probably trying to make him jealous. Knowing Cesar, she might have been trying to pin him down.

Proving what I'd heard at the castle would be really easy. I had to walk past Our Lady's Gemstones to get to the Hat House. What could it hurt to stop in and ask about Andre's purchase?

True, Chase wouldn't like it. And I had promised to report back to him before taking any action. On the other hand, I'd made that promise when I was going to visit Eloise. This could be construed as something totally different.

I wasn't sure what it would prove. Beth had a thing for Andre, who was in love with Eloise. He bought the tart an expensive piece of jewelry. Beth thought it was for her.

It seemed to me that if anyone would have been murdered out of that situation, it would be Eloise or Andre, killed by Beth in a jealous rage.

Still, being able to verify the information about the jewelry might be good. My wayward feet wandered past Eve's Garden and into Our Lady's Gemstones.

The shop had been taken over by a brother and sister last year. The original owner, Captain Jack Russell, had decided it was time to quit the business and retire to Florida. He used to spend all his free time fishing in Mirror Lake—but there were no fish, a fact he complained loudly about every chance he got. He was a character was Captain Jack, with his peg leg and large sea captain's hat. Surprisingly, he never got along with the pirates. He fancied himself more the English admiral sort.

Anyway, I hadn't been in the shop since Captain Jack

left. I had considered cutting and setting gemstones as a possible craft, but it was down on my list. I don't really know why since I liked sparkly, shiny things as much as the next person.

I was surprised to see how dark the shop had become. There were never many windows in Village shops but the few here were covered in deep purple velvet. No outside light—or breeze, for that matter—reached inside.

The lights were all on the gemstones. It was like walking into a dark cavern and being surrounded by sparkling, multicolor jewels waiting to be picked up. Only in this case, there was a high price to pay for pocketing any of the stones.

The idea was for visitors to pick out the kind of stone and setting they wanted and the jeweler would create the masterpiece as they walked around the Village or it would be shipped to them.

The settings were very nice, too. More than I could afford on my assistant professor's salary and my Village paycheck combined. I enjoyed looking at them, though, and had to admit the rather creepy atmosphere was perfect for them.

"May we be of assistance, milady? I am Rene and this is my sister Renee."

I jumped and dropped one of the sapphires I was admiring when I heard the voice and saw two ghostly faces coming toward me from the back of the shop. I hastily picked up the sapphire and put it back on its velvet bed—hoping it wasn't damaged.

"I was just—er—looking around," I stammered, totally thrown off by the pair. No one had told me the brother and sister were twins like me and my brother, Tony.

But there the likeness ended. These two looked exactly alike. I could only tell them apart because the woman had long white hair and the man had very short white hair. Not that either one of them looked to be much older than me.

Their eyes were an unearthly color of blue. Their perfect, pale faces were beautiful, like they had stepped out of a Botticelli painting or were sculptures come to life.

They were both dressed in matching purple velvet, despite the heat. What was even weirder was that neither one was sweating.

"What did you have in mind?" Renee asked me.

"I'm not really sure." Confronted with these two, I almost forgot why I was there. I mentally shook myself and began again. "I admired the necklace you made for Andre Hariot. I was wondering if you had something like it."

Rene nodded to his sister. "None of our work is exactly the same. We would be happy to make something similar, perhaps."

"That sounds fine. What would that price range be?"

"Around five thousand dollars," Renee replied. "We would need half up front and the rest when the piece was finished. Have you chosen your stone and setting?"

Wow! So now I'd confirmed that Andre had a very expensive necklace made for Eloise. Where would a former Hollywood hatmaker get that kind of money? I didn't think anyone in the Village could afford something like that.

Then I thought about Chase. His family was wealthy, though you wouldn't know it to look at him. Plus he worked as a patent attorney in his spare time. If he had the money, anyone could have it, including Andre. Who knew what secrets lay in people's pasts?

"I'm not really ready for that yet," I stalled. "I was hoping maybe my boyfriend might buy something like it for me."

"The bailiff?" Rene nodded. "The sapphire would be a wonderful choice, Lady Jessie."

Apparently they knew me even though I didn't know them. That was kind of scary. I was glad I hadn't seen them the first time on a dark night somewhere in the shadows of the Village. They reminded me too much of every evil vampire movie I had ever seen.

"Thanks. I'll have to see what I can do. I appreciate your time."

Both of them nodded solemnly, not so much as a trace of a smile on either face. "Of course. You know where to find us."

"Yes. I have to go now. See you around."

I backed out of the shop, afraid of not making it out alive. I knew Chase would tease me about it (once he got over being angry that I was there in the first place), but the two really creeped me out.

When I was outside, I felt like kissing the ground, only there was too much animal poop and sawdust to make that appealing. Regardless, I was glad to be out in the sunlight again. It was probably stupid to feel that way about them, but I couldn't help it. I ran all the way back to the hat shop.

Andre was alone when I got back. I told him Olivia was happy with her hat and that it fit her like it was made for her—which it was.

"Good. That's very good."

He seemed distracted. I wasn't sure he heard what I'd said. So I repeated it. This time he kind of muttered but didn't say anything I could understand.

"Is something wrong?" I asked.

"Have you ever wondered what your life would be like if you could remove all the mistakes from your past, Jessie?" He laughed and sat down at the window again. "Of course not. You're too young to have made those kinds of mistakes. I wish I hadn't, but life isn't always the way we think it will be. I wish I could change some of those things."

I wasn't sure if he was talking about the near past or distant past. Did he regret dumping Beth for Eloise? Was he sorry he'd put out that much money for the necklace he'd given the tart?

I didn't know him well enough to say. Andre was a different man under his trendy tunics and fastidious ways. "It's not always easy knowing what to do." I shrugged, feeling a little lame.

He smiled and seemed a little less tense and melancholy. "It's true. It's always easy to look back and see the mistakes you wish you hadn't made. Tell me, Jessie, how did our good queen seem when you visited her? I know there must be some juicy gossip floating around the Village by now."

I told him about Livy's unhappiness and Harry's rude question about the birth father. He rubbed his hands together. "This reminds me of when I was working on the set of *Ghostbusters* and we found out one of the script girls was pregnant. The rumor was that the baby belonged to one of the stars of the movie. No one could ever prove it and the script girl decided to leave. The next time I saw her, she was driving an expensive sports car and had traded up in the apartment arena."

We were both laughing about all the crazy antics he remembered from the *Ghostbusters* set when Chase came in. I was happy to see him until I noticed that little frown between his eyes that always gives away his more serious mood.

I was formulating my explanation for visiting Our Lady's Gemstones—I thought he'd heard about it somehow and now we were going to argue. I didn't question how he found out. It was bad enough that he did.

But that wasn't the problem. Chase nodded to Andre, ignoring me completely. "I'm afraid I have some bad news. Detective Almond is on his way to see you. He knows about your past."

Eleven

I would've asked but there wasn't time. Detective Almond and two officers were already following Chase in the Hat House door. "Manhattan! Why am I not surprised to see you here? I told you we could handle it."

"The deal is that I take care of the Village. That makes it easier for you. You don't have to come out here every five minutes to see what's going on. But I take it seriously when one of my people might be accused of murder."

I felt Andre's hand creep around mine. I squeezed his back for good measure.

"Fine." Detective Almond looked at me. "But we don't need your girlfriend here, right?"

"I'd rather she be here, if it's all the same with you," Andre said. "And I assume it is, since you're visiting me instead of taking me down to the station."

"That's right. You know the drill, don't you?" Detective Almond smiled slightly but his eyes were steely in his chubby red face. His shirt collar was dirty, like always, and there was a stain that looked like spaghetti sauce on his tie. "Okay. If you don't mind your little friend knowing the kind of man you really are, that works for me."

Andre smiled and patted my hand. "I've lived with what happened for a long time, Detective. It won't bother me."

"Well then, Mr. Hariot, I see from your police file that came in today that you were once a suspect in a murder investigation in Hollywood. Care to elaborate on that?"

"Not really. Since I assume you're here to question me about Cesar's death, what happened back then doesn't matter—except to prejudice you against me."

I wished someone would say what happened. I was about to explode with curiosity. I'd been thinking and telling everyone that Andre wasn't the right kind of person to kill anyone. Yet here he was, a suspect in another murder.

"That's your prerogative, of course." Detective Almond nodded. "What about you and Cesar Rizzo? You were both seeing the same woman, Eloise Santee. That couldn't have been easy, considering you're you and Rizzo was himself. Not to put too fine a point on it, he was younger, a little more apt to have someone like Ms. Santee go out with him."

Andre smiled. "If you mean by that comment that Cesar was a demon womanizer who never truly cared about anyone he ever dated, you're right, Detective. Eloise is in love with me, but Cesar kept pestering her. He wanted her for himself. She only wants me."

Detective Almond glanced at Chase, then said, "That's not the way we've heard it. Miss Santee and Rizzo were a couple when you started forcing yourself on her. You bought her gifts and tried to take her away. It's my supposition that when those things didn't work, you decided to take Rizzo out of the equation."

"You have no reason to assume that," Andre charged. His upper lip was quivering a little, making him look agitated.

"Maybe I do. The handmade hat pin—your signature, I

believe. But to clarify things, what exactly were you doing the night Rizzo died?"

"I was working on the new hat Queen Olivia ordered."

"See, that's what I mean about being out here." Detective Almond did a monologue for his officers. "It's crazy. Nothing makes any sense. The queen needed a hat. Anybody else believe that?"

Chase stepped into the discussion. "Were you alone, Andre?"

"As you know, Sir Bailiff, I frequently work at night after the Village has closed. So I suppose I was alone, yes."

"Can anyone verify that they saw you here between the hours of midnight and two A.M.?"

"I seriously doubt it," Andre responded. "But that doesn't mean I killed him."

"Like you didn't kill your wife in Hollywood either, right?" Detective Almond nodded to his officers. "I think you were right. We should continue this conversation at the station. If you'd come with us, Mr. Hariot. Maybe we can get to the truth in this matter."

There was nothing else to do but let the police take Andre. They didn't handcuff him or anything. He meekly walked between them out of the shop.

"That was unbelievable!" I sank down into the chair behind me again. "They think he killed Cesar *and* his wife in Hollywood?"

"It looks like it," Chase replied. "I don't know all of it yet, but whatever happened thirty years ago was bad enough that the police feel like he's a slam dunk for killing Cesar."

We kind of looked at each other for a moment then the same idea hit both of us.

"Google!" I yelled, getting to my feet.

"If there was a murder investigation, it should be out there somewhere," Chase agreed.

"I love Renaissance Village," I said, lifting the hem of my skirt to go past him. "But I'm glad we have the Internet."

The rest of the day and into the evening was cloudy and rainy, which meant fewer visitors until the Village closed and we had time to ourselves in Chase's apartment over the Dungeon. It didn't take long to locate the information about Andre. The whole scandal was chronicled in the newspapers and Hollywood insider magazines.

"So the police think Andre murdered his wife because she was sleeping around," I told Chase as he worked on his patent attorney paperwork and I perused the Internet while I ate cheese curls.

"How did Andre's wife die?" Chase asked.

"I know you aren't going to believe this—"

"Try me."

"There was a hat pin involved. The woman drowned in the pool, and the police would've gone with an accidental death because she'd been drinking. But there was a hand-made hat pin shoved in her eye."

"Sounds familiar."

"They had to let Andre go because the DA refused to indict him. He said there was insufficient evidence. But no other killer was ever found. The case is still open."

"And that's why Detective Almond thinks Andre killed Cesar." He nodded without taking his eyes off the screen where he was working. "I don't blame him. It sounds too similar not to be the same person."

"It's kind of spooky thinking about it." I shivered. "I could've sworn Andre wouldn't be capable of doing anything like that. You know him better. What do you think?"

He paused and shook his head. "It's an awfully big stretch between Myrtle Beach and Hollywood for the same basic crime to happen—and coincidental that Andre was involved in both cases."

I turned off the laptop and lay back on the bed. "Back to the frog catapult for me."

"Maybe not." Chase got up and lay down beside me. "Mayhap I can convince the powers that be that I need a lackey or a pretty minion. You could help me keep the Dungeon clean and get ripe vegetables to throw at evildoers in the stocks."

I sighed. "Like I said, back to the frog catapult."

"You'd rather help people throw frogs and win prizes than be with me?" He wrapped his arms around me. "I think I'm hurt."

"Wounded nigh to death you are, sir." I did my best pirate impression learned from my summer spent on the *Queen's Revenge*. "And in truth, I pity ye for falling for such a wench as meself. It can only bring ye trouble."

"Oh, lass," he whispered before he kissed me, "but a right pleasurable trouble it is."

Twelve

It was later, when we were sharing a snack, that things got ugly between me and Chase. All I asked is if he was going out to see the knights later, and he got angry.

"I wish everyone would understand that there's not much I can do about the knights. They sell tickets and they look good on brochures. That's all Adventure Land cares about. Everyone forgets that before the knights came, they were all complaining about Robin Hood stealing toaster ovens and snacks. Now it's the knights. That's the way it is."

I felt sorry for him, but he had a duty to the Village. I couldn't believe he was willing to shirk that responsibility. He never had before. "You know, Bart and some of the other guys would be willing to go out there with you. It's not like anyone expects you to confront them alone."

He laughed in a snickering kind of way. "I'm not afraid of the knights, Jessie. But there's not much point in me going out there and confronting them because the girls in the

Village want to be out there with them. They haven't broken any rules."

"I'm not saying you're afraid."

"Yes, you are. And I don't know why. Did someone else say I was afraid?"

My poor Chase. It was becoming even more apparent to me that he really dreaded going out there. I hugged him and told him it was okay. "No one blames you. They have big horses and everything."

"Jessie! I'm *not* afraid of the knights. I can get a big horse, too. It's not necessary. I'm not going out there unless one of them actually breaks the rules. Can we talk about something else?"

I immediately changed the subject. There was no reason to antagonize him. I started formulating a plan that would include a group of people from the Village, maybe a few of the more impressive guild heads, confronting the knights. There was a guild for each of the groups such as the Craft Guild, Weapons Guild, Magical Creatures Guild, and the Knave, Varlet, and Madman Guild. The Pirates, Nobility, and the Brotherhood of the Sheaf were all separate groups with their own heads.

I shouldn't have pushed Chase, I thought as I closed my eyes to go to sleep. Yes, he was big and, yes, he was usually good at telling people what to do. But anyone can face a foe too terrible to handle.

I lay there for a few minutes, listening to Chase's even breathing—he suddenly whispered my name. I was drowsy and comfortable, so I didn't answer right away. Imagine my total surprise when he got carefully out of bed, got dressed, and left the apartment.

I couldn't imagine where he was going or what he was doing. Obviously, he'd called my name to see if I was asleep.

If there was a problem, I would've heard the radio go off. What surprised me even more was that he'd left his radio on the bedside table when he went out. Now I was really curious. Where could he be going? Why didn't he want me to know?

I sat there for a few minutes, not sure what to do. Finally I got up and slipped my feet into sandals before I bounded down the stairs. Yes, I was wearing my pajamas, but they looked like a tank top and shorts. It was more important for me to find Chase than to bother with what I looked like.

I could barely make out his dark tunic as he walked down the cobblestones toward the Stage Caravan. A dancer! I should've known!

But then he suddenly veered right toward the privies. Okay. Maybe he wasn't cheating on me. Maybe he was inspecting the privies and didn't want to bother me. Usually that wouldn't be his job, but Chase didn't mind doing whatever needed to be done.

That wasn't right either. Chase walked past the privies and toward the edge of the forested area. A man dressed like one of the Templar Knights was waiting by the large sign that proclaimed the beginning of the encampment.

I hung back. This was something more than a woman. *Thank God!* It was probably something interesting instead of devastating. The fact that he didn't want me to know that he was going out here, and let me think he was afraid to confront the knights, made it even more of a priority to learn the truth.

Chase and the knight talked for a few minutes. Most of the normal sounds from the Village were silenced by the lateness of the night. I could still hear some of the animals calling out and some laughter probably coming from the Pleasant Pheasant. There was also a little music from somewhere that drifted by me toward the pine trees Chase and the knight were getting ready to enter.

I hung back, giving them time to get ahead of me. There were a few real torches scattered along what looked like a path leading into the forest. Normally, fire was discouraged in the Village, but no one cared what went on after the visitors went home. Robin Hood never had any lighting along the path to his tree house encampment at all. It was hard to get in and out without scratching or stubbing something.

When I saw Chase disappear along the path, I slowly began to follow him. I hugged the darkness away from the torches. The smell of freshly cut pine was strong as I crept along at the edge of the tree line. The torches heated up the already hot night, making it hard to breathe from the fumes as they burned.

As I left the Village behind me, I began to hear sounds and see flickering lights coming from the deeper part of the forest. The music was loud here and mixed with extravagant laughter. Obviously, someone was having a good time. Since it wasn't me, it made me angry. It was too hot to be out with dive-bombing mosquitoes swarming around me. There were already pine needles wedged in my sandals. Nothing about this trip to visit the knights was making me feel better.

I heard movement in the brush close to me and dropped down, breathing quietly. Two knights passed barely a few inches from my position. I looked the way they had come and saw the lighted area around the huge, black tents. Large fires were burning in pits, keeping the area well lit. As many as a dozen knights were standing around like they were waiting for something.

Once again, I had to admire their wonderful costumes and nicely made swords. No wonder everyone hated them and Chase didn't want to come out here. Everyone probably wanted to be them or was afraid of them.

But what was Chase's angle? He didn't seem afraid for his life when he met the knight at the entrance. If he wasn't afraid, why not come out and talk to them sooner? I'd seen him lay down the law on Robin Hood, the pirates, and every other group of miscreants in the Village. Why hold back on the Knights Templar?

I moved to get a better view of the knights and what they were doing, but a branch cracked under my weight. It sounded like cannon fire to me because I was so nervous. I waited for several minutes to see if anyone else had heard. The men in the encampment didn't seem to notice, and I took a deep breath of relief.

That was before a sword found its way to my back and a deep voice said, "What are you doing out here?"

Thirteen

"I demand that you release me," I shouted, hoping Chase would hear me. "The bailiff will hear of this! You better let me go."

All of these demands were made from a bad position—sitting on the ground by the fire, trussed up like a turkey and blindfolded. No wonder everyone hated the knights. I was starting to lean that way myself.

The music had stopped, but I could still hear muted talking. They were out there, just ignoring me. Or worse, trying to figure out what to do with me. I didn't like that part at all.

Where was Chase? I hoped he wasn't close by in the same condition. I knew it would take a lot more than being surprised by an attacker to tie him up and blindfold him. I wanted to kick myself for not putting up more of a fight— but I couldn't move my legs.

I kept reminding myself that this was Renaissance Village. Nothing really bad would happen. The knights might put on a good show, but I'd been kidnapped by pirates and the Merry Men before, not to mention the monks. It might seem scary but, in the end, it was all just good theater.

The smell of pine smoke from the fire was strong. It was getting a little too warm. I hoped they remembered I was here. While I didn't believe anyone would purposely hurt me, there were always accidents. I didn't want to be one of those.

I was about to start screaming again when I felt someone testing the rope that held me. "Sit very still, madam, if you value your limbs. I am going to free you now. I hope you won't make me regret my decision." The voice was very low and husky. I didn't think it was the knight from the morning Cesar died. But I couldn't be sure.

I felt something cold touch my skin as a knife cut the ropes that held me. I sat very still for that moment. I planned to get up and run as soon as I could. Maybe I could find a weapon and still give them a good fight.

"The blindfold stays on," the deep voice told me. "We can't have everyone knowing what goes on out here."

"I demand to see your leader."

"I am the leader of the Knights Templar."

"Oh. Well in that case, I demand to know where the bailiff went." I was feeling a little more courageous since I wasn't tied up.

"I think you should be more worried about yourself," the deep voice told me.

"I'm not leaving until I know where Chase is. I saw him come out here with one of your other knights. Where is he?"

I felt him lean closer to me. His voice was a whisper near my ear. "You may have given him away. Did you think about that? What if he came out here to spy on us and now we know about him. It's much wiser to think before you speak."

I hadn't thought about that. And I didn't believe it. Chase is always upfront. He might be afraid to confront the knights, but I had no doubt that he'd do it face-to-face when it happened.

"Thanks. I appreciate the advice. Can I leave now?"

"I thought you wouldn't leave without the bailiff?"

"Are you mocking me? If you are, you should know that I am the queen of retribution. You don't want to mess with me. Just ask the pirates, if you don't believe it."

"Time for you to leave." He helped me to my feet. I must have been sitting there cross-legged longer than I'd thought. I felt the pins and needles in my legs and would've fallen back to the ground if he hadn't caught me. "Careful. Don't be in such a hurry."

As I held on to him, I felt him moving away, clumsily taking me with him. I smelled horse and, before I knew it, I was up on the beast with the knight. "Where are we going?"

"You're going back to the Dungeon, where I feel sure the good bailiff awaits you."

"What about Queen Crystal and the other missing women from the Village?"

"They are not your concern, Lady Jessie. Don't return to our encampment. The next time could be your last."

Even though the large horse only walked down the trail between the trees, we were back in the Village in no time. I could tell because the smell of wood smoke and pine were replaced with popcorn and barbecue being made for the next day.

He slid me down the side of the horse like a sack of beans. I rushed to remove my blindfold and have a good look at him, but he was gone too quickly. I felt like shaking my fist and cursing him for good measure, but it wouldn't do any good.

I had to admit it was an interesting, if infuriating, experience. All that leather and wood smoke is very attractive. I could tell he was strong—I was nothing for him to lift, and I'm no lightweight. I also understood why the women of the Village were headed out to the black tents. Not that I'd be one of them since I was totally committed to Chase.

"Jessie?" Chase asked when I finally got upstairs (it took me a few minutes to get the pine needles out of my sandals). "Where have you been?"

"I could ask you the same thing." I nudged him as I walked by. "You ran off in the middle of the night, making me think you were seeing someone else. Then you left me in the encampment."

"You followed me out there?"

"I just told you—I thought you were with a fairy or a dancer. What did you expect me to do?"

"You knew I was going to talk to the knights. I can't believe you thought I was seeing someone else."

"So what happened out there?"

"Not much. I told them they had to stop interrupting shows. That's really the only thing they've done wrong, at least as far as I'm concerned."

"And then you just left."

"I didn't know you were out there. You shouldn't have followed me. The knights get a little testy when they find strangers sneaking around."

I didn't tell him about my return trip from the forest. I threw my sleeping bag (I always bring it to the Village just in case) on the floor and grabbed a pillow from the bed. I also didn't tell him about the man who brought me back. There was no point, even though I could still feel his lips whispering close to my ear.

"You don't have to sleep on the floor," Chase said. "I can't believe you're making such a big deal about this. I get called out all the time during the night. What's the difference?"

"The difference is that you purposely sneaked out. That's the difference. Good night, Chase."

He sighed but didn't argue. When the light was switched off again, he said good night. I ignored him and closed my eyes. It wouldn't hurt him to realize how upset I was. Maybe next time, he'd tell me what was going on so I'd know it was okay.

I didn't plan to dream about the knight with the smoky voice, but it happened. In the morning, I shrugged it off. I wasn't attracted to him—just angry at Chase. It made me feel guilty anyway.

Chase and I had breakfast and parted ways in better spirits than we had going to sleep. I wasn't sure what I should do since Andre was at the police station. I didn't want to take another job until I knew what was going to happen. So I walked over to the Hat House anyway, thinking I could hang out there while I waited. To my surprise, I found all the little assistants were there working on the hats.

"Good morning, Jessie." Andre smiled and wiped his forehead with a clean white handkerchief. "You're running late again, I see. I know watches aren't allowed while the visitors are here, but surely you and Chase have an alarm clock."

"I didn't think you'd be here," I confessed. "What happened at the police station?"

"Suffice it to say, the police don't have any real proof that I was involved with what happened to Cesar. My hat pins are available to anyone who comes in the shop. They don't have my fingerprints anywhere at the crime scene. There was nothing to hold me on."

I understood then what Detective Almond meant about Andre knowing his way around the procedure. I didn't think most people would realize their fingerprints needed to be somewhere around a dead body. Andre was very calm and understanding of the whole thing.

"Sure. Sorry. What do you want me to do?"

"Since you're the last warm body here, I'd like you to clean the shop a little. Some ladies are coming by for fittings. I thought it would be nice for them to be able to get in the door."

I shrugged. Such is the life of an apprentice. I thought

Andre and I had reached a different level yesterday, but apparently I was wrong. "I'll take care of it."

He nodded, not taking his eyes from his assistants.

I opened the door to the shop from the work area and took a deep breath. Andre was right. The place was a total wreck. It looked like a tornado had gone through, leaving bits and pieces of fabric and hat material everywhere.

I started with the larger pieces of silk, satin, and felt that were still on the bolts and got them up on the worktables. The rest had to be swept up and gone through carefully since I knew Andre saved all but the tiniest scraps. I finally discovered the counter and cash register and knew I was on the right track.

In an hour, I could see the rough floor boards. The larger scraps were in cloth bags (no plastic here), and the smallest ones were in several barrels where they belonged. I was tidying a massive stack of stiff hat brims for the large, plumed hats when I was reminded of the fact that Cesar had been found covered by his large, red hat.

It made me think about the handmade hat pin, too. If Andre wasn't guilty of killing Cesar, whoever was wanted everyone to think he'd done it. The clues were set up to make sure that fact wouldn't escape notice. Why would anyone want to frame Andre?

What the castle wenches said about Beth came to mind. What if Cesar's death was more about getting even with Andre than about killing Cesar? The chocolatier may have been collateral damage.

Could Beth be capable of trying to hurt the man who'd rejected her? Her motive—despite my own self-interest— was much stronger than Eloise's. The tart had been getting everything she wanted, a devoted slave with money and a handsome stud who could keep her happy.

I didn't like thinking about Beth that way. I liked Beth. She was hardworking and a nice person. I didn't want her to be guilty of anything. Portia, on the other hand, would be okay to take away in chains.

Unfortunately, the more I thought about Beth—rejected and humiliated as the man she loved pursued a bosomy tart—the more it made sense. Beth wasn't a dainty woman. She could have hit Cesar over the head, stuffed his face in the liquefied chocolate, and crammed a hat pin in his eye.

Maybe she knew about Andre's past, too. Chase and I had found the information easily enough. Anyone with that information would know how to make Andre look guilty by using the hat pin idea from the previous murder.

I stopped sweeping and sat down on one of the chairs I'd found buried under piles of material.

Andre was in the clear, according to the police. Cesar wasn't the most likeable of men. Maybe his death could be one of the thousands of unsolved murders that happened every year. Not everything was fair and just. If I never said anything about Beth, the police would probably never think to question her.

It was a heavy weight on my conscience. Maybe if I went and talked to Beth, she might have a great alibi for the time Cesar was killed. Then I wouldn't have to feel guilty and it would be obvious that she had nothing to do with this.

I put down the broom and would've left the shop, but Andre came to look for me. "I need you at once. Hurry, Jessie."

The emergency was a visit from Princess Isabel. She looked like she'd been crying—no doubt worried about her royal position in the court now that the king and queen were going to have a real child. Isabel was just an actress hired to play the part. Her fate was anyone's guess. They could decide to keep her on as she was or they could turn her out of the castle to do menial labor if she wanted to stay in the Village.

There had been several princesses who hadn't lasted in

the part. Isabel had been there for a while, but that didn't guarantee anything. Major characters were recast sometimes.

I couldn't say I'd miss her since she always insisted on flirting with Chase, but I felt sorry for her that morning. She looked awful. I knew how hard it was to be out of a job.

When I got in there with Andre, I could see my duty was to help her calm down enough to buy a hat. Shopping was always therapeutic—it didn't surprise me that she'd taken that route to alleviate her stress.

Several of her waiting courtiers were already at her side to give her comfort. They patted her hand, offered her chocolates, and generally tried to make her feel better. She might not be Olivia and Harold's daughter in real life, but she certainly sounded like the queen. Maybe she was rehearsing to take Livy's part in case the queen had to leave after her pregnancy.

Andre watched her in frustration. "You there"—he pointed to one of his assistants—"get me some lemon balm tea from Mrs. Potts. And don't forget the honey cookies. Maybe those will help."

"Is there something I can do to help?" I hoped it would be something more productive than watching Princess Isabel cry. It was too hot to be so irritated.

Andre nodded and had me follow him out of the room. "You know, one thing about the great actresses, they worked when they were supposed to work. I know everyone isn't 'on' twenty-four hours a day around here, but a little professionalism would go a long way. I really think some of the actors in Renaissance Village have forgotten that they're acting!"

I couldn't disagree with him. Of course this place wasn't a movie set with start and stop times. It was easy to get lost in the part. I didn't bother saying anything since it seemed he just needed to vent.

"I need you to pick up a few things for me. I'll give you a list. Everything is paid for, so all you have to do is fetch it."

"Okay." I didn't mention that fetching wasn't really learning how to make hats. Things were tense enough without putting that out there.

He gave me the list, written in his flowery script, and waved his hand impatiently when I didn't leave the shop right away. "I need those things yesterday. Don't dawdle."

Thus dismissed, I went outside and took a better look at what my master needed. Some of it made sense—silk flowers from Eve's Garden, a crocheted scarf from Lady Cathy's Crochet, a scarf from Sarah's Scarves, and some material from Stylish Frocks.

Yes! Just the place I needed to go if I wanted to talk to Beth.

The other things were more personal. He wanted scented oil from Cupid's Arrow where my good friend, Adora, sold love potions, lingerie, and incense. He also wanted me to pick up jewelry at Our Lady's Gemstones. *Eww!* That meant I'd have to face the twins again.

There was no getting around it. I started along the cobblestones toward Stylish Frocks first. I'd probably visit the gemstone shop last even though it was next door to Beth's shop. Maybe if I did it last, it wouldn't be so bad.

Stylish Frocks made costumes for the entire Village. Residents wore their garments every day. Visitors bought their costumes for elaborate prices and paraded them around the Green. Every costume imaginable, from fairies to dragons, horses, and elegant ladies and gentlemen, was created here. Beth Daniels was at the heart of it all. She was amazingly talented. I'd seen her look at a picture of a wedding gown and create one exactly like it. She always seemed tireless and had a good sense of humor.

But not today. Beth stood in the middle of twenty-five seamstresses whose sewing machines were always humming. If Andre's Hat House was messy, Stylish Frocks was always neat. There was never any excess material lying around. Not even a colored thread would dare be out of place.

Today, there seemed to be some problem with a multi-colored gown that had sixty layers swirling with lace and satin. Beth was frowning as she looked at it with the seamstress who was putting it together. "This sherbet color can't go here," she told the other woman. "It has to be blue here."

"That's not what they gave me," the seamstress objected. "It'll take me the rest of the day to rip it out."

"Then you better get started," Beth snarled.

Was this the result of a guilty conscience? I wondered. I'd never seen her this way. I hated to even catch her attention and tell her what Andre needed. She was carrying a pair of large scissors in her hand as she walked toward me. I hoped they wouldn't end up in one of my body parts.

"Hello, Jessie," she greeted me nicely enough. "What can I do for you?"

"Hi, Beth." I dragged out my words, wishing I didn't have to say them. "I need some material you're holding here for Andre."

Her face contorted. If ever I could imagine a look from someone who wanted to kill a person, this would be it. Of course, she hadn't killed her ex-lover. Could she have killed Cesar to set him up?

"That slimy little weasel." She threw her scissors down on a perfectly organized worktable. "He should've come himself. I'd like to have the chance to give him a piece of my mind. But every time I go to look for him, he seems to vanish. Or at least that's what his assistants say."

Without the scissors, Beth just looked tired and sad. She raked her hand through her short red hair and adjusted her multipocketed coat that was always full of buttons, needles, and thread. She wasn't exotic like Eloise or even particularly attractive. She looked like she'd had a hard life without much happiness in it.

"If you went over there yesterday, he was probably at the police station." I offered the information carefully like

I was giving food to a wild animal. I watched her face and waited for her response.

"The police?" She sighed. "What did he do now? Did he start running after a fairy who reported him?"

"They were questioning him about Cesar's death." There it was. On the table. What would she do with it?

Fourteen

"I need a cigarette," Beth said. "I gave it up this year, but that was before Andre decided he could live without me. Want to come outside?"

We stood near the back door where smoke wouldn't go inside but Beth could see what was happening. I could see the mermaids flirting with passing visitors. They could seriously become more obnoxious than the fairies even though they were trapped in their lagoon. I smiled as I imagined them dragging their colorful tails through the Village streets to pursue one of the knights or a Merry Man.

"I've known Andre for years," Beth said between puffs of smoke. "You think you're safe with someone like that. I even thought with all of the hunky men in the Village, the girls would leave him alone. Not a chance."

I didn't want to point out that Eloise hadn't pursued Andre. He just fell in lust with her like so many other men. "It's only physical." I tried to help her feel better. "Andre probably still loves you."

"Well, he's got an odd way of showing it." She threw the cigarette to the ground and crushed it with her foot. "So they think Andre killed Cesar so he could be the only man in Eloise's life. Is that about right?"

"That's the working theory, I guess." I cautioned myself against saying anything about the other murder Andre might be involved in. If Beth told me about it, I'd know that she knew.

Beth laughed. "Waste of time, huh? Somebody needs to enlighten them. Andre would have to kill off half the Village to get rid of all the men who want Eloise, including *your* man. Don't think Chase is above eating a piece of that pie."

It was a zinger I wasn't expecting. It was mean-spirited for her to bad-mouth Chase just because Andre had dumped her. I knew she was in pain, so I pretended not to notice. "The police decided Andre wasn't guilty anyway."

"Even with the hat pins in Cesar's eyes?"

So she knew, at least about that part of it. I guess that answered one of my questions. "It was only one hat pin. Of course, that made him a good suspect. But it could also make other people in the Village suspects. Andre isn't the only person who uses hat pins."

"You're right," she agreed, staring at the mermaids. "I can come up with at least a dozen people, not including all of the nobility. But you weren't talking about them, were you, Jessie? You were talking about *me*."

Well, since you mentioned it— "I suppose in an odd sort of sense, you could be a suspect. I mean, you could've wanted to make Andre look guilty for killing Cesar."

"Honey, if I were gonna kill someone, it would be Andre. I wouldn't mess around trying to make him look bad. I'd flat-out put my scissors in his chest. Or maybe lots of hat pins in his eyes. I'd hurt him like he's hurt me. What good did it do to kill Cesar? That just left the field wide open for Andre to continue doing what he wants."

I admitted that she made sense. I'd feel the same way

about it—except with a sword instead of scissors. "I don't think Andre killed Cesar. He really believes Eloise loves him and would choose him over anyone."

"He's a snake, Jessie. Watch out he doesn't decide he's in love with *you*." She smiled halfheartedly. "I have to go back in now. We're running full blast with a lot of crazy complicated costumes this summer. And now with Livy being pregnant, she's going to want all new clothes."

I went back in with her and picked up the material Andre needed. I wasn't sorry I'd talked to her. I felt even more strongly that she hadn't killed Cesar. Just the passion in her face when she talked about killing Andre was convincing. I could see her envisioning Andre lying dead at her feet. A woman doesn't feel that kind of emotion and settle for framing a man.

I dreaded it, but the gemstone shop was staring at me when I walked out of Stylish Frocks. It would be stupid not to go there next, then drop both items off with Andre before continuing on with my other errands. I clutched the emerald green taffeta closer, like a shiny shield, and advanced into the shop.

It was disorienting again, going inside, but this time I knew what to expect and didn't bother looking around at the gemstones. I told Rene that I was there to pick up Andre's purchase. He nodded and disappeared behind one of the dark curtains.

I didn't notice that Eloise was also there (it takes a few minutes to see anything in the dark after coming in from the bright sunlight), but her laugh caught my attention. She was sitting at a table with Bernardo, trying on jewelry. He was inspecting the necklace around her throat while his eyes dropped to her cleavage. Renee was saying how wonderful the ruby necklace looked on her, no doubt encouraging a lucrative sale.

And the police took *Andre* in for questioning? Obviously they didn't realize that at least two of the Three Chocolatiers had been seeing her. Probably Marco, too. I knew that didn't make them guilty of killing their brother, but their alibis must've been the best in the world for Detective Almond to dismiss their involvement so quickly.

Eloise, like she could feel my eyes on her, looked up and smiled brilliantly. "I think this will do nicely, Bernie. You have the best taste. And I'm not just talking about your chocolate."

They giggled in a disgusting manner that made me want to strangle both of them, and I had no emotional investment. Imagine how disgusted Andre would be if he knew.

"Here it is." Rene returned with a wrapped package. "It's a piece of art, really. We should have charged much more. But since it was for Andre . . ."

Which implied some kind of more personal relationship between the twins and the hatmaker. Or he was just a good customer. I wanted to stay and chat but I could feel Eloise and Bernardo listening intently. I didn't want them to know what I was thinking, even if it meant I had to wait until later to talk to him.

"Thank you." I gave him a brief but respectful head nod.

"I'm glad you came in to pick this up," Rene continued before I could make my exit. "I thought we might have gotten off to a bad start when you were here last."

"What makes you say that?" I didn't want to be the focal point for the evil twins. The idea was frightening.

"Renee just had a feeling that you had some problem with us," he said. "She's a little fey, you understand. She gets impressions from people."

Great! They look like vampires and read people's minds. What else? "No. No problem. I was surprised to finally meet you. I hadn't been in here since Captain Jack left. You've done wonders with the place. I was seriously thinking about applying here to be your apprentice."

I was babbling. I knew it, but I couldn't stop. It's kind of my reaction to stress. Rene didn't interrupt me, just waited

patiently for me to tell him my whole life story. When I was
finished, he smiled a little and said, "We would love to have
you apprentice with us, Lady Jessie! It would be our pleasure
to teach you what we know of the fine art of gemstones."

"You would be most welcome here." Renee joined us
and added to the conversation even though she'd been
across the room only a moment before.

I shivered and tried to keep my response short and to the
point. No way was I ever going to get that involved with
them. The idea was terrifying. "Thanks! That would be
great."

I didn't mean it. It's just what came out of my mouth. I
seem to have little control of that at times like this. I hoped
it didn't involve writing my name in blood on some old
parchment.

"We hear the police questioned Andre about Cesar's
death," Rene said. "Do they think he is responsible for what
happened?"

"I'm not sure." I managed to keep my mouth mostly shut
on this one. "But they let him go."

Renee made a hissing sound, not unlike a snake. She
stared at her brother. "The hatmaker is lucky—*again*." She
glided back to Bernardo and Eloise, leaving a trail of questions I wanted to ask.

"My sister isn't feeling well," Rene said. "She didn't
mean what she said."

Even his ghostly demeanor couldn't hide the fact that he
was lying. They obviously knew about the first murder.

I walked back out of the shop consumed by the tiny bit
of information. I was so busy turning it over in my mind
that I didn't even notice the rather large black horse with an
equally large knight on it until I was almost under them.

The Templar Knight was a good horseman—he was
able to pull the horse up quickly and avoid crushing me
under its hooves. Just the thought of lying on the ground,
broken and bleeding, drew me out of my Holmesian trance-

like state. I realized I'd dropped my packages and bent to retrieve them.

"Have you no regard for your own personal safety?" the dark, helmeted knight demanded.

I recognized the husky voice from the night before—or at least I thought I did. My heart skipped a beat. "I was blinded by the sunlight, Sir Knight." I curtsied low to show him that I was sincere. "You have my thanks for saving me from your horse."

Of course, our conversation began to draw a crowd. Anything could be a play for visitors. They reacted by taking photos of everything they saw and posting them on the Internet. It was our job to keep the fantasy going.

The knight inclined his head stiffly in my direction. The helmet wouldn't allow him to do any more. I wondered why he didn't at least pull up the visor so he'd be able to breathe in there—and I could see his face.

"Your pretty apology is accepted, Lady Jessie. Pray thee be more careful in the future."

He started to ride away, the melodrama between us over. I should have let him go. Not just because of the crowd either. I didn't want him to think I was flirting with him. Of course I *wasn't* flirting with him. I loved Chase and didn't want to be with anyone else.

"Good Sir Knight." I yielded to the tiny zing of attraction that teased my senses. "Will you not allow me to fetch you a dipper of water from the well? You must be thirsty in this heat. It is the least I can do."

The visitors were eating it up (that's the excuse I'm using). The women stood spellbound and clutched the arms of the men who were with them. The hot sun beat down on us all. My heart beat faster as I contemplated what I'd done.

"That would be most welcome, my lady."

There was a water fountain nearby. Cold water shot out of a dolphin's mouth twenty-four/seven from a deep well tapped beneath it.

I removed my cup from my side and filled it, then held it up for the knight. He took it from me and sipped carefully, then swallowed it. Because of the small aperture, I could see his lips. A few drops fell on him, running down the black armor across his lean, hard body beneath.

What was I thinking? What was I doing?

I swallowed hard and took the cup from him to an explosion of applause from the crowd. The knight continued on his way down the cobblestones, and I picked up my packages.

Why was I so attracted to him? Maybe I had heatstroke. Something had to be wrong with me. I vowed there and then that it wouldn't happen again.

I took Andre's items—and my exasperation—to the Hat House. I wanted to question Andre about his relationship with Beth. Couldn't he see what a great woman she was?

Can't I see what a great man Chase is?

I felt too guilty to even question him when I gave him his packages. Andre only opened the box I'd brought him from the gemstone shop and exclaimed over the gorgeous earrings that matched the necklace he'd had made for Eloise. He tossed the taffeta to the side.

"Have you ever seen anything more beautiful? Except for the woman who'll wear them, of course."

I couldn't answer. I could hardly stay there. I was as bad as Eloise. I wasn't taking expensive jewelry from every man in the Village, but anything was possible. How could I be with Chase when I was flirting with the Templar Knight? Someday I'd be old and alone and no one would want me. Chase would be gone from my life because I hadn't treated him right. It was a depressing thought. I needed chocolate. Nothing else could make it better.

"We're going to have to make twelve green hats with this taffeta." Andre was continuing to speak despite my misery. "Why don't you take a break and come back ready to work?

I noticed you forgot my other packages. Please pick them up while you're out."

I went for chocolate first. It was the only way I could handle the events of the day. Without thinking, I headed toward the Three Chocolatiers, then remembered that the shop was closed until further notice.

There were other places to get chocolate in the Village—their chocolate was just the best. Frenchy's Fudge was close by and would have to do.

I spotted Bernardo and Marco at an outside table by Sir Latte's. They were there with Chase and two men in suits who looked as out of place as fur coats on a hot day.

Chase might tell me later what happened—but maybe not. I decided to browse a display of delicate glass animals at the Glass Gryphon next door for a few minutes while discreetly listening to their conversation.

"We aren't asking you to give up your shop," one of the suits was saying. "Just the opposite. We want you to stay open."

"But we need you to take on a partner," the second suit said. "Think of it as a new brother. Obviously, you can't be the Three Chocolatiers if there are only two of you."

The brothers looked at Chase, who nodded and sat forward at the table. "Can't they call the shop the Two Chocolatiers?" he suggested for them.

"I'm afraid that won't work," the first suit said in a long-suffering tone. "You get the idea. Three Chocolatiers—Three Musketeers. Two Chocolatiers—not so good."

Marco glanced at Bernardo. "Is that why we called the shop that name? We named it after a candy bar?"

The two suits shook their heads. Chase looked away, but I could see the deepening smile lines near his eyes as he tried not to laugh out loud.

"I don't know what else we can say," Suit Number Two responded. "You have to hire someone to be your brother if you want to keep the shop open. We know this is painful for you, but we must all move on."

The brothers appeared dazed by the request to hire someone to replace Cesar. That kind of thing never comes easy.

When the two suits had picked up their briefcases and started toward the castle, the brothers appealed to Chase. "There must be something you can do to help us. How can we get a new brother?"

"Why would we want to?" Bernardo continued. "We'd have to split the profits three ways again. How would we know a new brother would be any good at making chocolate?"

"I'll talk to management about it," Chase said. "I can't promise anything, but I'll try. Maybe the best thing right now is to keep an open mind."

"What about Cesar's body?" Marco asked again. "When can we bury him? Mama is going to fly over from Naples for the funeral, but we don't know when we can have it yet."

"I'll check on that, too."

"Can we reopen the shop yet?" Bernardo asked.

"Not yet. I'll ask the police about that, too." Chase answered a call on his radio and had to leave the brothers.

I made sure the glass animal display was between me and him until he was out of sight. I didn't want him to think I went around spying on him all the time. Or at least that I was stupid enough to get caught at it all the time.

I started to leave and head toward Adora's shop when I noticed Bernardo and Marco were still at the café table. Maybe another few minutes might yield another answer or two about what happened to Cesar.

"I don't like it," Bernardo said plainly. "They don't have any right to tell how many people I need in my business."

"I think we signed something when we moved in that said they do," Marco reminded him. "But Cesar always handled that stuff. I miss him already."

"Cesar!" Bernardo shot to his feet and adjusted his cape.

"We can do very nicely without him. He thought he was more important than us. I guess he knows better now."

As far as admissions of guilt went, it wasn't a total confession. But when I added it up with Bernardo buying jewelry for Cesar's girlfriend and his attitude about the shop, maybe it meant something. I needed to find out what his alibi was that totally took him off Detective Almond's hook for that night. It had to be something unquestionable. Detective Almond knew nothing about the Village—his alibi might be a lie that the police didn't understand.

"Jessie!" Roger Trent, former bailiff and owner of the Glass Gryphon, greeted me. "Looking for anything in particular?"

"Not really. I was just admiring the glass. How's Mary doing?"

"She's across the street making baskets as usual. I told her we should put in a bid on one of the bigger shops and move our businesses together. That way we'd have a larger living space, too."

"What would that be called?" I thought about the combinations between Wicked Weaves and the Glass Gryphon.

"I was thinking Wicked Glass and Weaves or just Glass 'N' Weaves. What do you think?"

"That sounds like a good idea," I said, though I really didn't think so. "Good to see you, Roger. I have to run over to Cupid's Arrow for Andre."

Roger spit on the ground. Fortunately, I was the only Village resident to see him do it. Spitting is a very popular pastime around here. Residents can indulge in matches for hours. Not a pretty sight. "Hariot? I can't believe that murdering scumbag is still out of jail! The cops today don't know what they're doing. When I was on the job, we would've arraigned him already."

"Anybody can get to those hat pins," I told him. "Other than that, most of the men and some of the women in the Village wouldn't have minded seeing Cesar dead."

Roger leaned in closer and whispered, "Were any of them arguing with Cesar right before he died? Did any of them threaten to kill him if he didn't leave Eloise alone? I don't think so. Put that with Hariot's past and it spells murder to me."

That put a new feather in my bonnet.

Fifteen

I discussed it with Adora (after eating fudge) between aisles of Renaissance lingerie, incense, and body oils in Cupid's Arrow. She hadn't heard anything about Andre confronting Cesar, but we both agreed that Roger was close enough to the chocolate shop to hear everything.

"What does that mean?" she asked me.

"I'm not sure yet. Maybe nothing. And I'm sure Roger already told the police. You know how he is."

"You mean, 'Hey! I'm Roger—I used to be a cop but now I blow glass.' Yeah, I know."

I picked up Andre's package, not thinking about the whole *eww* factor.

"Andre has to know he's not the only one Eloise sees," Adora pointed out. "She's not exactly known as a one-man woman."

"Yeah. He's kind of like Don Quixote."

"Does that make Eloise the nasty mule slut or the wind-mill?"

"I don't know—the windmill, at least from his point of view. No question what I think!"

We both laughed, and I said good-bye. I started back across the King's Highway after visting Sarah's Scarves and Lady Cathy's Crochet. My errands were complete and my chocolate craving satisfied.

It made total sense that Andre killed Cesar. There was so much going against him. Knowing that he'd threatened Cesar before he died was icing on the cake. No wonder the police took him in for questioning.

But it was also beginning to make sense that Bernardo could have given his brother the chocolate bath, too. He had motive, it seemed. Maybe not opportunity, since Detective Almond had already questioned him. I had to find out what his alibi was. Otherwise, Bernardo was going to be on the top of my list.

"Jessie!" Chase came up behind me and put his arms around me to stop my forward motion. "I've been looking all over for you. How's everything going at the Hat House?"

"Good, I guess. I've been running errands and cleaning the shop. Not much actual hat making going on."

"Sounds interesting. Anything else you've gotten into today?"

He knew about the knight. "No. Nothing I can think of." The Village grapevine was a powerful tool for good and evil. It probably only took five minutes before Mrs. Potts at the Honey and Herb Shoppe was telling Sam Da Vinci, who relayed it to Mother Goose, and now the whole Village knew. I felt guiltier than ever.

He smiled and hugged me again. "I was at the gemstone shop a little earlier. Rene said you're going to be his apprentice."

"Oh. Yeah." He was talking about *that*. What a relief!

"I was surprised, that's all. You didn't seem too crazy about them yesterday."

"That was yesterday." I told him what Renee had said

about Andre getting away with something again. "I think they know about the Hollywood murder."

"Since Roger knows about that, it's a good chance the whole Village knows by now." He kissed me and smiled. "Can we forget about Cesar for a while? How about a nice romantic dinner at home tonight instead of going out?"

"That would be great! Would you like me to pick something up?"

"You choose what sounds good for dessert, and I'll take care of the rest. Okay?"

I kissed him and held him close for a few minutes. "Okay. I'll see you later."

"I'm looking forward to it."

I remembered as he started to walk away that I needed to know Bernardo's alibi. I stopped him again and asked if he knew why Detective Almond had let the two brothers off the hook.

"Marco said he was home with his girlfriend. Bernardo wasn't in the Village." Chase raised his left brow. I love it when he does that. "Why? What have you heard?"

I couldn't exactly relate the conversation I'd overheard between the two brothers—he'd know I'd been there when he was talking to the suits from Adventure Land. "Roger told me about the confrontation between Andre and Cesar."

"Roger told everybody else about that, too," Chase replied.

"Well, that's it then. I'll see you later. For that romantic dinner."

We actually parted on that note. I wished I could just stay with him the rest of the day, but I was sure he had fights to resolve, visitors to appease, and animals to take to the Main Gate because the vet wouldn't come in the Village anymore. I had things to do, too. But I couldn't wait for tonight.

To keep myself occupied, I went back over everything I knew about Cesar's death. Andre seemed guilty—really guilty on so many different levels. Bernardo seemed guilty, again on many different fronts. Beth, not so much. I thought she would've killed Andre. Eloise was a less likely suspect, as much as I wanted to think it was her. The evil twins? Maybe not involved at all except as a link in the gossip chain.

Maybe I was wrong about Andre. I hadn't known him for long. It was more a gut feeling, the kind cops and private detectives rely on to find the truth, at least on TV. But maybe my gut was wrong. He had motive. He had opportunity. And, probably worst of all, he might have done it before. In a lot of ways, I wondered why the police hadn't already arrested him, like Roger said.

Bernardo was the dark horse. Chase said he was out of the Village when Cesar was killed. Maybe he was—or maybe he'd gotten someone to lie for him.

There were musicians playing at the Village Square in the middle of the King's Highway. There was a crowd of people around them, sitting and standing in the lush green grass. I stopped and listened to their music for a few minutes. Susan Halifax from the Merry Mynstrel's Stage was playing her harp. There was also a lute player and someone on the reed pipes.

They made beautiful music together. I knew the real Renaissance wasn't like this every day. Renaissance Village represented the best and most romantic ideals of that time. Let's face it, not many visitors would come here if it was dirty, plague-ridden, and full of church doctrine like the real thing had been. There was no way to really be historically accurate and still make money.

Seeing the musicians made me realize that I was running late again for the hat-making process. *Chase was right,* I thought as I ran the rest of the way to the Hat House. I needed to get my mind off Cesar's death and focused on hat making.

"Where have you been?" Andre demanded. "I needed you an hour ago."

"You sent me to have lunch and get your packages." Maybe stress was affecting his memory.

"You know, Chase described a different woman to me when I agreed to take you on as an apprentice for the summer. I'm feeling very let down, Jessie. You're always late. I never know what you're doing. I don't know if we can continue this way."

My Renaissance fantasy bubble burst, at least temporarily. Andre's temper tantrum roused my temper—not a difficult thing to do.

"Look, I know you're busy with everything. I know it hasn't been easy being accused of murder. But I was expecting to be treated like an apprentice and not an errand-running, shop-cleaning lackey. An apprentice learns things, Andre. I already knew how to sweep and pick up packages. Let's say we're both disappointed and move on."

I could tell right away that he was surprised when I said something back to him. His little mouth hung open and his eyes bulged. Maybe I'd said too much, but it was the way I felt. Sometimes I open my mouth and the words just fall out.

"I think you should leave, Jessie. Maybe your talents are better served helping small children throw frogs at targets."

"That's fine," I retorted. "You have enough lackeys to go around."

"Good-bye then." He turned his back on me.

"Bye."

"You can leave now."

"I'm leaving."

"Not fast enough."

If this was a contest to see who could have the last words, Andre was going to find he could never best me. "Is this a race?"

"It might be. You're standing in the middle of my shop."

"Not for long."

"The sooner that changes, the better."

"I'm sure."

Andre stared at me. "You are one of the most stubborn women I've ever known. You remind me of Sigourney Weaver. I worked with her on *Ghostbusters*. The first one— the real one, as far as I'm concerned. She was stubborn, too. But a great actress."

"Yeah?" He almost took the wind from my sails with that remark. "Well, you remind me of Joel Gray in *Remo Williams*. I can imagine you dodging bullets and dancing away."

He looked pleased. "I know Joel very well. I worked with his daughter on the set of *Dirty Dancing*. He asked for me personally. We had lunch every day."

I wasn't sure where to go from here. The contest to see who could have the last word seemed to be over. I was already feeling the loss of my apprenticeship—such as it was. I wasn't looking forward to possibly waiting tables or helping visitors in any game capacity again.

"You should stay, Jessie," he said. "You and I are cut from the same cloth. We may have our disagreements, but we make a good team. I'll try to treat you more like an apprentice."

"And I'll try to be on time," I conceded, glad to have my job back. "Thanks, Andre."

He waved his hand in a dismissing gesture. "Not at all. You've paid me a deep compliment without realizing it. What more could I ask?"

We cleaned off one of the long tables and started work on the new hats for the dancing girls at the Stage Caravan. They were like small boxes with trailing veils that matched the costumes they wore. Some of them were pink and purple while others were blue and purple. In most cases, the hats were the biggest part of their skimpy costumes.

Andre and I worked well together. He talked constantly as he worked—small hands moving quickly as he cut the material and pinned it to the stiff backing that created the shape of the hat.

"Making hats has always been in my blood," he said as the scissors slashed through the material. "My grandfather made hats during Hollywood's heyday. My father took over from him, and I followed suit. My son or daughter should be taking over for me right now. I guess that isn't going to happen."

I held the material in place as he pinned and then basted it. "It must've been hard to leave your life behind that way. How did you end up here?"

He sighed and wiped a tear from the corner of one eye. "Please don't get me started. There's nothing worse than an old hatmaker no one wants anymore." He paused for a moment, then explained. "I hated leaving Hollywood, but my life there was over. Even though they never found me guilty of anything, they never said I was innocent either. No one would hire me. Friends in the industry I'd known since I was a child turned their backs on me. I made a lot of money there—more than I could keep track of, truth be told. I'm still trying to figure out what happened to some of it."

I thought about Cesar's death and hoped it wouldn't end up being the same way here. Most of the residents in the Village had something to hide. Maybe it was part of why they were living here in this make-believe world. Secrets were layered on secrets in the shops and apartments that lined the cobblestones.

But when those secrets were revealed, many times it went badly for the resident. I recalled being here one summer when everyone found out that dear old Paddy at Paddy's Pub was a member of the Irish Republican Army.

He was arrested by the FBI early one morning. After that, Hephaestus came in and changed the name of the place to Peasant's Pub.

That was one of the more dramatic secrets—but it seemed to me like everyone who lived here had one.

"And ending up here," Andre continued. "That was a fluke, my dear. One of my old pals was working for Carolco and took pity on me. He let me come in on one of the last movies made at that studio. It was a bust that only went to video, and the studio closed down. I had sold my house in the Hollywood Hills, and I knew I couldn't go back. I heard about Renaissance Village and I've been here ever since. It may not be Hollywood, but there's a need for me here—a purpose, if you will."

"I know everyone appreciates your efforts." I tried to cheer him up.

"Everyone except whoever murdered Cesar and wants to pin it on me." He paused and stared at me. "Excuse the bad pun. I didn't mean it that way. But I'm not leaving this time, Jessie. They'll have to arrest me or Adventure Land will have to kick me out. I made that mistake last time."

By this time we had the shells for a dozen little hats. The long, sparkling veils came next. The hats and veils were too delicate to sew with a machine. We sat in chairs and stitched until a few of them were done.

My fingers were starting to get sore when Andre called a halt to the work. "Take these over and have a few of the girls try them on. Check the length of the veil and make sure they don't look like little monkeys without organ grinders. I wouldn't have created these for them, but they're made to their specifications. Let me know what happens."

I gathered the finished hats into a cloth carry bag, brown, of course, to fit in with Village dress requirements. No shocking colors that didn't exist during the Renaissance.

"That's not too errand-like, is it?" he asked.

"Not at all. And we made these hats. I feel like a real apprentice. Thanks, Andre!"

He smiled at me in his sad way. "Thank you for listening to my meanderings. In one way, I can't believe this has happened to me again, this thing with Cesar. In another way, it doesn't surprise me. Life isn't finished with me yet, I suppose. Thank goodness it wasn't my darling Eloise who was sacrificed to the evil gods of conflict. Even if I end up going to prison for Cesar's death, at least I'll know she's out here and safe."

When he put it that way, what could I say? Knowing me, there had to be a reply. "Why Eloise? What happened between you and Beth? You seem perfect for each other."

He thought about it for a minute. "I suppose you're right. Beth and I make a good couple. But there's no spark, no fire. When I look at Eloise, when I touch her, I feel young again. I feel like nothing else matters."

I couldn't let that stand. "You know she goes out with almost *every* man in the Village, right? She even acted like she'd go after Chase when I'm not here. Doesn't that bother you?"

"The question, my girl, should be, doesn't that bother *you*? Eloise is a wild, passionate creature. Of course she isn't happy with just one man. My wife was the same way. We can never truly expect to hold these creatures. They are only with us for a short time. But what magic they make!"

I thought about Andre's explanation for wanting to be with Eloise. It was stupid, really. I was glad my relationship with Chase wasn't so flimsy.

I left the Hat House for the Stage Caravan, which was close to the Dungeon, on the other side of the big tree swing. I thought I might go home and shower, get cleaned up for the big night, then go out and find dessert for dinner.

"Hey, there." One of the madmen who I'd noticed around the Hat House stopped me. His face and hands were dirty (no surprise), and his clothes were mismatched and torn. He had the usual madman pan and other paraphernalia on his side like most of us wore our cups for free drinks. He was an older man with graying hair and sharp eyes above sagging jowls. "Jessie, right?"

"Lady Jessie," I reminded him. There was a certain protocol that needed to be observed when dealing with knaves, varlets, and madmen. "What do you want of me, sir?"

He glanced around uneasily as visitors walked back and forth around us. "My name is Neal Stevenson. I'm a reporter for the *LA Times* here on assignment. I was wondering if I could have a few minutes of your time to talk about the murder of Kathleen Hariot."

Sixteen

We went into Peter's Pub and found a secluded booth in one dark corner. The lunchtime rush of visitors had cleared out, and it was too early yet to be busy with residents stopping in for dinner.

I signaled Peter for my usual, and Neal Stevenson—reporter and madman—ordered ale when Peter brought mine. I was interested in what Neal had to say. It might shed some light on Cesar's death.

"Look, I got a job as a madman in this crazy place so I could fit in. I've been hanging out, waiting to see what breaks ever since I heard about Hariot's involvement in another murder," Neal said. "I've been waiting for some kind of break in this new case, but everything seems to be on hold. I've talked to the police and they don't seem to know what's going on."

"But you think I do?"

"You live with the closest form of law enforcement around here *and* work for Hariot. I'd say that makes you a good source."

I looked into his face—middle-aged, eyes still bright with the need to find the next story. "I don't really know anything you can't get from the police."

He sipped his ale. "Come on, Jessie. Level with me. I'll make it worth your while."

I squared my shoulders and nodded at him. "Let me repeat, sir, my name is Lady Jessie. You will find yourself in the stocks facing vegetable justice if I have to tell you again."

"You're as crazy as the rest of them."

"Quite."

"But you know something. I've seen you skulking around the Village. It reminds me of myself. What's between Hariot and the tart on the other side of the Village? Why did he kill the chocolate maker?"

"Even if I had answers for these questions, you'd be the last person I'd tell." I smiled, finished the rest of my ale, and got up to leave.

"Wait!" He got up and took my arm. "Just tell me what you've heard. I don't care how small it seems. I want to know."

Peter, good tavern keeper that he is, sensed my distress and came to my aid. "You'd better pick up a copy of the guidelines for correct behavior in the Village, madman. Your kind doesn't grab ladies—unless it's part of a skit or something. Be glad it's me telling you this and not the bailiff."

Neal moved his hand. Peter nodded and left us.

"I need someone inside," Neal continued as we walked out of the tavern. "I need *you*, Lady Jessie. You could be my eyes and ears in Hariot's shop. What do you say? I know you people don't make much here. I could pay you if I bring in this story."

I stopped in the middle of the cobblestones. "You need to leave Andre alone." I punctuated my words by poking him in the chest. "He's suffered enough."

"The man killed his wife! Doesn't that mean anything

here? He's gotten away with it all these years. Don't you want justice for Kathleen Hariot and your friend that he murdered?"

We were standing face-to-face with my finger almost permanently wedged in his chest. As the day was drawing to a close, most visitors were finding their way back to the Main Gate. I could hear the music and laughter as the jugglers and musicians said good-bye to our guests as they were leaving.

I glanced up as I caught sight of Robin Hood and some of his men coming out of Sherwood Forest. They approached quickly when they saw me and surrounded Neal.

"Having a problem, Lady Jessie?" Robin asked.

"Nothing a night in Sherwood Forest wouldn't help," I told him.

"You hear that, good sir?" Robin's right-hand man, Alex, asked the doomed reporter/madman. "We have a special treat for you! Huzzah!"

Robin gave his loud, obnoxious laugh—head back, mouth open. "Back to the trees, my Merry Men! I believe we have a good deed to do and a hardhearted knave to vanquish!"

"Hey! Wait a minute!" Neal tried to stop them as they got him up between them and started back into the forest. "I'm not really part of all this. Put me down! I'll sue!"

Alex bowed deeply, his forest green hat in one hand. "A pleasure, as always, my lady. Until next time." He kissed my hand and followed the Merry Men and Robin off the cobblestones.

"Jessie, Andre's a killer!" Neal yelled before he disappeared into the trees. "Don't trust him!"

Seventeen

The hats fit perfectly when I gave them to the dancers at the Stage Caravan. The delighted belly dancers even did a few turns in them and declared them exceptional. We were all set to finish the rest.

It only took a few minutes after I got back to the Dungeon to look up Neal Stevenson on the Internet and find out he really was a reporter for the *Times*. He'd worked on the story about Andre years ago, too. Still it seemed like a long way to come to follow up on a story. What was his game?

I tried to put it all behind me, at least for the evening. I wanted everything to be as perfect as I knew Chase wanted it to be. We didn't really set up a lot of dates, like real couples. It warmed my heart that he still thought of me this way.

After I showered and changed into a new sundress Chase had never seen (backless, short skirt, sexy bodice—take that, fairies!), I walked down to the Pleasant Pheasant and picked up some apple pie with rum sauce for dessert. It was Chase's favorite.

It was that dusky time of evening when it's not really dark but not daylight either. Someone told me once that this is the best time to see ghosts. There were plenty in my life that I dragged around with me, but none I actually hoped to see.

I was thinking about Chase and our future together when a group of Templar Knights came riding out of the forest. There were about twenty of them—all mounted on large, black, magnificent horses and dressed in those ridiculously awesome costumes. Each of the knights carried a black shield with a red cross on it.

Residents stood to the side of the cobblestones and watched them go by. Visitors were long since gone, the Main Gate closed for the night.

Maybe people didn't like them, but they couldn't deny they were an inspiring sight. And the Village ladies seemed near to swooning when they went by. I wasn't the only woman who was a little swept away by them.

I followed them along with several dozen other residents. They were headed for the Field of Honor.

"Should be quite a contest," Mrs. Potts said, standing at my side when I reached the field.

"Contest?"

"Where is your head, Jessie? There are posters everywhere. Look! There's the TV news people over there."

Indeed there were several hundred posters stapled to the gates. And there were TV cameras at the opposite end of the field. I guess I'd been too busy to notice this event. The posters said the Knights Templar were going up against the queen's personal knights for the honor of her majesty the following day.

"That should be something all right," I agreed.

Something like a massacre. The Templars were well trained, fast, and knew how to work together. I could tell they'd make mincemeat out of the queen's knights. Most of those loyal gentlemen were older, not too sure of their seats in the saddle, and unwilling to be placed in any possible jeopardy from a lance coming their way. They weren't the daily show knights who fought regularly on the Field of Honor for visitors.

"They'll get their tails whipped for sure!" Mrs. Potts said in a way that kind of scared me.

Most of the residents that had followed the knights to their practice had crowded on the bleachers where visitors usually watched the jousts. This was entertainment after a long, hot day of playing storybook characters or keeping their shops open.

"I'm seriously lusting after the big one over there," a young wench who serves ale at the Pleasant Pheasant said in a dreamy voice. "They say his name is Neil. How hot is that?"

I glanced the way she pointed. The knight looked like the same one who'd brought me home from the encampment in the forest, the one I'd flirted with outside the gem shop. At least I thought it looked like the same one. He was big like him anyway. Otherwise, they all looked the same in their costumes.

"He's got a good seat on his horse," I added to the conversation.

"That's not all he's got," the tavern wench said.

"Who are they?" one of the fortune-tellers asked.

"No one knows," Bo Peep responded. "They have a secret society. Someone told me they can never say their names aloud."

"Wow!" the serving wench said again.

Did I say residents followed the knights to the field? Perhaps I should be a bit more specific. I looked at their audience. There were no men, not even boys, in the group watching them practice. And all the women had lustful expressions on their faces.

"Have you been out to the encampment yet?" Bo Peep asked.

"No," the fortune-teller replied. "But I'd like to. What's it like?"

"Like them," Bo Peep answered. "All black and hard and male. Lots of leather and smoke."

This was getting kind of weird, even for me. I decided to head back to the Dungeon and hope Chase would be there soon. It was almost eight P.M. already. My nerves couldn't stand much more.

The knights' practice began to break up, too. It was just a teaser for the real thing tomorrow. The show was over, and the residents sighed as the horsemen left the field. There was still a lot of admiration going on in quiet conversation. It was clear everyone (female) loved them.

I turned back from the fence and skirted between the shops that made up Armorer's Alley. It was quiet, cool, and dark now. The lights from the Village glowed softly as they would have if we were really living during the Renaissance.

I heard the sound of a horse coming toward me. This time, I stood still on one side, thinking he'd pass me by on his way back to the forest. But he slowed and stopped, gazing down at me.

"Good evening, my lady." He inclined his head. His deep, raspy voice sounded the same. My heart did a little dance, and I told it to stop.

"Good evening, Sir Knight."

"A lovely lady like you should not have to walk through the night to her house." He dismounted in a heartbreakingly elegant fashion—especially considering he was wearing armor. "Allow me to see you to your domicile."

It was only a short walk past the blacksmith's shop and Stage Caravan to reach the Dungeon. I should have said no thanks. Instead, I kind of nodded and simpered. He swept me off my feet into his arms and settled me on his saddle, then proceeded to walk beside, leading the horse.

I was more than swept away—I was blown away. My heart was pounding, breath coming fast. I couldn't even think of anything to say to him. It was almost unimaginable.

"Your clothing is most provocative, my lady," the knight filled in for me. "Mayhap you should be more careful when alone in the dark."

"I'm fine," I assured him, but my voice sounded a little squeaky. I cleared my throat and tried again. "I mean, I'm done working for the day. Time for some fun, right?"

"A Templar Knight knows no fun."

"How . . . sad. You must do something to relax after a hard day of—well, riding and whatever else you do."

"Indeed."

I wasn't sure what that meant, but I didn't ask him to explain. The horse moved slowly beneath me, a perfect angel. It was amazing considering the power I'd witnessed in the animal during practice.

"Look up! The stars attempt to rival the gleam in your eyes this night, my lady. I fear they are doomed to disappointment. No light, even a heavenly one, can achieve that unworthy goal."

"Uh—excuse me?" Was he really flirting with me? I thought—well, maybe.

"We have reached your home." He came to my side and lifted me off the horse. I felt like a doll in his grasp. His hands were strong at my waist.

"Thanks. I appreciate the ride."

"You are most welcome, my lady fair."

This was going too far. I was attracted to him, no doubt. But this couldn't continue. It was fun, but I wouldn't do this to Chase. "I'm sorry, Sir Knight, if I've given you the wrong impression."

"Indeed?"

"Yes. I'm—with someone. There are hundreds of fair maidens who would love to ride around with you and enjoy— your horse. But I have someone waiting for me and I'll have to bid you good-bye."

He seemed surprised at first. Kind of taken aback. Finally he bent his head and kissed my hand. His lips lingered on my skin, making it sizzle. I definitely didn't need to see him up close again.

"The loss of your company saddens me, lady. This man must be extraordinary to enjoy such loyalty."

"He is indeed, Sir Knight. Farewell." I took my hand away while I could and ran—not walked—into the Dungeon and shut the door. I stood with my back against it for a long time, breathing hard. I went upstairs to take another shower and get rid of the telltale horse smell from my ride home.

When I got out, Chase was there with food from Polo's Pasta that smelled wonderful. "Sorry I'm so late. I'm going to jump in the shower, then we'll eat."

"Never mind that." I grabbed him and brought his face close to mine. "I need some affection."

He pulled away. "Sorry, Jessie. Just a minute and we'll be fine."

I sat on the bed and waited for him. Chase isn't usually that particular. I mean, he showers regularly but usually he can manage to kiss me without getting cleaned up. What was he in such a hurry to wash off? Maybe just good honest sweat. It had been a long, hot day. And this was a special night. I reassured myself out of my sudden funk.

He came back out in snug jeans that clung to him in all the right places and an old Renaissance Village T-shirt that hugged his damp chest. His dark hair was loose around his shoulders as he put pasta and salad on plates and lit a candle.

"I have wine, too." He poured each of us a glass, then sat on the bed beside me. "To us," he proposed a toast. "Happy anniversary."

I thought about it for a long moment, then looked at him blankly. "What?"

"It's our anniversary. We met five years ago today."

"Oh."

He put down his glass. "You don't sound very excited."

"I'm more—surprised. That's all."

"Okay. You still sound kind of funny. Is something wrong?"

"No." I held up my glass and smiled. "You just have a better memory than me." We clinked our glasses together and kissed before we ate our pasta.

I stopped thinking, speculating. This wasn't turning out to be what I'd expected. But that was okay. Chase remembered that we met five years ago. That was good, right?

"So ask me," he prompted.

"Ask you?"

"Ask me when I knew that I loved you. That's what everyone wants to know."

I took a big drink of wine. "When did you know?"

"The minute I met you. You were working as a kitchen wench, carrying a platter of food. You asked me if I wanted corn or potatoes. Remember?"

I didn't remember, and it made me feel guilty. "You really do have a better memory than me."

"When did you know, Jessie?"

I looked into his clear brown eyes, loving his lips and the little imperfections in his handsome face. "I don't know. It just kind of happened, I guess."

He frowned and took a big drink of wine. "Really? No magic moment?"

"I'm afraid not. I remember liking you a lot—admiring you. But I don't have a specific moment. I just knew I loved you one day. I don't think you were even around. I think I was at the university."

He made a noise somewhere between a *hmm* and a *humph*.

"Is that okay? I mean, maybe everyone doesn't have a magic moment, but it doesn't mean they aren't in love, right?"

Chase's radio went off. There was a problem with the water at the Good Luck Fountain in the Village Square. It was shooting up fifty feet in the air, according to Chase's security minions.

"I have to go." He got up, found other pants to wear that weren't as cute, and gave me a quick peck on the lips. "Don't wait up. This might be a long night."

I wasn't happy about the situation. We didn't resolve the magic-moment issue. I still felt kind of out of the loop. He'd looked so hurt when I didn't remember when I first knew I loved him. I probably should've made something up—but it was such a surprise.

I couldn't just let it go like this. I didn't want to go to sleep knowing he was out there battling a menacing fountain, thinking I didn't love him the way he loved me.

Part of this was guilt over my lustful feelings toward the knight who'd brought me home. I had to show Chase—and myself—that our relationship was important and special to me.

I got rid of what was left from dinner as fast as I could. Dessert got stowed away for later. I pulled on jeans, a tank top, and sneakers and left the Dungeon headed for the Village Square.

I could hear the noise from the center of the Village. A few residents had lined up to watch maintenance deal with the geyser that the Good Luck Fountain had become. Some off-duty security men watched them work, too. People without TVs will watch anything for amusement.

"Have you seen Chase out here?" I asked one of the Lovely Laundry Ladies.

"No. If I had, I wouldn't be watching the fountain, would I?"

Ignoring her, I went to ask Shakespeare if he'd seen Chase. It had only been, at the most, thirty minutes since Chase had left the Dungeon. Someone had to have seen him.

"He was here," Shakespeare (Pat Snyder) said. "He left maintenance in control. Sit down, Jessie. Have some wine with me. The night is young and the fountain is flowing. There must be an ode there somewhere. I'll think of it to-morrow."

I was completely baffled. I knew I hadn't passed him on the way from the Dungeon. The rest of the Village was quiet. Where was Chase? Why wasn't he here? If he'd gone back and found me missing, surely he'd think about me following him. I walked back toward the Main Gate.

"Maybe I can help you find your lover," a man I didn't know said. "I can at least point you in the right direction."

He was dressed like another madman. His pants were baggy and threadbare. He had the customary pan and utensils on his side. His face was hidden by his large flowered hat, but I knew it wasn't the reporter from this afternoon. This madman was taller and thinner even with the baggy clothes.

"Thanks. But I can find him on my own." What was with the extra madmen this summer? Did Beth make too many madman costumes and decide to hand them out to anyone passing by the costume shop?

"That wasn't necessarily a request."

I felt something hard and angular pushed into my side. "Are you serious? That better be a gun or I'm going to hurt you."

Eighteen

"Oh, it's a gun all right, honey," he whispered. "Let's walk away from the event here and find someplace quiet to talk."

The madmen truly were quite mad this year. I wasn't sure if I should put my hands up or not. The gun in my side nudged me toward the back of the manor houses at Squire's Lane. It was dark, unusually dark even for the Village, in the shadow of the large, brick houses.

I'd never really thought much about it before, but it struck me as odd that no one lived in these houses. They were empty shells made to impress the visitors. I wondered why they never put shops or Village housing inside. Too bad, since if someone actually lived here, I could call for help.

"This is good," he grunted at me. "You're Jessie Morton, right? You work with Andre Hariot at the Hat House."

"Is this some kind of weird survey thing?"

"You people all have a strange sense of humor down here.

Is it normal, or something that comes from living here with all these freaks?"

"Excuse me. You're dressed like a madman and you're holding a gun on me. I think you might be one of those freaks."

"Is that what this is supposed to be?" He chuckled. "I was wondering. What's the idea of the pan and spoon?"

"You're supposed to sit along the street and bang the pan with the spoon, all the while making either witty or disgusting remarks to visitors as they pass you. Don't they give out character guides anymore? When I started here, everyone knew what their job was. But they also knew not to bring guns into the Village. Knives, daggers, swords, bow and arrow, lances—"

I was stalling. I thought if I could keep him talking, someone else might walk this way. People with guns made me nervous. How did he know my name? Why single me out to harass?

"Never mind all that." He made a snorting noise and shifted position a little like his feet hurt. "I want to know what's going on with Hariot. I think you're the one who's going to tell me. I need to hear whatever that little murdering weasel has to say. I want to know his schedule and how you fit into all of it. I've been watching you come and go, skipping around in your little costume. It's time to get real."

Boy, had he come to the wrong place. "This is something else about Andre and the murder in Hollywood, isn't it?"

"You got it."

"And you're a reporter?"

"No! I'm a private detective. I was hired by Kathleen Hariot's children from her first marriage. They're tired of waiting for justice. They want to see that snake who killed their mother go to prison."

"That sounds like justice to me!"

"Don't get smart, missy. Just tell me what I need to know and nobody will get hurt."

I wasn't in the best of places, standing in the dark where no one could see me with a madman who had a gun in my side and didn't know what to do with his pan and spoon.

I didn't know what to do either. There were no weapons within reach—not that a sword, shield, or catapult would help me out. A gun was top of the food chain when it came to weapons. It was faster, easier, and deadlier in most cases. I know a little self-defense but not enough to take on someone who was ready to kill me for information.

"I don't know what to tell you," I said honestly. "I'm Andre's apprentice. We make hats for the Village. I don't know anything about his role in either murder. You said you were watching me today. You know what I do. I run a lot of errands for him. That's about it."

"You spend time with him. He confides in you. Tell me what he says."

"He hasn't confided anything in me unless you count that thing about the script girl getting pregnant on the *Ghostbusters* set. We talk about movies. That's it."

There were actually spotlights in the Village—giant, eye-rending lights that were only turned on during emergencies. They kind of destroyed the whole Renaissance atmosphere. The fountain must have suddenly been designated as an emergency, thank goodness, and the stadium lights, disguised as trees, came on.

The man who held the gun on me was facing the lights. He made an *argh* sound and covered his eyes, but not before I kicked him in the leg and brought my knee up into his groin.

As he fell to the ground, I ran. I didn't wait to see if he was getting up again or not. I was immediately glad that I'd worn my tennis shoes instead of my sandals.

I stopped the first security man I saw and told him what

happened. He followed me back to the manor houses, but the private investigator was gone.

"I could call Chase," he offered, betraying his knowledge of our relationship.

"Do that," I said a little harshly. "I'd like to know where the hell he is. He was supposed to be out here helping with the fountain."

But there was no answer from Chase's radio. The security man shrugged. "Sorry. Maybe he's busy."

"Maybe," I agreed. "Thanks anyway."

Was that pity I saw in his eyes? Did he feel sorry for me? Worse, did he know something I didn't know about Chase's weird disappearances?

I hoped not, for Chase's sake. Between being held against my will at gunpoint and Chase not being there to save me or even prevent it from happening in the first place, I wasn't feeling very charitable toward him at that moment.

"Would you like me to walk you back to the Dungeon?" the security man asked.

"No. I'm fine." As I walked away from him, the fountain with the dolphins where I'd gotten water for the knight that day, sprang a gusher. "Looks like you're going to have your hands full."

I was too angry to sleep. I wandered around the Village, daring that stupid man to come at me again. I was armed with a heavy wooden stake that had been used to anchor part of a sheep enclosure. Maybe it would've been better against vampires, but it wasn't Halloween and I was convinced I could do some damage with it.

There were always some lights left on in the Village at night. Most of them were small and had something to do with security—not like the big lights at the Village Square. I was used to them and ignored most of them as I went by. But when I reached Da Vinci's Drawings, I noticed a larger, more commercial light at the Three Chocolatiers Shoppe.

As far as I knew (like Chase said to the Rizzo brothers),

no one was allowed in the shop. Someone was messing around in there where they weren't supposed to be. It made me angrier thinking about it. Poor philandering Cesar couldn't even be buried, but someone could go through his shop. Maybe nobody else was around to take care of it, but I decided to put my foot down. Enough was enough.

Nineteen

I sneaked around the back of the shop, clutching my solid piece of wood in my hand. Maybe I'd get lucky and find the killer trying to cover his tracks. I knew it was unlikely—not to mention a little too late. Detective Almond and his men had been over the shop several times since Cesar had died.

I was wondering what else someone could want here. A chocolate craving came to mind, but I couldn't think of anyone that desperate.

The back door was open—yellow, non-Renaissance light spilling out into the back courtyard where the brothers used to come out and practice their sword play. I looked at my wood and wished it were a sword. But my fairy godmother was apparently out on another call. I was stuck doing the best I could with what I had. *Where is Chase?*

Without backup or reinforcements, I knew I was crazy to approach the shop at all. But after the stupid man who'd held me at gunpoint disappeared, running for help would probably mean not catching this person in the act.

I'd seen the movie *Lady Hawk* and admired Matthew Broderick trying to convince his would-be attacker that there were several people with him. It seemed like a good plan for this occasion.

As I approached the open door, I lowered the timbre of my voice, trying to sound more masculine, and said, "The door's open over here, Jack! Someone might be breaking in!"

"I'm almost there, Chase." I tried to sound a little different again. "I'll take care of it."

"I'll get it," I volunteered in my own voice at the same time that I pushed the door. It swung open and smacked against the back of the shop, making me jump.

"Who's there?" Bernardo called out into the darkness.

"What are you doing here?" I looked over my shoulder and called back to my make-believe friends that it was only Bernardo. "I'm patrolling with Chase and Jack tonight. You're lucky we're not the police. They don't like their crime scenes messed around with."

Bernardo was clutching a big, wooden stirring utensil as though he planned to use it against his would-be attackers. "Is that Jack with the beanstalk or the piper's son?"

"Neither," I told him in what I hoped was an offhand way. He still hadn't put down the sturdy-looking utensil. "He's a new security man. You probably don't know him. He's from Ireland. He just got here tonight."

Bernardo shrugged and put the utensil back on the cabinet. "I hope we can keep this to ourselves. No need to involve the police."

I glanced back like Chase was coming right up behind me. "That works for me, but you better tell me what you're doing in here before Chase comes in. You know he can be a real stickler for the law."

"It wasn't anything, Jessie, really. You know I never made chocolate while Cesar was alive. I'm not even sure I *can* make chocolate. He didn't leave any instructions. What kind of cook does that? What's going to happen if we reopen and I don't know how to make chocolate?"

It was a valid question. "Have you looked through all of his belongings?"

"Everything the police haven't taken. I don't think he ever wrote the recipe down. You know, our father made chocolate. Cesar learned from him. I was never included—too young, I guess. But now, here I am. I don't know what to do."

Part of me was moved by his confession of ignorance about the chocolate-making process. But part of me was still a little unsure that Bernardo hadn't killed his brother. Maybe there was something else to find here that he believed the police had missed in their searches. It could go either way.

"Well, you better wait until the police tell you it's okay to come back in here. I'll get Chase to look the other way on this for right now."

"Look the other way on what?" Chase's real voice (not even close to my copy of him) said from behind me. "What are the two of you doing in here in the middle of the night? You both know the shop is off-limits until the police investigation is over."

I fell back on Bernardo's excuse. "I was helping Bernardo look for Cesar's chocolate recipe, right, Bernardo?" I could only hope he'd pick up on the lifeline I was throwing him.

"That's right! I ran into Jessie down by—" He flailed in his story like a witch in a duck pond.

"—at the Village Square where the fountain is shooting up," I finished. "And since *you* weren't there, Chase, I decided to help him."

For better or worse, that changed the tables and put me back in control. I was still angry about his disappearance. I hoped Bernardo wasn't the killer and had found something overlooked that would keep him from being caught as I pushed past Chase and headed out the door.

"Jessie!" Chase said as he followed me. "You know these things are part of my job. It's never bothered you before."

I saw Bernardo turn off the light and close the shop door before slinking away into the night. "That was because you were still answering your radio, and you didn't get up in the middle of the night and sneak off every time you got the chance."

"Just because I don't wake you up—I'm trying to let you sleep. We don't both have to be dragged out of our bed."

I turned around and poked my finger into his broad chest. "You're lying to me. I know it and you know it. If you're seeing someone else, just spit it out. I won't hold it against you. At least we'll both know where we stand."

There was mist swirling around on the damp ground beneath our feet. The stadium lights from the Village Square suddenly went out again. We were back to Village lantern light, which made it difficult to see anything but Chase's outline.

"I can't believe you'd think that about me," he said. "I remembered our anniversary. I was the one with the magic moment. You couldn't even remember when you fell in love with me. Maybe that's because you never really did."

It was hard watching his silhouette turn away and walk off toward the Field of Honor, visible only by the lanterns on the fence posts. A couple of years back they'd put those lanterns in place when one of the residents hurt himself on the fence posts after drinking too much ale and saying he wasn't able to see where he was going.

I wanted to call Chase back. But I was still mad. Apparently he was angry, too. Maybe we both needed to cool off. Maybe we needed a little space.

It broke my heart to go back to the Dungeon, stuff my clothes into my bags, and look for somewhere else to spend the night. We might be able to talk about this tomorrow. There had to be some way to make him understand how I felt. I wasn't as afraid of the man with the gun as I was of the idea of living my life without Chase.

Twenty

Somewhere else to spend the night wasn't as easy as it sounded. Village housing was always overflowing even if it wasn't the middle of the night. I didn't want to tell everyone I was moving into the castle—at least not yet.

I ended up in the Romeo and Juliet pavilion with my head on my bag, shivering in the chilly, damp air. I looked at the stars for a long time and wished I could see the ocean that I knew was so close.

Maybe tomorrow, I'd take a drive to the beach and lie out in the sun. Maybe I'd meet someone more fabulous than Chase—though I doubted it. Maybe I'd—

Sheesh! I was beginning to sound like the Chicken Ranch girls leaving Dolly Parton in *The Best Little Whore House in Texas.* I had to get a grip.

I could smell the bread baking at the Monastery Bakery long before the smell of coffee drifted by me. I got my stuff together and wandered that way, feeling like a homeless person without a shopping cart.

Brother Carl, head of the Brotherhood of the Sheaf, was totally sympathetic to my plight. He led me to a small room with a cot and a blanket. I lay down, thinking I'd never be able to sleep on the uncomfortable bed, but I passed out and I didn't wake up until almost nine.

Three young monks were watching me as I woke up. They were wearing the black robes of the brotherhood, but I could tell they hadn't been there long—no flour on them. Only the more experienced monks were allowed to bake.

"How long have you guys been standing there?" I asked when they didn't say anything.

"Only a few minutes," the smallest one, in the middle, replied.

"Great. Why are you still here?"

"Brother Carl told us to serve you in any way necessary. We're waiting for your commands, Lady Jessie."

Three monks at my command. It was different. Not exactly waking up next to Chase but better than waking up next to some maintenance guy who was about to hose down the Romeo and Juliet pavilion.

"I really need a shower. Also a large, triple shot mocha. And a cinnamon roll would be nice. Not necessarily in that order."

My squires led me to the communal shower area while they went to fetch coffee and a roll. The water was freezing—the monks didn't have the perks of living in the Dungeon. I guessed I didn't either anymore. I knew I'd have to find some corner to sleep in that night or I'd have to go home. I wasn't sure which choice sounded worse.

But there was coffee, strong and hot, and a cinnamon roll melting with gooey goodness waiting for me after I toweled off and got dressed. I sat down by myself out in the dining area and contemplated the events of the previous night.

It's funny how when you argue with someone you love, you can never really understand how it happened when you look back on it. It's like everything is fine one moment then everything falls apart. I felt like I'd been blindsided by a runaway carriage. There weren't any wheel marks on my face, but I felt broken up inside.

I knew Andre would be waiting for me. I was late for work after my promise yesterday not to let it happen again. I knew the little hatmaker was a romantic, however, so I knew my story about fighting with Chase would get me out of it. Maybe he'd even be able to help me find someplace to stay for a while.

I thanked Brother Carl and his monks for their compassion. Carl took my hands and told me to come back and stay there if I needed to that night. I hugged him and he turned a bright shade of red. It was nice to think I had some real friends in the Village.

But it was awful to walk past so many of them on the way to the Hat House. I could tell all of them already knew what had happened. My friends looked at me with pity while those other people who weren't all that crazy about me were laughing. I was sure many of them—especially the fairies, Eloise, and two of the Lovely Laundry Ladies— were measuring themselves for a place in Chase's bed.

I didn't let it bother me. I held my head high and clutched my two heavy bags as I walked to the Hat House. Let them think what they would. They could guess what happened. I didn't care.

I knew Andre had heard when I opened the door to the shop and he rushed to hug me. "My poor darling! You should've come to me last night. I would've taken you in. What kind of man lets the woman he loves sleep outside? I've always thought more of Chase than that. I'm planning to give him a piece of my mind."

"I'm fine," I told him. "I'm sorry I'm late, but I fell asleep on the monk's cot when I went for coffee."

"Have you eaten?" he asked. "Don't worry about being late. Don't worry about anything. If there's anything I know, it's being dumped. Let me know what I can do for you—except kicking Chase's behind, which I'm sure he deserves but I don't think I could pull off."

I had to smile at that picture. I knew Andre would take my side.

After I'd assured him that I'd eaten and we found someplace for my bags, we got down to work finishing the little veiled hats for the dancers at the Stage Caravan. Andre promised to have one of the other assistants deliver them so I wouldn't have to go past the Dungeon. I appreciated his kindness. I wasn't sure not going by the Dungeon was the answer—it was a small Village. I was bound to run into Chase if I stayed. That would be more difficult than anything else.

Chase and I had argued before. We probably would again. But Chase wasn't just another man. Our relationship was longer than one summer like the others had been. My heart wasn't broken yet. We'd have to find some way to get past this disagreement. I knew that Chase loved me. I felt sure he knew I loved him, too.

We started working on a new project after the hats for the dancers were out the door. These were three large, plumed hats, which reminded me in many ways of the Chocolatiers' hats. But these were for three sisters who were planning to visit the Village. All three hats were a deep purple satin, but each had a slightly different design.

"You see how the brim on this one is deeper," Andre pointed out. "And this one has a large bow as well as the plume. The sisters wanted the same color and the feather but didn't want to look exactly the same. I think they'll be pleased, don't you, Jessie?"

I did, and it was fun working on the new designs. If I kept drifting away to think about Chase, it was because I was still exhausted from the night before. Not sleeping could do that to you. It could make you question if you should go running through the Village shouting Chase's name until he came to find you. It could make you forget that the things that were wrong were still wrong.

We worked all morning. At lunch, everyone went out. I needed to turn in my costume and get a fresh one but I didn't want to leave the shop. Suddenly the idea of facing all those people who thought that Chase and I had broken up was too much for me. I felt like hiding underneath all the reams of material cascading around the room. If I was lucky, no one would know I was there.

"Aren't you going out?" Andre asked as he brushed threads from his purple tunic.

"I'm not really hungry. I was thinking I might stay here and take a nap, if that's okay."

"That's fine." He tried to put his arm around my shoulders. It was a stretch for him. "But you have to go out sometime. I know it's hard. But you can't hide away forever."

"I can leave the Village." I heard myself blurt out these terrible words without realizing I'd said them. How could I leave the Village? This place was the only thing that kept me going.

"You don't mean that." He patted my shoulder and told me to get some rest. "I'll get you something to eat while I'm out, and later we'll talk about finding you another place to stay."

I hugged him tightly, careful not to hurt him. I could see he was surprised but not unhappy at the gesture. "Thanks, Andre."

"I frequently take naps over in that chair by the window. There's an old blanket over there somewhere. Curl up and close your eyes. I'll be back soon."

I found the chair and the blanket. It was a very comfortable chair. Most of the window was closed over with large pieces of cloth and other hat-making accessories. There was only one little corner I could look out and see what was going on in the Village. I watched the ladies and their gentlemen stroll by, assailed by minstrels, sheep, and beggars as part of the Renaissance experience.

As I drifted off, thinking they were lucky not to have to watch out for chamber pots being dumped from upper-story windows, I heard the shop door open and close. I started to tell Andre that his chair was very comfortable and that he'd gotten lunch too quickly. I wasn't ready to get up yet.

Then I noticed it wasn't Andre.

I kept completely still, hoping the yards of fabric would hide me from the private detective who'd held a gun on me. I only saw him for a moment the previous night when the stadium lights came on, but I recognized him. I don't forget people who hold guns on me.

He moved stealthily around the congested work area, obviously looking for something. Maybe this was why he'd wanted to question me. I wondered what he thought he'd find here that would help him. I'd been all over the shop and hadn't seen anything that I thought was suspicious.

I wondered if he knew there was a reporter in the Village looking for information about Andre and the Hollywood murder. Maybe they were working together. I might be wrong, but I had a feeling Detective Almond wouldn't appreciate two outsiders stirring the pot.

I dived down a little farther under the blanket—still managing to peek out. If he found something, I wanted to know.

Apparently there was nothing downstairs, or he couldn't find it in all the scraps from every hat Andre had ever made. He went upstairs to the living quarters above the shop, and I heard him rummaging around up there. The pan and spoon clattered on his side as he walked across the squeaky wood floorboards above me.

I waited, hardly breathing, until he came back downstairs again. He left right away—which made me think he'd found something up there. I threw off the blanket as

soon as he stepped out the door. Two (or three) could play
this game. He'd stalked me like the reporter had. It was my
turn.

It was really easy to follow him even through the crowd of
visitors milling around the Village. I was so familiar with my
surroundings that I could concentrate on his weird, mustard-
colored shirt and floppy hat as he made his way down the
cobblestones toward the castle.

"Oh, Jessie! I heard about Chase. I'm so sorry." Lady
Godiva was taking a break from riding her horse around
the Village. She was lounging in the shade of the *Queen's
Revenge* as it rode at anchor.

I ignored her. I wasn't even sure if I knew who she was
this year. I certainly wasn't going to let her get to me.

I focused on my nemesis as he continued toward the
castle, then suddenly veered back on the King's Highway.

For a brief moment, I was afraid he knew I was following him. I darted into Eve's Garden just in case. The smell
of herbs and flowers perfumed the air as I watched him
through the open doorway.

He surveyed the area like he was looking for something,
then changed direction again and walked in the back door
to Our Lady's Gemstones. He was either in a sudden mood
for jewelry or there was something else afoot.

I waited until I thought he'd had enough time to get
inside and feel safe, then I followed him in. Knowing Rene
and Renee might be watching me almost made me turn
back—but I had to know what the detective had found at
the Hat House that had brought him here.

The back of the shop was a work area with none of the
eerie lighting or props of the front. The tables were cluttered
with a rainbow of gemstones, settings, and jewelry-making
paraphernalia. It was fascinating looking at everything. It
would be a great place for an apprenticeship—if the twins
left and someone took their place.

I could hear people speaking in the front showroom and

found a place to get behind the black velvet walls so I could listen. This was even creepier and made me wonder if it was worth being there or not. What could he have found that would matter?

"We specifically told you that we didn't want to meet with you here," Rene said in a voice that reminded me of Mr. Smith from *The Matrix*.

"You were only to contact us by phone and we would meet you off premises," Renee added.

Not enough sleep and too much imagination made me wonder if we'd find the private detective in a trash can later, shot by the twins for his ineptitude.

"I knew you'd want to see this right away," he defended himself. He obviously pulled something out to show them, and there was silence except for some paper-rustling sounds.

"A hat pin?" Rene queried, no expression in his voice.

"A *handmade* hat pin," he explained. "Just like the one they found in your mother. I'll take it and have it analyzed—"

Renee corrected him, "Andre Hariot has thousands of hat pins. He probably made hundreds of them himself. That hat pin is in a lockup somewhere inside the LA police crime lab. The hat pin that killed Cesar Rizzo is also in police custody. What did you hope to gain by this?"

I didn't know what the private detective had hoped to gain, but I learned something important—Kathleen Hariot was the mother of the evil twins! That's why Renee had said that Andre was getting away with murder again. They knew all about what had happened—without the Internet.

Already images of Captain Jack Russell lying dead at the bottom of Mirror Lake came to mind. The evil twins had killed him and taken over his gem shop to be close to Andre so they could kill him, too. They probably set this whole thing up to make Andre look guilty for killing Cesar. Then they could kill him and make it look like suicide. Or put him in the lake with Captain Jack—although it could get crowded down there pretty quickly. But at least the whole thing made perfect sense.

My hand itched for my cell phone, but it was back at Andre's with my stuff. I took a deep breath, trying to be patient and very quiet. I didn't want to end up on the evil twins to-do list.

"How many people have handmade hat pins?" The hapless, clueless PI persisted. "This means something."

Rene (I think) sighed quite heavily. "You said you knew about this case. You said you were an ace detective. You said you could help us privately. All hatmakers have hat pins, sir. Please find another angle."

This was all said in a completely flat monotone. I would've been yelling at the idiot. I hoped they weren't paying him much money. What *was* his problem?

"I understand." He got it at last (about time). "I made a mistake. No reason to get personal about it. I'll still solve this and prove Andre killed your mother. I just need more time."

"Time is all we have at this point," Renee said. "Please don't come here again. You have our phone number. We will only meet you again off-site. It wouldn't be good for people to know who we are."

He mumbled something, then left the shop, slamming the door behind him. I wished I'd known he was going to leave so quickly. I was trapped here without a diversion to get away. What was I supposed to do now?

"He's no help at all," Rene said.

"Patience, brother. We're in the right place at the right time. We'll find justice, one way or the other, for what the hatmaker did."

"We should have paid Jessie Morton to snoop around. At least she seems intelligent and has a reputation for finding out what's going on in the Village."

"Lucky for us that she's distracted by the loss of her lover."

I really expected to hear evil, maniacal laughter and maybe a little pipe organ music. Clearly the twins were even more evil than I thought. It wasn't a figment of my imagination.

Now I had to get out of the gem shop—preferably while still alive—and find Chase.

Lucky for me, the front door to the shop opened and the twins greeted a customer. It was the diversion I needed to get out of there.

I made it to the back door before the black velvet curtain parted and Rene saw me. "Lady Jessie? May I serve you? We don't allow people in our work area." He paused, and his evil little eyes stared at me. I could see he was figuring the whole thing out. "Let me call my sister so we can sort this out. No reason to panic."

My hand was on the doorknob. "Thanks, Rene, but I think I can sort this out by myself."

Twenty-one

He yelled for his sister at the same moment that I jerked open the door and ran outside. There were lots of visitors and Ren folk to blend in with, but I didn't want to risk the evil twins catching up with me anyway. I ran as fast as my long legs and size twelve feet would take me. The world around me was a blur. I kept running until I ran headlong into the proverbial immovable object—Chase Manhattan.

We both fell on the ground, realized what had happened, then grabbed each other.

"I've been looking for you everywhere, Jessie. Where the hell have you been?"

I clung to him like a sea urchin. "I'm sorry I didn't believe in you. I'm sorry I cared if you were sneaking around. I'm sorry for anything in the future that keeps us apart ever again."

"Oh, God, Jessie, I'm the one who's sorry. I don't know what I was thinking, not telling you the truth right away.

They asked me to keep it a secret—very hush-hush—and I thought I could do it but that's just not me."

"They?" I moved away from him a little.

"It's a long story." He kissed me, and that made any story better. "But no matter what happens again between us, promise you won't leave. The Dungeon is your home, too. Okay?"

"I'll never leave again," I promised. "Who are *they*?"

But there wasn't time for him to explain. The evil twins were coming our way like Frankenstein or the Green Slime. They didn't have to move fast. I knew they'd catch up with us.

There wasn't time for me to explain about them either. "Get up!" I urged him. "We have to run."

"What are you talking about?" Chase looked up at Rene and Renee. "What's wrong?"

Like all evil entities, they reached us before we could get ourselves together and get away from them. They looked like vampires in the bright sunlight—pale skin and hungry eyes.

"Don't worry," Rene said. "We won't press charges against you, Lady Jessie. We understand that your circumstances are desperate."

"Yes. We all know how hard it's been for you after your breakup with the bailiff," Renee added in a sympathetic voice.

"Press charges?" I yelled, not caring if it drew a crowd. "For what? Eavesdropping on your plans to kill Andre?"

"What?" Chase got up, taking me with him. "I think we should all go inside before this gets any bigger."

"Not in the gemstone shop." I shuddered. "We can go in the bakery or in the privies, but not in *their* shop."

"That's fine," Rene agreed. "As I was saying, if Lady Jessie will return the diamond she took from the back of the shop—no charges. But it is quite valuable and we have to insist on getting it back."

"Seriously?" I glanced at Chase to see if he was as

outraged as me. "They're accusing me of stealing from them?"

The crowd I'd foreseen was growing—visitors and residents. I should've realized good theater when I heard it. Both evil twins were almost shouting when they called me a thief. They knew everyone would want to get involved. I couldn't believe they outsmarted me in my own Village.

Everyone knew Chase and I had had a fight. They probably knew I'd spent the night outside. They didn't have time to find out that we were back together. The grapevine was good but not that good.

Now Rene and Renee were accusing me of stealing. Like they said, I was desperate. As far as real-life drama went in the Village, it was pretty tasty.

"We demand justice!" Rene managed to sound loud and convincing as he turned to face the crowd. It turned out he was as much an actor as the rest of us, especially to save his own skin. "We demand justice at the stocks!"

This was suddenly bigger than all of us. The crowd sensed blood, even though the best they could get at the stocks was tomato juice.

Chase couldn't deny Rene's right to present his case, according to Village rules. Cameras flashed, and the crowd roared its approval as he nodded. "All right. Let's take this to trial."

I knew I couldn't ask him not to do it. He had no choice. I couldn't imagine what the evil twins would gain by this except the barest reprieve from me telling everyone about them and their relationship to Andre.

Despite not wanting to be labeled a thief (a little late for that), I knew I had to go along with the justice system. It would look bad for Chase if he let his girlfriend go. The twins couldn't prove I took anything any more than I could prove I didn't. It could still mean a turn in the stocks for vegetable justice, since an accusation was almost as good as proof in this kingdom.

It didn't even have to be a real accusation to cause fun for the audience. That's why if someone doesn't accuse their friend, sister, or cousin of a crime to see them put in the stocks, Chase grabs residents and makes something up. Most of the time, it's fun and exciting—at least for the visitors. It gave them something to talk about when they left the Village.

It was a brilliant plan. I had to admit it as we all walked down the cobblestones toward the Dungeon. The twins looked mysterious and angry. Camera flashes continued to go off like sunspots. Chase held my hand as we approached the stocks, their wood frames stained from squishy tomatoes and other vegetables thrown at perpetrators.

"I have to get my wig and robe," Chase whispered. "Will you be okay out here for a minute?"

"I will. Go ahead. Believe me, when this is over, I have something major to tell you and Detective Almond."

"That's why they're doing this?" He threw the evil twins an angry look, left brow raised. "Don't worry. It will be over quickly."

I knew better. Already, King Harold and Queen Olivia, attended by most of their court, were out in carriages to see the spectacle. There had to be four or five hundred people gathered around to watch—which is why we *usually* do resident justice before the Village opens.

"What's going on?" Lord Dunstable called out from his place behind the king and queen in the carriage. It was his job to announce events at the King's Feast and to ask questions that Livy and Harry didn't want to ask. It might sound vulgar coming from the king and queen.

"Lady Jessie Morton stands accused of stealing," someone from the crowd yelled out. It sounded like Fred the Red Dragon, though I couldn't see him to be sure.

"She took some diamonds from the gem shop," someone else yelled out. That sounded suspiciously like Bawdy Betty from the bagel shop. If anyone belonged in the stocks it was her. She was always hitting on Chase, right in front of me. Of course, I'd have to start a list for that offense.

"Impossible!" King Harold actually stood up and roared back. "We do not believe Lady Jessie is a thief. We demand she be released as a member of the nobility. We shall handle this problem ourselves."

I appreciated the sentiment and was surprised by it. Of course it drove the common people in the crowd crazy. I suppose that's what happened in the French Revolution. At least we didn't have a guillotine in the Village.

"She was sleeping on the cobblestones this morning," one of the Lovely Laundry Ladies added. "She was alone. Nowhere to stay. Not a crust of bread to eat. Desperate, she was. Have mercy on her, Sir Bailiff."

"Wait!" Brother Carl called out from behind me. "This is not true. The Lady Jessie was with us. She was neither desperate nor alone. I do not believe she has committed the crime she stands accused of."

"Thanks," I whispered as he put his arm around my shoulders.

Chase appeared at the Dungeon door to loud cries for justice from the crowd. Even the little kids were yelling for me to be put in the stocks. He looked stern and very un-Chase-like in his big white wig and long black robe. "Justice will be done this day, I vow!" Again loud cheers went up from the crowd.

"I would speak on behalf of the Lady Jessie," Roger from the Glass Gryphon said. "I have known her well for a long time. She was my apprentice at the glass-making shop, where all our blown glass figures are half off for today only. She is a good woman. If anyone belongs in the stocks, it is her lover, Bailiff Chase Manhattan, who abandoned her to this fate. And there is free gift wrapping for all purchases before closing time today."

The crowd seemed unsure if they should yell *huzzah* or

repeat the cry for justice after that infomercial. Of course, Roger thought Chase should be in the stocks. He'd disliked Chase since Adventure Land decided he should be bailiff instead of Roger. It was nice for Roger to speak up anyway—even if it was only to take advantage of the crowd.

Chase finally held up his hand for silence. The crowd fell quiet, waiting to see what would happen next. "The plaintiff—speak your piece, and mind you tell the truth or face our justice yourselves."

Rene and Renee made their way to the front of the crowd. "We request a moment alone with the bailiff and the accused."

Chase nodded and the four of us stood by the Dungeon door. I hoped we could wrap this up before the crowd got restless. There were three large bushels of ripe tomatoes within hands' reach of too many people. They were as likely to pelt Chase and the evil twins as me if they had to wait too long.

"Let's settle this quickly," Chase echoed my sentiments. "You made this a sideshow, Rene. What do you want?"

"I want Jessie's word that she'll keep her mouth shut about what she may have overheard today in the shop. In return, we'll pretend we found the diamond and everything will go back to normal."

"You must be crazy." I glared at both the evil twins. "For one thing, this crowd isn't leaving without seeing someone get hit with tomatoes. They won't care who it is. Ask Chase if you don't believe me. You haven't been here long enough to know about these things. You should've considered it before you dragged all of us into it."

Rene started to speak and I stopped him. "Besides all of which, this, in case you haven't noticed, isn't real. The worst that would happen is we all get covered in tomatoes and I go upstairs and take a shower. You two hired someone to ransack Andre's shop, possibly set him up to take the blame for Cesar's murder, and who knows what else. Not to mention that you believe he killed your mother, Kathleen Hariot. He's your stepfather."

Rene's upper lip showed a sheen of perspiration. He looked very put out. "And while we're talking about real-life events, Jessie, what will happen when we call the Myrtle Beach police and Adventure Land to accuse you of this theft? We might never successfully prove it in court, but your time here would be at an end. Your reputation would be ruined. Is it worth all that to tell everyone that Hariot is our stepfather and we hate him? That, after all, is all you have. The private detective came here on his own, as he would testify. Consider your choices carefully."

I knew he was right. He could make my life bad, both here and at the university. In the meantime, all I had was the basic information that he wanted to blame his stepfather for his mother's murder. I wasn't sure if it was worth it. But I was too angry to let it go. At that moment, I didn't care what happened after everyone knew the truth about them.

"I've heard enough," Chase decided. "Let me tell you what's going to happen here. Because someone is going to end up being pelted with tomatoes no matter what any of us say, we're going to go forward with the idea that Jessie was homeless and desperate. Rene, you'll tell everyone—right now—that she's given the diamond back to you."

Rene and Renee looked incredibly smug. I knew Chase had to do something to appease the crowd. I wasn't sure I was happy about it. Forget it—I *wasn't* happy about it. But there was no way around it.

"But let me add that I'm going to recommend that Detective Almond question the two of you in regard to Cesar Rizzo's death. You better be ready to come forth with the man's name that you hired and I hope for your sakes that he tells the same story. That's my judgment. Any questions?"

The evil twins knew they were bested. They shook their

heads, then we all turned to face the crowd. I was glad I wasn't wearing my own clothes. Tomato stains are hard to get out. Even Portia couldn't fault me for what was about to happen.

"Good people of Renaissance Faire Village!" Chase got everyone's attention, his hands held high. "We have reached a verdict."

The crowd had swelled again while we were talking. They cheered loudly, then waited to hear Rene tell them that I had returned the diamond to him. "My sister and I hold Lady Jessie in the greatest respect. For us, this trial is over."

The evil twins pushed their way back through the crowd. In the meantime, the large group was beginning to sense that they might be cheated of their diversion. I didn't want to think about the stampede for tomatoes that could ensue. I started to step forward and let them know that vegetable justice was coming. The sooner it was over, the better, as far as I was concerned. I'd been in the stocks several times. It wasn't really that bad. The hardest part was getting the tomato smell out of my hair.

But before I could take my place in the wooden frame, Chase removed his wig and robe. "Good people," he called out. "Lady Jessie is not to blame for losing her home. I am the culprit behind this situation. I was the one who put her out on the cobblestones. As such, I reserve the right to take her place in the stocks."

I don't know where Diego and Lorenzo, the Tornado Twins, came from, but they were up there with us, telling everyone that they would dispense vegetable justice. Roger put Chase in the stocks before I could raise a word of protest. The crowd shifted position to avoid any tomato residue, then waited for the end of this drama.

There were loud cries of *huzzah* before the tomatoes began to fly. Ladies wept and gentlemen acknowledged Chase's sacrifice on my behalf.

Only a handful of tomatoes actually hit Chase before the

crowd began to lose interest. The Village Crier came by to let everyone know that the Templar Knights were about to meet the Queen's Champions on the Field of Honor. Within five minutes, everyone had dispersed to one end of the Village or another.

I ran to Chase's side and released him. A tomato caught me square in the side of the face. "Oops!" Diego grinned. "Sorry! My bad."

"Time to leave," Lorenzo said, his hands red with tomato juice. "We were happy to help you out here, Chase. Please remember us for any future tomato-throwing needs that might come up for you."

I looked at Chase's tomato-stained face and laughed, kissing him with my own tomato-stained face. "Why did you do that? I was prepared to take it. You're the bailiff. You aren't supposed to be in the stocks."

He put his arm around me. "I wasn't going to let you go through that in front of all those people. Give me some credit."

"Never mind. Thanks for trying to rescue me from the tomatoes anyway. I'll get Diego later. Right now, I think we both need a shower."

"I agree."

"What about Rene and Renee?"

"They aren't going anywhere. We'll deal with them later."

Twenty-two

After we were both clean again, Chase left a message for Detective Almond on his voice mail, then apologized to me. "I have to go over to the pirate ship. Someone dropped a cannon ball on deck and the ship might be damaged. Everyone is a little paranoid about rebuilding another ship.

The good ship *Queen's Revenge* was in its second incarnation after its maiden voyage, when someone thought it would be a good idea to use real cannons. The fire that resulted burned the ship to the water.

"That's okay. It's your job, right?" I kissed him, hoping he was telling me the truth this time. "I have to get my stuff from Andre's. I'll see you later. We'll talk about the private detective the twins hired who stuck a gun in my side last night."

"He had a gun on you?"

"He got away after he reported to the evil twins. There's so much going on in the Village that you don't know about.

Whatever they have you doing is taking too much time away from being bailiff. And from me."

"I'm sorry, Jessie. I didn't know it would come to this. I promise I'll explain everything later."

"Yes, you will."

"Jessie?"

"Hmm?".

"No more sneaking around looking for killers. I don't know if Rene and Renee are hands-on with this, but they could've hurt you."

"They weren't holding me at gunpoint asking me questions," I reminded him. "And I wasn't sneaking around when that happened. I was looking for *you*."

"You know what I mean."

"I do."

"Next time, call me before you come up with any scheme that could put you in danger."

"I will."

"Really?"

"Yes. Really." I smiled. "But I don't have a radio."

"Let's not start that again. Radios are only for Village security. I have to go."

"I'm just saying—you want me to call you? It's hard to yell over everything going on around here. How am I supposed to call you without a radio?"

"Leave the investigation to me or the police and you won't have to."

"Okay." I ran a comb through my hair. "I'll see you later. Looking forward to hearing all about why you were sneaking around the Village."

I'm sure we both knew what he was asking me wasn't going to happen. We both knew about Rene and Renee being related to Andre and possibly Cesar's death because I snooped where I shouldn't have been.

I was a valuable asset to both Chase and Detective Almond

even though I was underappreciated. Sometime it would dawn on both of them that I made all the difference. Chase would want to give me a radio—Detective Almond would command him to do so. I would finally possess the only modern-day invention allowed in the Village besides the cash register.

I tried to imagine what Chase was keeping from me but couldn't. *They* were asking him to do things without telling me. At least he didn't say *she* was asking him to do things. It had to be Adventure Land. It was his mistress when I was there or in Columbia. I'd be jealous if I didn't love her so much, too.

My best bet might be to question Merlin, who wasn't very good at keeping a secret. Yes, he was CEO of Adventure Land and not many people knew that. But if everyone went around asking him directly if that was his position, the entire Village would know. He had looser lips than a Saint Bernard.

From the lack of people on the cobblestones as I walked back toward the Hat House, I knew the Queen's knights were still at the Field of Honor with the Templars. Nothing gets the crowd moving like a good joust. I could hear the *huzzahs* and applause coming from that direction. I wanted to go and watch, too, but I didn't want Andre to worry after he'd left me at the shop before lunch. That was almost two hours ago. I owed him some kind of explanation.

So I ignored the frenzy of the crowd as they watched the knights face each other and kept moving toward the Hat House. I was a little more aware of my surroundings, since the private detective was still on the loose. He might be capable of more than the twins, for all I knew. It made me sorry I didn't tell Chase all about him before we parted ways.

Andre was happy to see me and glad that I was back with Chase. He was surprised when I told him his stepchildren were in the Village. "It's been so many years—they were only children when their mother died. I didn't recognize them," he said. "But moving here, hiring a private detective to set me up—that's a lot even for them!"

"You've had trouble with them before?"

"Yes, they've tried to come after me legally a few times. I guess this is a new tactic for them."

He sat down hard in the little chair by the window. "I never did a thing to them. They hated me from the time I married their mother. I was a few years younger than she was, and they never had any respect for me at all. Do you think they could've killed Cesar for some kind of twisted revenge?"

"I think it's possible—although if it were me, I would've killed Eloise."

"Don't even say such a thing! Thank God they didn't hurt her."

"I don't believe Bernardo and Marco would agree with you."

"Of course you're right. It was a shallow, self-centered thing for me to say. I hope the police will deal appropriately with Rene and his sister. I can't believe they've been right here in the Village and I didn't even realize it."

I looked at the soggy sandwich Andre had gotten for me. It was basically inedible, but I ate most of it anyway to show him how much I appreciated him taking the trouble to get it for me. "Maybe you should talk to them. Maybe you could work things out—saying they didn't kill Cesar, that is."

"I think I'd be best served waiting until we know that for certain, don't you?" He got up and we began work on the hats again. This time I was helping him cut fabric for the crowns of the big, splashy hats. We talked about movies we'd seen and actors we both admired. The time passed quickly, and we were both surprised when Detective Almond poked his head around the shop door.

"Have you seen Manhattan?" he asked me, frowning at

Andre. "He was supposed to meet me at his place, but no one's there."

"That's been his MO this summer. The last I heard he was trying to save the pirate ship from sinking."

"His MO, huh?" He kind of snickered. "You watch too many police shows. I'll see you later."

I told Andre I'd be right back and ran out after him. "Did you question the twins?"

He paused, and I wasn't sure if he was going to tell me. Then he nodded and sat down on one of the benches near the Good Luck Fountain, which was splashing happily again instead of pretending to be a geyser.

"Tell me about this thing with Manhattan. This isn't the first time he's set something up to meet him and didn't show. Is he drinking or doing whatever it is you all do around here?"

I was sorry I'd said anything. I didn't want to get Chase in trouble, though it sounded like he might already be there. "I just meant they have him running around in all different directions. I think they might be putting too much on him instead of hiring someone else to take care of some of the responsibilities."

I hoped that would help explain without making it sound like it was Chase's fault.

"They? Who's they?"

"Exactly! I want to know the same thing. Obviously, it's not another woman, though I had my doubts about Eloise. Of course, I have my doubts about most of the women in the Village at one time or another. I think it has to be Adventure Land, though I won't know for sure until I talk to Merlin."

He looked confused, his heavy chin sinking down to his chest. "You mean Manhattan is seeing some other woman?"

"No. I don't think so. It appeared that way. But now I don't think so."

He shook his head. "What are you people doing out here anyway? If it were up to me, I'd close this whole mess down.

It's not worth the trouble. But Manhattan is a good man. If anybody is giving him a hard time, they'll have to answer to me."

I was so touched by his heartwarming support for Chase that I gave him (including his dirty shirt and mustard-stained tie) a hug. "He *is* a good man. But sometimes people take advantage of good men."

"That's true."

"What about the twins? Are they responsible for Cesar's death?"

"I'll give you a break this time, Miss Jessie, and tell you that they aren't. They have a solid alibi, since they were out of the Village when Rizzo was chocolate coated. I think they wanted their ex-stepdaddy to be guilty of this crime. Hell, I wanted him to be guilty so I wouldn't have to work so hard. But I don't have anything on either of them. Does that make you happy?"

"What about the private detective?"

"The twins aren't talking about any PI."

"I met him last night and followed him into the shop today, which is where I got into trouble. But he's real."

"What's his name?" Detective Almond took out his mangled notebook.

"I don't know. It's not like he gave me his card or anything." I told him about the incident the night before and again at Andre's that day. "He seemed kind of stupid when he was reporting to the evil twins, but he was pretty intense last night with his gun in my side."

"The evil twins, huh?" He put away his notebook. "Well, if you come up with a name for this person, let me know. Until then, I can't do anything."

"Which is what the police always say, and then the hard-working, beautiful apprentice is killed and suddenly everyone believes her, but then it's too late."

He laughed. "You're kind of cute, aren't you? And perky. I don't really like cute or perky, but I guess Manhattan does."

He got up from the bench. "Take care of yourself. I'm going to find your bailiff."

So the evil twins had an alibi, I thought, going back to the Hat House. And they denied knowing about the private detective snooping for them. That was interesting.

But Andre was right—it was a lot of work to go through unless they had something important in mind to torment their stepfather. Of course, they weren't going to admit to their devious plot. I was going to have to keep my eye on them.

I told Andre what Detective Almond had said about his stepkids. "They didn't kill Cesar, but that doesn't mean they aren't responsible in some way. Maybe the private detective did it."

"I don't feel safe here anymore, Jessie." He cut at a wide bow with frantic movements, ruining it. "I think I should leave."

"I don't blame you. But won't they just come at you again—unless we take them out this time. Make sure they can't do it again."

He smiled a little like Jim Carrey as the Grinch. "What did you have in mind?"

Twenty-three

It wasn't so much a plan as enthusiasm for creating a plan. Really, I had no idea what to do. The evil twins seemed capable of anything—including murder. I was scared to walk past the gem shop again.

But it was enough that Andre and I could talk about it and laugh maniacally from time to time (to the consternation of the other assistants). Planning ways to catch the twins or the private detective in their nefarious plots took us through the day as we worked.

Andre didn't seem to have a clue either, but we were both excited about the idea, whatever it was.

"We could create a trap for them," I suggested as I pinned purple satin in place.

"What kind of a trap?" Andre asked.

"Maybe we could make them think Cesar left behind a clue that the police are keeping secret. If they thought we knew what it was, they might come after us and we could call the police."

He paused and seemed to think about it, then went back to cutting. "These things can get out of hand, Jessie. Not to mention that the police are quite far away. We could be dead before they get here. I'm not a young Harrison Ford."

That was true. And it was only a random suggestion. We were kind of brainstorming. Maybe enticing the evil twins to want to kill us wasn't a good idea. "Maybe we could use one of their resources against them."

"I'm listening."

"Okay—there's a private detective and a reporter wandering around the Village. I think both of them are on the twins' payroll. I don't like the private detective. He's kind of stupid and he has a gun. Neal Stevenson is just looking for a good story. Maybe we could use him to get at the twins."

"That sounds interesting and a little Hitchcockian to me," Andre said. "I like it. How do we use the reporter to get at the twins?"

I wasn't sure about that. I told him I'd have to think about it and get back with him. "In the meantime, watch out for the private detective. I don't know how stable he is."

Andre said he would be careful and advised me to do the same. "They seem to gravitate to you more than me. I don't think the twins want to kill me. They would rather embarrass me and see me go to prison."

"Well, we just won't let them do that."

We closed the Hat House as the last of the visitors were heading toward the Main Gate. The mermaids were going for a last swim and waving sad farewells to the huge number of teenage boys who'd gawked at them all day. That attraction seemed to be a hit.

I saw a group of Templar Knights riding through the Village toward the forest. They were a magnificent sight. Each horse and rider seemed in tune with each other and all the other riders. It made me sorry I'd missed their afternoon performance with the Queen's Champions. But I had no doubt who'd won that meet.

Robin Hood stood watching them go, leaning against one of the manor walls at Squire's Lane. His arms were folded against his chest, a sly smile playing across his good-looking face.

"I know that look," I assailed him. "What have you got up your gauntlet?"

"Not much," he answered as his smile grew bigger. "Our normal ways of getting justice don't seem to be working right now. But we have access to another way of putting those arrogant knights in their place."

"You're going to prank them." I nodded. I've been there. Sometimes it's the only way to get back at someone here. The knights had usurped the Sherwood Forest band as the most popular attraction. I understood the need for vengeance.

"Just a little reminder of who the *real* king of Renaissance Village is."

"I take it you don't mean King Harold."

"Nope. See you. Remember this conversation tomorrow when you wake up and the tables have turned. Good evening, Lady Jessie." He kissed my hand and swept me a formal bow.

Whatever he had in mind must be really good. I couldn't wait.

As I walked down the cobblestones past the Monastery Bakery, I was curious exactly what Robin would do if the mermaids became the most popular attraction. I had a feeling he would resolve that issue in a much different way. Or he wouldn't mind at all because it didn't involve testosterone or tight pants.

"Good evening to you, Lady Jessie." Mistress Mary Quite Contrary sauntered by with her mobcap-covered curls held high. "Have you heard that the king will only accept the queen's child as his own if she agrees to a paternity test?"

"No, Mistress Mary. I hadn't heard that yet, but it doesn't surprise me. Dost thou believe the child to be his?"

She shook her head. "I do not. The queen has refused the

test thus far. I believe she will refuse and the king will openly proclaim the child to be a royal bastard."

That was harsh. "Perhaps their majesties will find a way to work this out. They are the heart and soul of Renaissance Village."

Mistress Mary laughed her pretty, tinkling laugh. "Thou art a dreamer, Lady Jessie. The queen has cuckolded the king once too often. Mark my words—he will banish her and take a new wife. It could be one of us."

I couldn't believe her attitude. Plainly, she saw herself in the role Livy had had for the last ten years. I knew King Harold had fooled around a little with Mistress Mary (I've heard she looks ten pounds smaller in leather), but her dreams of succeeding the queen were beyond her station.

I wondered where Chase was and if we'd really have a chance to talk tonight. I'd already decided that if he sneaked out again, I was sneaking out after him. No more secrets. It was getting to where I couldn't believe what he was telling me. That wasn't going to work. I didn't believe he was seeing someone else, but whatever he was doing had to stop.

As I passed the Dutchman's Stage, I saw Neal Stevenson sitting on the stairs that led up to the stage. The magician who'd been the last act was cleaning up his props. Neal was drinking from a bottle of scotch, almost unheard of in the Village. We mostly prefer ale. I thought about the plan Andre and I had discussed earlier and decided to go and talk to him. Maybe he could help.

"Mistress Jessie." He nodded so low that he almost fell off the stairs. "It's very good to see you again."

I didn't quibble about being Lady Jessie. Instead I sat down next to him and started talking. "You're here at the Village because of Rene and Renee, aren't you?"

He waved his bottle as he swallowed a mouthful of scotch whiskey. "You have me at a disadvantage. You know why I'm here. But how did you get involved?"

I told him about looking everything up on the Internet.

"How did you know Andre's steptwins were here? Did you hear about Cesar's death and that Andre was living here? Did you follow all of them here?"

"You're good at guessing. Kathleen Hariot's murder is still open. I'd like to help close it. I keep tabs on all the players. That's why I'm here."

"Are the twins paying you to work for them?"

He laughed. "I wish they were. That would be sweet, wouldn't it?"

"But you want to write the story, right? That's what you said when you asked me to spy on Andre for you."

"You're right. That was it. But I got my pink slip today. It seems my editor decided they could live without me, even if I'm working on the biggest story of my career."

I studied his craggy face and large, fuzzy eyebrows. His nose was a little red at the end and his eyes looked as if he'd been crying. It was probably a major blow for someone his age to look for another job.

"I'm sorry. Maybe if you finish the story, your editor will be so impressed that he'll want you back again." I knew what it was like to be out of work.

"That's very nice of you. But people are being laid off left and right these days. I don't think the story will matter."

"You can always sell it to someone else," I reminded him.

"Because so many people are going to remember the death of Kathleen Hariot or care about the death of Cesar Rizzo? I don't think so. I think I'm a washed-up old hack who doesn't know enough about the Internet to blog or tweet or whatever they call it right now. I'm used to paper and ink. That's all I know."

I felt truly sorry for him. It would be like getting a notice from the Village that I was too old to come back again. Not coming here would be devastating. Old professors keep on teaching—but old Rennies might not be so lucky.

Despite my feelings toward him, I still felt like he could be useful in trapping the evil twins. "You know, the Village hasn't had a newspaper in a couple of years. It closed down and no one wanted to reopen it. Maybe you could start another newspaper. I could help you."

"Maybe. But this place"—he waved the bottle in the general direction of the area around us—"it's like bizarro land. I don't think I'd fit in here. Thanks for the offer."

"I know it wouldn't be permanent, but what if I could offer you a job for a while?"

"You mean doing something besides hanging out on the street beating this pan with a spoon? I don't give a damn what it is—I'll take it."

We talked for a while longer about the Village and I tried to think where I could find a job for him, now that I'd offered. I hoped something would come to me. There was always something extra to do here. Maybe Chase could take him on as help during vegetable justice. He usually had an assistant.

"I'm sure we can find something for you." *I hope.*

"Thanks. You know, I always thought it might be fun to be a truck driver. That was before I started writing. Maybe I'll go to truck driver's school. I could get into driving one of the big rigs."

I didn't mention that we didn't have any of those in the Village, but what I could find for him would only be temporary anyway. I encouraged him to follow his dream, then promised again to check around for a job. We arranged to meet first thing in the morning.

I felt good about myself as we parted company. The evening was settling in but remained hot and humid. It would probably rain again tonight. I was glad to escape into the Dungeon and turn the air-conditioning on full blast upstairs.

I was a little anxious about Chase not coming home— I didn't want to break our fragile truce, but I knew I'd have to say something neither of us would like if he didn't show up.

Lucky for me (and him), he walked in the door at the stroke of seven P.M. Life was good!

"Tough day," he said, changing clothes. "How's Andre holding up?"

We made polite conversation as I waited for Chase to tell me what was going on. Whatever it was, it still wasn't easy to say. I knew procrastination when I saw it. But it didn't matter, I reminded myself, we had the whole evening. He could take his time.

It wasn't easy listening to all the minute details of his day, knowing it was only a distraction. But I smiled and nodded, anxious for the answers I knew he had.

When I thought the last of my patience would burst out of me—there was a knock at the door. Chase seemed relieved when he went to answer it and found Detective Almond outside on the stairs.

I tapped my foot on the floor with a growing amount of impatience. What was he up to now?

"Sorry if I'm interrupting something." Detective Almond came in and sat down at the table, his action belying his words. "Just wanted to catch you up on the Rizzo case."

"Soda? Beer? Water?" Chase asked him, opening the mini-fridge.

"No, thanks. But you go right ahead and help yourself."

"Anything new?" Chase opened a bottle of water and sat opposite him.

"A little. Nothing has changed as far as Hariot is concerned. He's my man for Rizzo's death. I don't know how he managed it yet, but I'll figure it out. In the meantime, we tracked down the PI from California who's been hanging around the Village."

He paused—it looked like he wanted to be sure I was listening.

"Private detectives have to register with the police if they want to work here. His name is Joe Bradley. He's from

Fresno. Good references from the police there. He completely denies holding a gun on your girlfriend or reporting to Andre's stepkids."

"Then why exactly is he here?" I asked in exasperation.

"He says he's here looking for a felon who jumped bond out there. He's licensed for that, too. The felon story checks out, by the way. Bradley says his man is working here under an alias. That's possible."

"I didn't imagine the gun episode," I said a little sharply. Between him and Chase, I wasn't sure I had any patience left.

"Maybe you thought he said something he didn't," Detective Almond suggested. "You know how that is sometimes."

"Maybe I imagined a gun, too?"

"I spoke with your security guys here." He shrugged. "The man you asked for help didn't see anyone with you. He says the only people he saw, besides other security guards and you, were maintenance men."

"He was busy watching the water spray out of the fountains," I explained. "Besides which, the whole area was dark until they turned on the stadium lights. The man held a gun in my side. Maybe it wasn't this Bradley character that seems to be the salt of the earth. Maybe you have the wrong person."

"You could be right. I'll keep you posted if I hear about another private detective working here—if I can tell him from the other weirdos out here." He nodded at Chase. "Let's focus on tripping up Hariot. I'd like to be the one to close both of these cases."

Chase didn't say anything. Detective Almond strolled back out the door. The silence in the little apartment was scary. Usually, there wasn't enough time for Chase and me to say everything we wanted to each other.

"You don't believe him, right?" I hoped my voice didn't sound as anxious as I felt.

"If you say someone held a gun on you, Jessie, I believe

you. Just because the man Almond talked to denied it doesn't mean he didn't do it. Or it could be a different man."

I was almost completely relieved—but still waiting for my long-overdue explanation about why he kept disappearing.

"Let's get some dinner, huh?" He got to his feet and held out his hand for mine. "We can talk about everything else while we eat."

But it was then that his radio went off with a security alert that someone had broken into the Three Chocolatiers Shoppe again. "I have to get this. I'll meet you at the Pleasant Pheasant," he said.

"Not on your life!"

Twenty-four

This time no one was there. The chocolate shop was empty, but someone had been there and had tossed around everything that wasn't nailed down. It couldn't get much worse.

"Maybe we should check on Bernardo," I suggested as we walked through the mess of chocolate, sugar, and candy molds that were everywhere. "He was here looking for something before. Maybe he came back to look again."

"You mean the chocolate recipe?" Chase asked. "Something else is wrong, Jessie. Whatever is lost in here, the person is going to keep coming back until they find it."

He had the security guards padlock the doors this time. Normally, that wouldn't be necessary, but since it seemed to keep happening, he had no choice.

"Are we going to check on Bernardo?" I wondered as we left what had been one of my favorite places in the Village.

"That might not be necessary." He pointed to a spot on

the stairs and another on the cobblestones, shining his flashlight there. "It looks like whoever did this walked out with some chocolate and sugar on their shoes. Let's follow the trail."

"Small feet, too," I remarked as we walked back toward Fabulous Funnels, where the trail led. Of course, with my giant clodhoppers, I tend to notice these things.

"I know Detective Almond really wants Andre for Cesar's death, but I think he's wrong. I think he's blindsided by the idea that both murders seem the same. Everyone is convinced Andre killed his wife, so he must be guilty here, too."

"Except you?" I was careful to watch my step as we talked. I didn't want to ruin the trail that could lead to Cesar's killer. The small footprints turned back toward the fountain near Da Vinci's Drawings.

"I guess." He smiled. "But what do I know?"

"You know more about the Village than Detective Almond ever will," I said in total support of his position. "And I agree with you. I don't think Andre killed anyone."

He hugged me for a quick moment. "Thanks. But you always see the best in everyone. It's one of the things I love about you."

"That might be true. Except for the evil twins. And Wanda. I don't think they have a best."

We followed the ever-decreasing trail of chocolate and sugar until it reached the fountain, where it dead-ended. I could see some sugar granules sparkling on the edges of the stone basin, but there were no more tracks.

"I think our prowler noticed there was a trail." Chase touched the sugar on the fountain.

"But we know whoever it was had small feet."

"Which leaves out Bernardo."

"It had to be a woman."

"Or a man with really small feet." Chase shook his head. "Don't worry. Andre is small but not that small."

"Who else could it be?"

"There are approximately three hundred women working here this summer. I guess you could add in a dozen or so younger men with small feet."

"I think it's Eloise," I decided.

"Big surprise."

"Okay. It could be Beth," I admitted. "Although I don't think this would be her style."

He nodded. "All right. Because Eloise is dating Bernardo now, we'll start with her."

"You aren't jealous are you?" I tried to see his face, but there were too many shadows.

"She's not my type." He put his arm around my waist. "I like my women tall, sassy, and curious to the point of getting themselves killed."

"I guess I'm jealous now because that doesn't sound anything like me."

He knocked on the door of the upstairs apartment shared by the three sisters who ran the tart shop. It seemed like such a perfect combination—three pie-making sisters paired up with three chocolate-making brothers. I would've bet my matchmaking skills on it.

But Eloise apparently wasn't happy with only one man. She wanted as many as she could get at one time. Which made her and Cesar a perfect match. Maybe they could've worked it out, except for Andre.

Belle, the youngest tart, answered the door. If I were going to like any of them, it would be her. She was very pretty but not so belligerent about it. She was also more quiet and shy. She didn't talk trash like Angela and Eloise. She also never acted like she had a right to every man in the Village.

"Is Eloise here?" Chase asked her with a smile.

Belle nodded. "I'll get her."

Since the room behind her was empty, I whispered, "Has Eloise gone out anywhere in the last hour or so?" I knew the chocolate and sugar would've disappeared completely in the damp weather if it had been longer.

Belle's cheeks turned pink, which I took to mean that Eloise had been out. But she replied, "No. Not that I'm aware of. Is there a problem?"

"We're not sure." Chase gave me his annoyed look. "Could we just speak to Eloise?"

Angela and Eloise came out of their bedrooms to join us in the cramped living room. Their apartment was bigger than the one Chase and I shared, but not by much. There couldn't be many secrets between them—no privacy either.

While Chase questioned Eloise about her whereabouts, I looked at her shoes. Why waste your time talking when you could go right to the source?

She was wearing sandals—the kind that cross over the top of your foot and tie. Very nice. But her feet were bigger than the tracks we'd followed.

"Did you know Bernardo broke through the police tape to look for something in the chocolate shop?" Chase asked point-blank.

"Does it matter?" she demanded. "It's his shop."

Good point. Score one for Eloise. Angela had on slippers. Belle was barefoot. Both of them could be contenders for the shoe size, but I couldn't see why either of them would be involved. If Cesar had been dating all three sisters, I think we would've heard about it.

Chase explained that the police investigation of Cesar's death wasn't over. Eloise shrugged her expressive, bare shoulders, not getting why we were there. "Bernie has a right to look through the shop," she defended her new lover. "Maybe he needed some chocolate. Or maybe he needed money from the cash register."

"He told me he was looking for his brother's chocolate recipe," I added, knowing it would make her angry to learn that Bernardo and I had been talking.

"There you go." She smiled in an awful way. "Why are you bothering me with this? I don't have a chocolate recipe."

"Maybe not. But these weren't Bernardo's footprints that we followed from the shop," Chase continued. "We thought they might be yours."

She laughed. "You must be kidding! Like I'd be out there looking for something Bernie could find on his own. Besides." She shivered. "*Eww!* Cesar died in there!"

Her reaction was genuine enough. I knew Chase was convinced, too, because he got up to leave.

"Look, if any of you played any part in this—the murder or the break-in—now is the time to come forward. Don't wait to get caught." He took his time staring down into each woman's face. None of them so much as blinked. If they were guilty of anything, we weren't going to find out that night.

Belle looked like she had something to say. Her eyes widened and she opened her mouth as she put her hand out to Chase.

Angela pulled her back.

It made me feel like the youngest tart might know something about Eloise, but she was afraid to speak up. The sisters were loyal to each other—I had to give them that.

"Well, that got us nowhere," Chase said as we went back down the stairs to the cobblestones. It had started raining again, a light sprinkle that was clearing away the terrible heat.

"Maybe not but—"

The yard outside the King's Tarts was filled with dark riders. The Templar Knights were waiting on their wonderful black horses, each carrying a burning torch.

Chase stopped and looked up at them. "Is there a problem?"

"Not any longer." The knight in front, who seemed to be

in charge, wasn't the same smoky-voiced leader who was usually with them. I wondered where the big knight had gone.

"What does that mean?" Chase asked.

"You have been alerted, Bailiff. Our job is done." As though there were an invisible signal between them, they all rode away together, their horses' hooves striking on the rainy night air.

"Those guys are just plain weird." I had to voice my opinion. "I think the other residents might be right. They need to get out of the Village. I know they're popular—"

"I'm not Adventure Land," Chase growled. "Talk to Merlin about it. Let's go home."

Talking to the wizard that night might've been easier than trying to talk to Chase as we ate frozen dinners. He didn't have anything to say, and even my best attempts to draw him into a conversation were met with stony glares.

I know it was cowardly of me, but I didn't bring up either of the burning questions in my mind—why did he keep disappearing and what was Adventure Land forcing him to do?

I know I should've been more demanding. I shouldn't have lain there and let him fall asleep in my arms, but I'm not made of stone. Whatever was bothering him would come out. I could wait. I knew I'd wait forever for him if I had to.

Just before dawn, Chase eased his large frame out of bed very carefully, trying not to wake me. But I was determined that he wasn't going out again without me. I waited until he was dressed and gone, then I followed him.

There were two security guards outside the Dungeon along with my brother, Tony, and one other man I recognized from Robin's pack in Sherwood Forest. The five of them stood outside talking quietly as the gray morning light crept up on the Village.

"Hey, Jessie," Tony said even though I was still inside the open doorway, trying to be inconspicuous.

I'd forgotten how good he was at knowing I was there without seeing me. Chalk it up to twin magic. I had a similar talent—I was always able to tell when he needed money.

"How long have you been there?" Chase asked me.

"Not as long as you. What's up?"

One of the security men laughed. "I'd say about twenty of the Merry Men."

Twenty-five

He wasn't kidding. The Merry Men of Sherwood Forest—including Robin Hood—were scattered through the forest, hanging from trees like trussed-up turkeys. They were carefully bound and gagged, gazing at us in anger and frustration when we saw them.

The security men laughed until Chase finally said, "Okay. I think we've all had our fun with this. Each of you take a tree. Make sure there aren't any visitors tied up. If there are, bring them to me. Don't just let them leave. I don't want to see anyone's personal experience hanging from a tree in Renaissance Village on the Internet."

I had a little pocketknife with me that I'd recently started carrying in the pouch on my side. It had already come in handy a few times. I went to help Robin first, recalling his words from last night. I don't think this was what he had in mind.

As soon as I cut his gag, a steady stream of oaths followed, all aimed at the Templars. "We didn't do anything,"

Robin swore to Chase while I cut him down. "Those guys need to be reined in."

I knew he was lying—I knew something was up last night. It just didn't work out the way he'd planned. When I saw the look on Tony's face—let's call it his lie-to-Jessie face—I knew I was right.

Chase knew, too. "Don't bother denying that you planned to teach the knights a lesson. I live here, too. If you want to keep something secret, you shouldn't tell everyone in the Village about it beforehand."

Robin glared at me.

"I didn't say anything," I defended. "But I suppose you told other people, too."

He started to deny it but tried another tack. "We have our pride! We were here first."

"This isn't just your forest anymore," Chase told him. "We've talked about this before. Stealing from or otherwise tampering with the Templars isn't a good idea. Play your games with someone else."

"Never mind that," Alex, Robin's second in command, yelled as he was released. "Why do you always take their part, Chase? These guys are marauders. They need to be stopped. Since when can't groups have fun together?"

"Your idea of fun is different than theirs," Chase said. "What was your plan, Alex? You thought you could sneak into their encampment and take it from there?"

"These were our trees first." Robin pushed on the tree that had recently been his home. "The Templars have been taking over everything. Ask any resident—"

"Except the women," Tony added. "Don't ask the women."

But Chase was done hearing their excuses. "I'm not your father," he told them. "I don't favor either of you. I'm here to keep the peace. That's all."

"At *our* expense!" Alex shouted.

"Get some sleep, all of you," Chase advised. "Leave the Templars alone."

"Are you sure this is what Adventure Land wants?" I asked as Chase and I left the forest. The security men were still cutting Robin's guys down from the trees.

"I don't know right now, Jessie."

"How about some coffee? We can talk over breakfast."

"I have a hundred things to do before breakfast," he said with an edge to his voice. "I'll pass for now. See you later."

I'd never seen Chase so stressed. Not even when the elephants and camels had gotten loose at the same time. Not even when his lance broke during the joust and the Black Knight kept coming after him. I knew it was time for me to get involved.

I got two coffees and two extra-large cinnamon rolls from the Monastery Bakery. It was still early, no visitors yet. The Village was waking up around me with chickens clucking and roosters crowing. The maintenance guys were cleaning out the privies, and the street sweepers were washing down the cobblestones. I watched as the new Green Man practiced his routine on stilts and the men who owned the Three Pigs Barbecue unloaded what looked like hundreds of pounds of coleslaw. Did people really eat that much coleslaw in a day?

The pirates were up early (probably still doing ship repairs), barking out commands that drifted out over the lake in pirate-speak.

I waved to Ginny Stewart, a tough, white-haired woman who owned the Lady of the Lake Tavern. She was sweeping out the courtyard beneath the Hanging Tree. She kind of waved her broom at me and kept going.

I finally reached Merlin's Apothecary on the far side of the castle. He didn't know it yet, but he and I were going to have a little talk about what was really going on out here with the Templars—and with Chase.

Merlin was dusting his motley, stuffed moose head, affectionately known as Horace, when I entered his shop. Everything in the apothecary needed a good cleaning.

There were years of dust and cobwebs on the colored bottles and the jars that held Merlin's magic potions.

Apparently the place looked exactly like visitors thought it should, though, because they spent hours there and loved to have their pictures taken with the moose and the wizard.

"Ah! Lady Jessie! It's very good to see you this morning!" Merlin greeted me from the ladder. "I see you have two cups of coffee. To my knowledge—which is as vast as the ocean—the bailiff is not about this place. That can only mean you've brought me breakfast."

"That's right. I have a fresh cinnamon roll for you, too. Would you like to eat in the courtyard? The minstrels are rehearsing next door. It should be a wonderful place to talk."

"I see. This gift of breakfast comes with a price."

"Nothing is free, wizard. You of all people should know this."

He didn't move from the ladder, instead looking like he couldn't decide if he wanted to come down at all. "Mayhap I will forego breakfast, my lady. A thousand pardons. The shop needs cleaning, as you can see. Perhaps another time."

"Perhaps not." I wasn't taking no for an answer. Maybe I couldn't bully Chase, but I could handle Merlin. "Get down here and eat this food or I'm telling everyone who you really are."

He tipped his pointy, purple hat with gold stars to one side of his graying head. "I don't believe this would make any difference to the everyday workings of the Village. Tell away."

"If everyone knew you ran Adventure Land, there would be a line waiting all the way to the Village Square with residents who have complaints. Perhaps you have never seen how angry they are every Thursday morning as they wait to complain to the bailiff."

"The next time I see Sir Bailiff," Merlin whined, "I shall

complain as well. He was not supposed to share his information about me with everyone."

"Lucky for you, he didn't. I'm the only one who knows."

He mumbled and complained all the way down the ladder, but the important part was that he ended up sitting with me at one of the tables in the courtyard. The morning was pleasantly cool after the rain the night before. The music from the practicing minstrels was sweet. The coffee was still hot—and I was determined to get my answers.

"What do you want, Lady Jessie?" he asked when we were seated and enjoying our cinnamon rolls.

"I want to know why you aren't doing anything about the Templars terrorizing the Village. That's for starters."

"What would you have me do? The visitors like the Templars. We've seen a three and a half percent growth in ticket sales since they set up camp. You can't argue with the numbers. They make shareholders happy. In turn, that makes me happy."

"They hung Robin and his men up in trees last night. They interrupt other residents trying to do their jobs."

He shrugged. "Robin Hood steals toaster ovens. I don't see any difference except that he and the Merry Men aren't bringing in any new business. We have to continue to grow, Lady Jessie. I'm a very old man and there are two things in life I still enjoy. One of them is being with pretty, young women and the other is living here as a wizard. The only thing that could keep me from enjoying my final years on this earth is bad ticket sales."

"What about Chase? How does he figure into this?"

"I don't know what you mean."

"You have him sneaking out at all times of the day and night. He's not doing what he's supposed to be doing. I know he's working for the Village somehow outside his duties as bailiff. What's going on?"

Merlin sipped his coffee and smiled at me. "Methinks

this may be a personal matter, my lady. What does a beautiful young woman such as yourself do when her man strays?"

"Don't give me that crap! What's his special assignment?" He wasn't messing with my mind—at least not this morning.

"I don't know what you mean."

There was an off-key lute player on the stage next door. We winced at the sound and the music stopped as the rest of the musicians waited for him to tune his instrument.

Unfortunately, I'd already used my only threat against Merlin. I didn't know what else to say. I knew he was lying, but I didn't know how to make him tell me the truth.

"A pleasant repast, my lady," he finally said as the music began again, this time in tune. "I hope you have the answers you require. I must take my leave now. I have matters to attend to in my apothecary before the opening of the Village."

"Fine. Don't tell me. But I'm warning you, wizard, you're going to lose Chase Manhattan as your bailiff if something doesn't change. I've known him for a long time and I've never seen him this way. I know you know he doesn't have to be here. He could be gone in a puff of your magic smoke."

He seemed to consider my words. I wasn't sure at first if it would matter. I knew it did when he sat back down. "If you tell anyone what I'm about to tell you, I'll deny it."

"Not that it really matters, but fine. Tell me what's going on."

"One of the big shareholders in Adventure Land came up with, and financed, the idea for the Templar Knights encampment. It seems to be a good idea—except that he insisted his son be one of the knights. The boy is a little hotheaded and high strung. There were problems right away."

"And?"

"We decided to give the riders a leader. Someone strong

and capable they could look up to. They aren't bad boys, you know. They just need a firm hand on the reins, so to speak."

"The big knight." I nodded. "I've met him."

Merlin laughed. "Of course you have, silly girl. You live with him."

Suddenly I totally understood everything. "You're making Chase do double duty as the leader of the Templars *and* the bailiff! No wonder he keeps disappearing." And many other aspects that I didn't plan to relate to Merlin. "It has to stop. Detective Almond said Chase doesn't show up for meetings. I thought he might kill Robin Hood this morning. You have to find someone else."

"Don't you think we've tried? Chase is a natural leader. The knights, including our young stockholder's son, look up to him. He keeps them in check."

"Or he could if that was his only job," I argued. "You can't have it both ways. Either Chase stays on as bailiff or he leads the Templars. I bet you aren't even paying him extra." I got up from the table and gathered the trash from breakfast. "This isn't going to go any further. But find another person to lead the Templars or I'll convince Chase to leave the Village forever."

With my final warning ringing in the cool morning air, I left Merlin with the breeze whipping at his purple robe. I heard one of the tavern wenches from Baron's Beer and Brats swear at him as his robe flew a little too high, and I didn't look back.

Twenty-six

I was so angry that Chase was being used by Adventure Land. No wonder he was so moody and not himself. After all he'd done for them, I couldn't believe they'd treat him this way.

I stopped and considered that Chase had agreed to take on this double duty. It was true that his personality lent itself to helping others. But I had to wonder why he hadn't told me the truth. I knew now that he was close when he said they'd made him do it and that it was hush-hush. Now that I knew the truth, it made me uneasy.

I'd told Merlin that Chase would quit working at the Village, but that probably wasn't an option. I wouldn't be happy about that for me or for Chase. There had to be a way to reconcile this problem with the stockholder's son. I just had to figure out what it was.

After looking everywhere for Chase to tell him that I knew what was going on, I finally saw the Templars practicing at the Field of Honor. It was still early, so there was no show for the visitors and only a handful of residents watching from the closed gates.

The Templars had doffed their heavy chain mail for loose black kaftans and pants. Their faces were still covered, but I knew that the leader, the biggest rider, was Chase.

It made me smile to think about him flirting with me, letting me think he was someone else. And was I ever glad I'd told his alter-ego that I was committed to my man, who ended up being the same person. You never know when you're going to say exactly the right thing. Too often, it's the other way.

I realized at that moment that I couldn't say anything to Chase about his role with the Templars. He obviously didn't want me to know—for whatever reason. I decided to honor that, at least until he was ready to tell me the truth.

That didn't mean I had to give up trying to help him with the knights. Robin had been too boastful of his plan for retribution. The knights (especially the problem stockholder's son) needed to be taken down. They needed to see that the Village was more important than any single attraction. I had a plan forming that would be better worked without Chase's knowledge—at least I hoped so.

Chase was hard on the other knights. They practiced every drill and horse maneuver I'd ever seen. Horses and riders became one on the field. No wonder they'd beaten the Queen's Knights. They were great riders with huge egos. I hoped there was a way to teach them a lesson without hurting Chase.

The group of riders circled the field then met in the middle, clanging their shields together, kind of like fist-pounding, to show their solidarity as a team. Only one rider didn't do his part with the others. He stayed back from the group, and when they started to depart the field, he attacked Chase from behind.

I gripped the fence post until the wood threatened to go through my skin. This wasn't good theater, as some of the residents around me thought. This was malicious, an attempt to take power by embarrassing and possibly injuring the leader—Chase.

But years working in the jousts as both the good knights and the bad made Chase ready for a sneak attack. It happens all the time during performances. The lance coming at him from behind was deflected by his shield. Chase pivoted in the saddle and pushed hard, knocking the lance from the other rider's hand.

I wasn't sure what he'd do next. It was Chase—I thought he might continue riding out of the field. I was surprised when he lifted his lance and rode back to take on his opponent. The other knights formed a corridor around him and the contender but didn't interfere.

Without a lance, the rider could only wait until Chase hit him. He successfully moved his horse to one side and deflected most of the blow with his shield. But he dropped his defense and the shield clattered to the ground.

"These guys play for keeps," Hans Von Rupp, the blacksmith, said in an admiring way. "I like to see them rough, you know?"

I didn't—couldn't—talk to him. Chase was riding down on the other man with his lance at the ready. The rider came back at him with a long sword that looked disturbingly real. I wanted to run out there and remind them that this wasn't really the Renaissance. We were here to entertain, not fight for our honor or egos. But I stayed where I was. I wasn't sure the other riders would let me in, and I had a healthy fear of getting underfoot when two riders were fighting.

The long sword hit Chase's shield, but the lance pushed the rider from the saddle. He fell heavily on the ground while his horse moved away from the attack.

The man on the ground didn't move. Chase turned his horse at the end of the corridor of knights and rode back to finish the job, at least that's what it looked like.

"What the hell is he doing?" Daisy Reynolds from Swords

and Such asked. "It's over. Somebody needs to tell them to stop. What's wrong with these guys anyway?"

"I'll take care of it," Bart volunteered. But the heavy chain and padlock on the gate kept him from honoring that vow. It would take a key or bolt cutters to get through in time to stop the fight.

Or you could be stupid and small enough to climb between the rails and run into the enclosure with your arms up—screaming at them to stop. "Hey!" I screamed, standing beside the man on the ground. "Honor is satisfied. You guys need to go home and cool off. No death by joust today or the *bailiff* will have your heads in the stocks tomorrow!"

Yes. I was that fool. I was the only one who could get between the rails fast enough from the group watching. Not to mention that I had a vested interest in making sure Chase didn't kill anyone—no matter how much they deserved it.

The rider brought the horse to a dead stop right next to me. The hot air coming from the horse's nostrils tickled the side of my head. I didn't move—didn't breathe. I was totally conscious of how close that huge beast was to me.

The man on the ground moaned and tried to lift his head. He finally lay back against the ground and didn't move. I knelt beside him and removed his black headpiece. I wasn't sure if the loudest sound of surprise came from the riders around me or the watchers at the gate.

The young man under the hood looked like he was in his early twenties. He was very blond, very good-looking, and very out of it. He opened his eyes and smiled at me. "You must be an angel. Are you here to take me to heaven?"

I wasn't sure how to reply so I tried to make him comfortable, then looked up at Chase—still behind his own disguise and on his horse hovering over us. "You better call for paramedics. At the very least, he has a concussion. Wanda can't handle this. I shouldn't have to tell you either."

I didn't care then if he knew that I knew who he was. This was reckless and irresponsible. Chase knew better.

"What's going on out here?" Chase demanded, running in through the now open gate.

I did a double take when I saw him. *Huh?* If that was Chase—who was the big guy on the horse?

"Call the paramedics," he said into his radio. He dropped down on the ground and checked out the fallen knight. "What happened, Jessie?"

I was too stunned to answer. I didn't have to, though, because Daisy, Bart, and Hans all told the story at the same time. The riders still remained in their columns. The knight who'd injured his friend on the ground saluted Chase mutely, then rode hell-bent-for-leather out of the field and into the forest.

The young man was starting to come around. The color came back to his face. I didn't want to think about the mass of bruises that were hidden under his black costume. Chase talked to him until the paramedics got there—keeping him alert and asking him questions about the date, his location, and other information he should know.

We all stood around as the paramedics took the rider away. Daisy and the others didn't know what I knew. I wasn't sure right then if I knew what I knew. Was Merlin lying to me? Wasn't Chase part of the Templar Knights? Was the big knight who'd taken me home on his horse Chase or not?

Once the paramedics were gone, Daisy and Bart went back to Swords and Such after throwing out a few warnings about the Templars. Hans did the same. Chase couldn't say he didn't know the knights were a bad element in the Village.

"I think I need that coffee now," Chase said. "Are you busy?"

By this time, I'd found my voice again. "Are you kidding me? I just watched one of those knights try to kill another one, all the time thinking it was *you*, and all you can say is let's have coffee?"

He glanced around the empty field. "Not here. We should talk in private."

"This is about as private as it gets here. Are you one of the knights or not?"

"I guess you talked to Merlin. I can't believe he told you."

"Merlin would tell his last secret for a cinnamon roll. Or anything else, for that matter. I don't know why everyone in the Village doesn't know he's CEO of Adventure Land already."

"Have you ever heard of loose lips sink ships?"

"Have you ever heard that one lie becomes many?" I glared at him, daring him to come up with another axiom.

"Jessie—"

"Don't bother making it worse."

"I love you. I'm sorry I kept a secret from you. I won't ever do it again."

"Like that makes it better." I would not be wooed from my righteous anger.

He put his arms around me. "What would make it better?"

"I don't think you know those words."

He kissed me and smiled. "I've been a total ass. Forgive me."

I sniffed and pretended that I was still mad, but I just can't stay angry with him for long. "I already had coffee while I seduced the information about you from Merlin," I whined. "You'll have to think of something better."

"I have just the thing."

Twenty-seven

"So you're the leader of the Templars." I wanted to make sure I completely understood the situation. "First of all—how did you let them talk you into doing it? And why is this stockholder's son—"

"Stewart Reiker, the knight with no scruples on the horse."

"Yes, him. Is he trying to take over your group or are you trying to take over his group?"

"Reiker's father gave Adventure Land the money to set up the Templar encampment. All he asked in return was that his son be part of the group. Stewart knows everything about the Templars. If he could, he'd be one in real life. This is as close as he can get."

"What's the problem?"

"He has a wild streak. And he thinks of himself as the leader of the pack. He's a bully and doesn't mind getting physical with the other knights when they don't agree with him."

I grimaced at the delicate term. "That's putting it lightly

after seeing him in action today. I thought he was going to kill the other knight."

We had retired to the Dungeon for a while but were back out at Fabulous Funnels for breakfast (second breakfast for me). The Main Gate was due to open in about twenty minutes, but I wanted to have a chance to talk about this with Chase before the day parted us.

Chase had received a report on the fallen knight. The young man was going to be fine—just a bad bump on the head.

"So they asked you to step in and keep the knights going while controlling this troublemaker. And you said yes."

He sipped his coffee and nibbled on a funnel cake covered in strawberries. "They had a problem. I was the right fit for it. I thought it would be over by now. That's why I didn't bother saying anything to you."

It made me wonder how many other things I was missing in the Village while I taught history in Columbia most of the year. "Disband them," I recommended.

"It's not that easy."

"You're the bailiff—the Village law. What you say goes."

"Reiker senior is the largest stockholder in Adventure Land, Inc., and he has a lot of friends who also own stock. I'm stuck babysitting Stewart and the knights until Merlin finds another way around the problem."

"Lady Jessie!" Sam Da Vinci waved as he went by. "Heard what you did on the Field of Honor earlier. Brave stuff, girl!"

"About that," Chase started. "What were you thinking darting out on the field? You could've been killed. You didn't see Daisy or Bart doing anything crazy like that."

"Not now!" I gave him my most serious look. "And anyway, I thought it was *you*. I was motivated."

"You thought I was riding down on a helpless man who'd already been thrown from his horse?"

I shrugged. "I thought you were trying to teach him a lesson and it got away from you. It could happen—even to you. They don't call it the heat of battle for nothing."

"Thanks." He sat back in his chair.

Time for a change of subject. "Have you ever—I mean as one of the knights—have you ever—"

"Ever?"

I couldn't find the words to ask. I didn't know how to say it, especially after I'd just accused him of trying to seriously harm another man. How could I ask if he'd flirted with me? What if it wasn't him after all—like on the field this morning? What if it was the other knight, Stewart, who'd brought me home and been there while I flirted back?

If Chase was upset that I thought he was ready to hurt that young man, he might be even more upset if I told him I was flirting with Stewart.

"Never mind," I said.

His radio went off anyway. A problem at the Mermaid Lagoon with less than five minutes before the Village opened. I was glad to be interrupted for once.

"I'll see you later." He swallowed the last of his coffee and kissed me. "Thanks for letting me make up to you for not telling you everything. I feel a lot better that you know about my knightly duties."

"Me, too—I think. I'm a little worried about you being out there with that crazy kid."

He shrugged his broad shoulders. "All in a day at the Ren Faire, my lady. My duties are extensive, including taking one lovely young woman home twice in the last few days and saving her from being trampled by my horse."

"It was *you*! I knew it was you!"

He smiled and kissed me again, his braid sliding over his shoulder. "Gotta go. The mermaids can't get to their air hoses underwater. See you at lunch?"

I nodded, too full of excitement and my love for him to

speak. My heart was singing. I spun around in the grass a few times, just glad to be alive. Chase and I were solid. Even when I didn't know I was with him, I knew it was him. I didn't have to feel guilty about being attracted to the smoky-voiced knight who sat his horse so well.

"A lovely sight!" Galileo said as he scurried to reach his tent before visitors began flooding into the Village. "A good morning to you, Lady Jessie!"

"And a wonderful morning to you as well, sir!"

That's one of the things about being at the Village—good and bad. You're always on stage. You never really know what's real and what's not. Drama abounds. We are all part of it, visitor and resident alike.

I knew I should run to the Hat House and get started on my day, but I saw the carriages lining up and thought about Neal and his job. My good friend, D'Amos Torres, was getting the animals set up for the rides, checking each line and ribbon. He was the animal keeper for the Village after a distinguished career at the South Carolina Zoo in Columbia.

The Village had lured him here with the promise of more freedom and less paperwork. He was a hands-on kind of person who'd been stuck in an office for too long. We'd spent many nights in one Village tavern or another, kindred spirits as well as native Columbians.

"Jessie Morton!" He greeted me with a massive hug. His close-cropped hair was graying above his black face, but his dark eyes still shone with his passion for animals. He didn't care what kind of animals, as long as he was tending to them. "I haven't seen you in a while. Did you just get down for the summer?"

"I've been here a few days." I told him about my new apprenticeship and the work I'd done toward my dissertation.

He laughed. "You're too serious! Don't you know life is

too short not to do what you love with the people you love? Move your butt down here today. Don't go back."

This was always the heart of our conversations. He'd made the transition to living here full-time. But of course, he had his degree in veterinary medicine so he could leave and still get a job at another zoo. I wasn't in that position yet. And I was too afraid to let go of my teaching career.

"It's too hot out here for these carriage rides," he said. "The horses don't like it. Drivers either, I guess. I lost another one this morning. That means I have a carriage, a horse, and no driver."

"Really? I came over here to talk to you about hiring someone I met that isn't happy being a madman. I think he'd like to drive a carriage."

"Who could blame him? I'd rather muck the stalls than sit around in the street banging a pan with a spoon! Send him over. Otherwise I'll have to drive this rig myself. And you know I'm not cut out for that."

"You got it! Thanks." I hugged him.

"Jessie? Times a'wasting, girl. Get out while you still can before the real life beats you down and you can't get up. You got a good man who loves you here. Don't be so scared. Take a leap of faith!"

I waved and started running toward the Hat House. It was ten fifteen and I was late again. It seemed like I couldn't ever make it on time this summer. I hoped Andre would overlook it one more time. I promised myself it wouldn't happen again.

But before I could reach my destination, Neal kind of crept out at me from behind the privies, taking me by surprise. I had news for him, and I'd promised we'd meet up, so I couldn't exactly keep going. Andre would have to be understanding for a couple more minutes.

"Sorry," he said as I stopped short. "I have some important information to share."

"Me, too. Let's sit by the fountain for a minute."

We sat on the edge of the Good Luck Fountain. Seeing all the coins in the bottom made me think of those long summer days when I'd tossed coins in here, wishing that Chase would notice me as something more than a friend he knew from jousting. And all the time, he had already experienced his magic moment and knew that he loved me. I agreed with him that it seemed unfair that I didn't have a magic moment, too.

"Some guy named Joe Bradley approached me this morning while I was eating breakfast," Neal said. "He said he was hired by that weird brother and sister pair at the gem shop. He was looking for information about Hariot. He said he knew me from my column every week in the *Times*."

"What did he want?"

"Anything I could tell him." He shrugged. "He bought breakfast, so I told him everything."

I guess some of us were easier to get information from— Bradley held a gun on me. He could've tried offering me cinnamon rolls instead. "Did he act surprised by any of it?"

"No. Not really. I tried to get some information out of him, but he was kind of closemouthed about why he was here. I'm sure he's trying to put Hariot away, like everyone else." He smiled at me, the sunlight picking out all the craggy lines in his face. "Except for you, Jessie. Andre has you in his corner. I hope he appreciates that."

I guessed I'd wasted another few minutes. I had to tell Neal about the job and get to the Hat House before I was driving a carriage, too.

He looked better this morning. When I explained about the job, he brightened even more. I noticed he wasn't wearing a madman's costume. Portia had given him a red juggler's trousers and shirt instead. D'Amos would probably want him outfitted in the required gold and blue the carriage drivers wore. But that was their problem. At least I didn't have to approach Portia for a change.

"That sounds great. Thanks, Jessie. I don't know what else to do right now. I guess I'll wait and see how this story plays out. I won't forget what you've done for me."

I smiled and hugged him, too. It was that kind of morning—except for being late. I ran the short distance to the Hat House, where Andre was yelling at his assistants, like usual.

I kind of sneaked in from the side, and he didn't seem to notice I hadn't been there the whole time. We started working on the trio of purple hats again. Unfortunately, Andre was in a good mood, too, and had to tell me all about his date with Eloise and her rapture over the new gift he'd given her.

"She loves me," he gushed, cutting purple satin. "I know she'll be receptive when I ask her to marry me. Can you imagine a real Village wedding? Not just a visitor getting married here, but a real wedding in the heart of Renaissance Village."

I started to tell him I could imagine it without any problem because Little Bo Peep had married the Big Bad Wolf last summer in grand Renaissance style. Andre apparently hadn't attended those festivities. Or he thought his would be much better—I couldn't tell which.

I didn't tell him that his beloved tart was also spending time (and money) with Bernardo. I didn't have the heart. And maybe Eloise would take pity on him or decide he had a bigger bankroll and want to be with Andre. Weirder things—much weirder things—had happened.

Through the morning, I thought about how to control Stewart Reiker. Chase was too nice, too concerned with how things looked and trying to find equitable solutions to the problem.

I knew one solution that always worked for people in the Village whose egos got too big—a good prank.

A good prank told the ego-ridden person that they weren't alone here, that other people had feelings and priorities, too. I'd seen some really good ones and been part of many others. I knew if I thought hard about it, I could come up with something that would solve Chase's problem.

It would have to employ someone from each of the guilds in the Village. This would help with the revenge factor as well as making sure no one ratted out anyone else. It was always good to spread the guilt wherever possible.

While I was thinking, I cut, stitched, and even hot-glued a couple of hats that needed repairs. These came from all across the Village—Mother Goose's storytelling hat, Lady Lindsey's hat where her songbirds rested, and the hat (helmet) worn by King Arthur when he removed the sword from the stone twice daily to the delight of visitors who always gathered for the occasion.

I never realized how important hats were to the costumes they supported. In essence, a hat could make or break a costume. Andre's work went largely unappreciated even though, without it, Village characters would be less recognizable.

My last task before lunch was to sort through and organize hundreds of hat pins. They were all about the same length, but there the similarities ended. The pins were made with gemstones or flowers, they were beaded or braided, their color and style specially created for each hat.

But while they had a specific function—holding the hat on the head—their colors and styles were made to enhance as well. They could've been plain, unnoticed. Instead, each one was a tiny masterpiece. And each pin went with a specific hat.

I thought about what type of hat pin went with the Chocolatiers' fancy, wide-brimmed hats. I shuffled through all of Andre's collection, each one meticulously marked for each character so it could be replaced with one like it if necessary.

I finally found them—they all matched and each had a red stone in a brushed-gold setting. I was sure Chase had mentioned that the killer hat pin had a green stone on it.

The killer had covered Cesar with his hat but the hat pin might have belonged to someone else. I looked at the three matching hat pins for the brothers that were still in Andre's collection. If I could find out what the hat pin they'd found in Cesar looked like, I might know who killed him.

Twenty-eight

Full of theories about the hat pin that was found in Cesar and how to sufficiently prank Stewart Reiker, I went to meet Chase for lunch.

The mild morning weather had stretched through noon, giving residents and visitors a respite from summer heat. Everyone seemed to be eating outside, covering the Village Green with picnics and blankets, taking up tables and chairs along the cobblestones.

Chase and I had a system for meeting. If he wasn't where I was at lunchtime, we met at the closest place—in this case Peter's Pub. Not having instant communications took some planning and getting used to. It was much simpler when my cell phone was in my pocket. But our system usually worked.

Not this time.

I was a little annoyed right away, thinking that Chase had made another run to the forest for the Templars. He probably couldn't stop to tell me. Sometimes emergencies happened. But the sooner I found a way to take care of the Templar problem, the better.

"Looking for the bailiff?" Peter Greenwalt asked.

"Yeah. Was he here?"

"He was here," Peter's sister, Maude, answered. "He had to go over to the Chocolatiers' shop when the riot broke out."

"Riot? I've been inside working all morning. What kind of riot?"

"It's that ad Adventure Land put in the paper." Peter produced his copy of the *Myrtle Beach Sun*. "I heard there were six hundred applicants when the Main Gate opened. No telling how many there are now."

"I heard something about a few of them getting out of hand," Maude added. "I think that's why they called the bailiff. He already ordered lunch if you want to go ahead and eat."

"No, maybe later, after I find him." I looked at the ad requesting young men in musketeer costumes to apply for a job in a chocolate shop at the Village. No wonder it was such a mess.

I didn't have to wander far toward the chocolate shop to see the long line of colorful musketeers waiting across the King's Highway. If there were six hundred this morning, most if not all of them were still left. Their bright red, green, yellow, and blue capes and hats stretched like flowers dotting the landscape. Carriages of visitors had to go around the line, while the Lovely Laundry Ladies were displaced from their well, watching from the benches near the fountain and Da Vinci's Drawings.

I followed the snaking line of every imaginable type of male—some young, some not so young. They all seemed to be carrying swords, most not peace-tied the way they should have been. Someone at the Main Gate was going to get in trouble for this.

Chase was with four security guards at the front of the

Three Chocolatiers Shoppe along with Bernardo and Marco. There was still no access to the interior of the shop, so they'd set up a place outside to speak with applicants for the part of one of the Rizzo brothers.

"I hear you ordered lunch but had to leave," I razzed Chase when I reached him.

"This is the worst employment fiasco since I've been here," he growled. "These guys started sword fighting to show they could handle the part. It kind of created a frenzy for a while, but I think we're okay now."

I noticed the large sign, handwritten, proclaiming No Sword Fighting that had been installed on the side of the chocolate shop near the table where Marco and Bernardo sat. "How are they ever going to choose someone to take Cesar's place? Management would've been kinder choosing for them."

"I agree. How do you hire someone to be your brother?" Chase folded his arms across his chest. "They should've worded the ad differently, too. It doesn't matter so much that they look like musketeers as whether or not they can make chocolate."

"We've got this now, Bailiff, if you want to go to lunch with your lady," one of the security guys told Chase. "Sorry we had to call you, but it was really getting crazy."

"Thanks. That's what I'm here for. We'll be at Peter's Pub if you need me."

Chase and I started across the King's Highway when Bernardo called him back to the table. The flat surface was full of applications and resumes printed in color, displaying pictures and qualifications for various actors who wanted the part.

"Can you make this go away?" Bernardo pleaded. "Please, Chase. We can't pick someone to be Cesar. This is cruel and stupid."

Marco agreed, his sorrowful eyes glancing at the line of men before him. "We don't need another brother. Bernardo and I can handle it. Maybe we can just hire an assistant instead of a brother."

"I wish I could help you," Chase said. "At least they're giving you a choice. Maybe there's someone in this line you can work with. Don't think of it as replacing Cesar. Whoever you hire won't even be a business partner. Call him an assistant if it makes you feel better. Just get through this and let's get things back to normal."

"That's not going to happen with the shop closed," Bernardo reminded him. "We need to have Cesar's body for burial and we need access to the shop."

Chase could only offer platitudes. It wasn't up to him. The police would decide when it was time to release Cesar. And Adventure Land had made their decision about the chocolate shop. When it came right down to it, they were the evil overlords, the real kings and queens of Renaissance Village.

Twenty-nine

I was bursting to tell Chase about my hat pin theory, but there was so much noise and activity between the chocolate shop and Peter's Pub that I held it in. It wasn't easy.

We were finally situated in a quiet corner at Peter's, eating the fries and sandwiches Maude had kept warm for us. Still not a good time.

For the first few minutes, Chase spouted anger at Adventure Land's treatment of the Rizzo brothers. That took almost half a sandwich and most of the fries, not to mention a pint of ale. He finished off by telling me about the snake in the mermaid's air line and closing down the climbing wall for repairs, leaving a large crowd of angry visitors.

Finally he took a deep breath and smiled at me. "So how was your morning?"

I immediately launched into telling him my plan for pranking Stewart to relieve the Templar problem. Then I told him about the hat pin that should have been in Cesar's eye.

"Slow down," he advised. "One project at a time, please."

Chase wasn't crazy about pranking Stewart. "I don't think this kid has any weaknesses to exploit. He's not like the usual residents here who play by Village rules, Jessie. It won't be as easy as getting revenge on the pirates for kidnapping you or teaching Robin Hood a lesson by loosening his bow string or even pranking the monks. I think we should wait and let him screw up—it's bound to happen. Then we can move in on him, with Merlin's blessing."

As plans went for vengeance, or even to end Chase's leadership of the Templars, it sucked. "If he's the way you say he is, it could take years. I don't want this to go on for the rest of my life. Or yours."

"Merlin and I agreed that this is the best avenue of attack," he said. "Let's stay with the plan."

I could see that Merlin and Chase had made the cautious decision and were standing by it. No problem. I could handle this for them. Chase never had to be involved.

Merlin was head of the Magical Creatures Guild, but I didn't need him either. There were plenty of angry magical creatures out there, waiting for revenge.

Chase listened carefully to my idea about the hat pin that implicated Andre in killing Cesar. "So if we knew whose hat pin it was that we found in his eye, we might be able to figure out who's responsible. I like it."

"Could we get the hat pin or at least a picture of the hat pin from Detective Almond? I could go through Andre's collection and figure out who it matched."

"There must be a lot of hat pins."

"Hundreds," I agreed. "I didn't say it would be easy. Andre could help me."

"I like him, too, Jessie. But he's still on the top of Detective Almond's list of suspects. Until we know for sure that he wasn't involved, I think we should keep him out of the investigation."

That made sense. I didn't like it and I didn't want to think about it that way, but I could see his point. "Well, I'll do the

best I can. If I don't get through all the hat pins by the end
of summer—"

"I'll help you," he offered. "In my spare time."

I rolled my eyes. "What spare time—unless you want to
prank Stewart."

"I'll make time for it," he promised. "Please don't try
and do anything to Stewart Reiker. Let Merlin and me handle it."

All the more reason—in my mind anyway—to find a
way to get Stewart. Then Chase might have some spare
time. Not that I'd want to spend it going through hat pins
with him, but at least he'd be away from the Templars.

I wasn't sure when or where that opportunity would
come from. Chase made Stewart sound like he was Renaissance superman. How do you prank someone like that? Yet
I knew there was a way.

I left Chase at Peter's with a big kiss and a hug—not
only because I loved him, but also to begin making up for
doing what he asked me not to do. He had been called away
to another emergency, but not until we'd finished lunch. I
could live with that.

Lost in thought as I wandered back to the Hat House, I
didn't even see the young man who approached me until he
fell prostrate at my feet.

"You must allow me to serve you, Mistress. You saved my
life on the Field of Honor. I am in your debt. Command me!"

I wouldn't have known him without his black costume, but
his words gave him away. It was the young man who'd lost his
patience and his horse this morning fighting Stewart Reiker.

"Aren't you supposed to be at the hospital?" I asked.

"'Twas only a bump, my lady." He smiled, his hand on
his heart. "Allow me to serve you. Command me!"

He was quite the charmer, even in green hospital scrubs.
I assumed he'd left quickly and without his clothes. He had
a cute smile and big blue eyes. A crowd with cameras began
to gather around us.

"Not here," I whispered, thinking fast. "I bid thee rise, sir. Accompany me to the Hat House for some ... er ... shopping."

"Aw, give the lad a kiss, lady," an older gentleman with a strong Australian accent pleaded as his video camera continued to film us.

"Yeah. He's a cutie," a bleached blond in a green tank top said. "I'd kiss him if my husband wasn't right here."

The crowd wasn't going to let us get away without it. It was either kiss the young Templar or stand there as the crowd got bigger. Deciding it was better to give in than try to fight the wave, I planted my lips on his and hoped that would be it.

Too bad I didn't have the chance to brief my gallant knight beforehand. He totally took advantage of the situation, wrapped his arms around me, and went for the dip.

In the Village, the dip was always the thing. No kiss was complete without it. The man dipped and the lady held up one foot behind her. It was one of the first things you learn in training.

But it was over quickly. The crowd applauded. And my knight held out his arm (part of an IV attached) and we walked away to a chorus of huzzahs. The crowd was happy and no harm done—except for seeing Wanda LeFay applauding with them. Her evil, cold blue fish eyes promised that everyone would know about this within the next hour.

I wasn't worried about it. Chase would understand once he knew the circumstances. In the meantime, my mind had come up with a true purpose for the young knight at my side. The possibilities spun around in my head like colored butterflies.

"What is your name, Sir Knight?" I asked as we walked.

"I am Lord Robert Johnson," he replied. "I wasn't sure if you recognized me."

"How could I forget?" I kept my hand on his arm, guiding him to the side of the shop. I needed to talk to him but not where we could be overheard. "You said you want to serve me, is that right?"

He dropped to one knee again. "I owe you my life, lady. Whatever I may do to clear this debt, I will do."

"That's what I thought you said." I smiled at him and urged him to his feet. "You're going to help me prank Stewart Reiker. When we've finished, he'll be a different person. Are you in?"

He smiled back, but his angelic face took on an almost evil aspect. "I would help you with this quest, my lady, whether I owed you my life or not. Tell me what you want me to do."

We arranged to meet later when I'd had a chance to think about my plan. Lord Robert probably knew some helpful information about Stewart that I could use to our advantage. This was the opportunity I was looking for. I'd have to get some others onboard with the project, but that should be easy. Vengeance went with Village like meat and potatoes.

Thirty

While I finished helping Andre make the purple hats that were due tomorrow, I thought about Stewart—and the hat pins. I couldn't help it. I had both things on my mind.

Pranking Stewart seemed easy, despite Chase's warning. Compared to figuring out whose hat pin matched the one in Cesar, it was a snap.

Once the last touches went on the bold purple hats, they were laid in elegant round hat boxes with Andre's special label. The whole aspect was satisfying and gave me a feeling of creation.

I asked Andre if I could stay and clean up the workroom while he and the other assistants went for a celebration ale at Peter's.

He glanced around the material-stacked room and nodded. "Is anything wrong, Jessie?"

"No. I'm just not ready to go back to the Dungeon yet."

"Man trouble again? I swear you and Chase are in and

out as much as Doris Day and Rock Hudson! But that's fine, dear. Take your time. I'm having dinner with Eloise tonight. She called *me*, you know. First time ever. Perseverance. That's the key."

"That's wonderful! I hope you have a great time."

"I know we will."

As soon as he was gone, I started looking at the hat pins again. Every resident who ever wore a hat, past and present, had hat pins. Who knew there had been twenty Bo Peeps with their distinctive blue hats? Thankfully there was still only one pin for that character. Again, with a special group of blue beads on it.

Surely a good picture of the hat pin they found in Cesar could be made available. It didn't have to be the real thing if Detective Almond didn't want me to have the evidence, as I felt sure would be the case.

There were so many hat pins with stones of various shades—green, blue, red, and yellow. There were too many pins with green stones or beads of one kind or another. I wasn't sure I could even tell them apart.

I gave up trying to separate them an hour later. I never realized how many characters with hats were in the Village. Some of them weren't here anymore, but Andre kept their particular style of hat pin anyway—maybe just in case they came back.

Feeling like I had to cover my tracks—Andre was still a suspect after all—I cleaned up the workroom until I could see the floor again. I wondered what kind of hat pin had been found in Andre's wife all those years ago. It occurred to me that it might have something to say as well.

To the police, it would only be a hat pin (not that they'd know the unique part by themselves), but Andre probably kept records for the movie stars he worked with the same way he did here. It might be possible to know something about the earlier crime by knowing about the hat pin.

I decided it would be cruel to ask Andre about it. But Neal might be a good source for that information. I knew he was involved, if only as an outsider. I was sure he had a lot of details he could impart.

I closed the Hat House, wondering where I could find Neal after a long day of driving a carriage. Someone fell in step with me as I was crossing the cobblestones near the Dutchman's Stage. I looked up with a smile, thinking it was Neal—but I was wrong.

Joe Bradley, the newly sanctioned private detective in the Village, was about the same size and height as Neal. Maybe the same age, too. He was at it again—stalking me. But this time it wasn't dark and there were plenty of people I knew all around. One call would bring them all running. At least that's what I told myself. Sometimes it was easier to get attention from the visitors than the residents, who'd seen it all.

I stopped flat near the Jolly Pipemaker's Shop. "What do you want now?"

"Look, you and I got off on the wrong foot, Jessie. And I'm sorry for that. But we've got something in common we should talk about."

"And that is?"

"Justice for the dead."

"If you're going to go on about Andre being a killer—I don't want to hear it."

"Wait!" He put his hand on my arm as I started to walk away.

Too fast to really understand what had happened, he was on the cobblestones with a large, booted foot on his chest and a sword at his throat.

Thinking it was Chase, I looked up and smiled at my rescuer. Wrong again! This seemed to be my day for it.

Instead it was Lord Robert, late of the Templar Knights. He was dashing once more in his black trousers and shirt but minus the head covering. "Are you all right, Mistress Jessie?" he asked, not taking his eyes from the man on the ground.

"I'm fine, Lord Robert. Please let him up."

"Of course." He moved his foot and sword. "I didn't want him to offend you."

"Not a problem. Thanks for the help."

Joe Bradley got clumsily to his feet, rolling off the cobblestones. He was a large man, like Neal, but the resemblance ended there. He had a tough face with a nose slightly to one side of where it should have been. Too much fighting, no doubt.

"Jerk!" He railed at my rescuer. "Do you know how hard it is to get a new costume from that crazy woman at the shop? If you've ripped this—"

"Speak not to me, knave! You accosted the woman I am sworn to protect!"

"Knave?" Bradley laughed. "I'm a madman, thank you very much. In more ways than one, I might add."

"Off with you." Lord Robert nudged him with his foot. "Your presence offends me."

"Yeah? Whatever. You guys are all nuts out here, you know that?" Bradley turned to me. "Listen, I have a story to tell that you should hear before you decide who's innocent and who's guilty in all this. Here's my cell phone number. Give me a call."

"You aren't supposed to use that here," I reminded him.

"Sue me!" he yelled as he walked away with a last glare at Lord Robert.

"Shall we meet now to speak of Stewart's downfall?" my knight asked eagerly. "I am disguised so that others might not know of my Templar identity."

"About that, Lord Robert," I began, glancing around, glad the visitors were gone for the day. "Only the Templars dress all in black. FYI."

"Oh." He stared at me like I'd said he was naked.

And no sooner was the thought in my head than he began taking off his shirt—exposing his pink and white chest.

"What are you doing?" I whispered, really concerned.

"I am disrobing to make myself less visible for our meeting." He sounded totally nonchalant about it.

"Never mind. The Dungeon is right here. Let's just step inside for a few minutes." I glanced around and unlocked the door. "And put your shirt on!"

When he was dressed again, we sat on the stairs that went up to the apartment in full view of the tortured souls who occupied the ground floor. Some fifteen or twenty men and women peered at us with plastic eyes and painted faces through the dirty cell bars. Straw covered the floors as it would have during the Renaissance to soak up bodily fluids. *Eww!*

It wouldn't have been a good place to be back then, certainly not easy to get out of. At least no one could charge Chase with abusing his prisoners.

I told Lord Robert about my basic plan to prank Stewart—and the history of past misdeeds at the Village being erased by pranks. "It's practically a lifestyle here."

He looked at me like he wasn't quite sure. "As far as I know, my lady, there is no prank you could perpetrate on Stewart to make him a better person. He is a product of his very rich, very snobby parents who've spoiled him all of his life."

Lord Robert was very well spoken for an underling. "What have you done all of your life?"

"I worked my way through medical school. I have an internship at Duke starting this fall. I thought it might be fun to spend the summer here. Big mistake, I guess."

"Cheer up. There's still plenty of summer left." I told him about my life teaching history to many students who thought the world began in 1975. "We won't let this rich bully ruin both our summers. We can turn this around."

"What has Stewart done to ruin your time here? I only saw you at the encampment once."

I couldn't tell him about Chase. I had to make up a few white lies about how the Village meant so much to me and all the residents were suffering. Maybe not lies exactly— people were kind of unhappy about the Templars.

"I wish I could be more help," he said. "I can't think of anything we could do to Stewart that would make a difference. You haven't met him. You don't know what he's like."

Maybe my brain was too full of hat pins and pranks. Maybe I was tired and not capable of rational decision making. But I got an idea—more like a cannon exploding in my head—and I knew what to do.

"Maybe you could help me get in as a neophyte knight. I could wear the costume and the headdress and find out Stewart's weaknesses."

"No offense, my lady." He smiled that cute little smile again. Reminded me of a little puppy my brother Tony and I had when we were small. "But women can't be knights. There's the physical stamina, not to mention the fact that there aren't any women at the encampment besides concubines."

I smiled right back at him. There wasn't any knight in the Village—except maybe Chase—who knew more about being a knight than I did. I was pretty good with a sword, excellent with the long bow, and a decent horse person.

"I think I could manage."

He didn't look convinced. "If I introduce you as a friend and you are unmasked as a woman, Stewart will have my head."

I got to my feet, dusted off the back of my gown. "As far as I can see, you're on the verge of leaving anyway. What have you got to lose? Let's keep this in perspective, Bobby.

This is Renaissance Faire Village and Market Place in the heart of Myrtle Beach, South Carolina. No matter what—things aren't real here. I think my plan would work."

He nodded slowly as he got to his feet. "All right. When do you want to begin?"

Thirty-one

Chase was home that night. I didn't ask what the Templars were up to or volunteer information about my plan. I did tell him about seeing Joe Bradley again. I gave him the business card with Bradley's cell phone number on it.

"I don't know what he's up to," Chase said. "But since he has Detective Almond's blessing, there's not much I can do about him—unless he steps across some Village law. Then I can boot his butt out of here."

"What about the cell phone?"

"You said the Main Gate was closed already. You could've used your cell phone."

"What about him holding that gun on me?"

"He denies it."

"And you believe him over me?"

He put his arms around me. "Not ever. But like I said, Detective Almond made it clear this is a personal favor to him to have this guy capture this fugitive. These people have all kinds of powers outside the regular law. He can come in here without a search warrant and search through everything if he thinks the guy he's looking for is here."

"All right. I'll find something else. I have a feeling he's not exactly adhering to Village law."

I made a point of not talking about anything else that pertained to law, the Village, or the Templars that evening. It was just me and Chase, the way it might be if we lived a normal life. Not that I wanted that life—but intervals of it were nice.

The next morning a crowd was gathered outside the Dungeon. It wasn't Wednesday, but residents wanted to air their grievances anyway. There wasn't much Chase could do but listen. It was early, so I stayed around for moral support.

Of course it was all about the Templars. They'd stolen one of Bo Peep's sheep and borrowed Galileo's eye piece from his telescope. The list seemed endless.

"We're not asking anymore, Chase," Alex from the Merry Men warned. "We're going to take things into our own hands."

Chase kind of snickered. "I think you've already tried that. It didn't work so well."

"Well, what do you suggest, Bailiff? The Green Man said that the Templars had broken a pair of his stilts. What are we supposed to do?"

"I'll talk to the knights," Chase promised.

"That's what you always say," one of the dancing men from the Stage Caravan said.

"Look," Chase addressed them. "If you weren't here complaining about the Templars, you'd be here because Alex and Robin Hood had taken your toaster ovens. Or the pirates had spent the night tying up half of what you have and taking the rest. This way, it's just the Templars."

No one liked that idea. They railed and promised vengeance. I knew most of them weren't sincere. A few were on my list for helping me prank Stewart. I needed strong-willed pranksters who could keep their mouths shut but had a grievance to avenge. I made a mental list of those who fit the profile.

"All I'm saying is that we've all done some things here that might not be what others wanted us to do." Chase tried to win them again. "I have complaints about loud parties at night. Bo Peep, your big bad wolf howls too late for the animal keepers. Diego, Lorenzo, people complain about you in general."

Diego hugged his brother. "Thank you, Bailiff. That means so much to us."

"Whatever." Chase sounded like he was getting impatient. "My point is that you've all decided that the Templars are the number one bad guys right now. But no one has gotten hurt, and all sheep and other items have been returned. No harm done."

Most of the crowd couldn't argue with his roundup of the situation. It was all true. I'd been living with the bailiff long enough to have heard it all. Some of the complaints were valid—most were stupid.

What he'd said was enough to disperse the early-morning risers back to coffee and breakfast. Chase watched them go, clearly unhappy with the situation. "I'm going to see Merlin. I don't know how much more of this I can take. I should only be a few minutes. Do you want to wait for breakfast?"

I knew it would take a lot more than a few minutes. And I'd seen a package with my name on it near the door as we came down the stairs from the apartment. "You know, I think I'll get an early start at the Hat House. Maybe we can meet for lunch."

He kissed me and didn't say much. "That's fine. I'm sorry about all this."

I promised him silently, as he started toward the other end of the Village, that I had the problem in hand. He wouldn't have to suffer much longer.

When he was gone, I went back inside and opened the brown paper–wrapped box. It was a black shirt, trousers, and headdress—the working garment of the Templars. There was a note from Lord Robert inside. *Meet me at the tree swing at ten tonight.*

I tried on my Templar gear—it didn't fit me as well as it did the knights. But that was a good thing, since I was trying to disguise myself. I hid the box away so Chase wouldn't find it. It might be tough to slip out tonight. If Chase was home, I'd have to think of something. Maybe a hat emergency. That wouldn't be any more stupid than some of Chase's calls.

It was for Chase's own good that I was undertaking this mission. For him and for me. Stewart Reiker had made my bailiff unhappy one time too many. I vowed I was going to make it better.

I went back outside in search of a new gown, caffeine, and possibly chocolate—it might require a lot of chocolate through the day to build my courage for tonight. It might be for the greater good that I infiltrated the encampment, but I was a little worried about it, despite my reassuring words to Lord Robert.

The day was warming up quickly with no rain the night before to cool everything down. I was glad it had been dry overnight though—less mess from mud and wet straw to put up with.

I met Neal on the way to the Monastery Bakery and invited him to breakfast. I really wanted to pick his brain about hat pins. I thought the least I could do was buy him something to eat before subjecting him to the painful brain-picking process.

He was dressed in his resplendent blue and gold livery, a little hat with a big feather on his head. I knew Andre had made that hat at some point.

"How's the job?" I asked when we were waiting for food at the bakery.

"Hot. And the costume is itchy. And I wish the hat fit better. It feels like a little box squeezing my head. I think it was made for a little boy." He swallowed some coffee. "But otherwise, it was okay, you know? I like horses."

"Good! You know, I could take a look at your hat. Maybe it could be altered."

"That would be great! Thanks, Jessie." He took the hat off (it was quite small for such a large man) and handed it to me. "I think D'Amos will understand, don't you?"

"He'll understand. And I'll find you and bring it to you later if it can be altered today."

Breakfast arrived—cinnamon roll for me, bagel and cream cheese for Neal. We talked about life in the Village and whether or not King Harold would acknowledge the queen's child—a major topic of conversation for everyone right now.

"This place is really something." He shook his head as he watched the monks praying over some loaves of unbaked bread. "It's like living in another world. They just think Hollywood is La-La Land. They should try it here sometime."

"Speaking of Hollywood." I used this segue as my jumping-off point. "I wanted to ask you a question about Andre's wife's murder."

"Shoot!"

"Did you notice the hat pin? The one they found at the scene of Kathleen Hariot's death. I know that might seem a little weird—"

"Hey. Not at all. I took the Three Pigs and some guy in a big tree suit around the Village yesterday. I know what you mean." He munched his giant-sized bagel while he seemed to get his thoughts in order. "You know, I think it was pink. Or at least had pink on it. I'm not sure if it had a gemstone or what. But I think it was a pink color."

I sighed—no thrill of revelation there. I'd have to have some reference for a pink stone on one of Andre's hat pins. "Did the investigation actually find that the hat pin belonged to her, Kathleen, I mean?"

"I don't remember. What's with the visit to the past when you've got your own murder to solve?"

"I'm not sure." I sipped my coffee. "Just curious, I guess."

I didn't want to explain my hat pin theory to him. Not yet anyway. I wasn't sure why. Maybe because I didn't really know him. Chase felt that Andre shouldn't be clued in, and I still wasn't clear about Neal's real motives for being in the Village—especially since the newspaper had fired him. I didn't want to give him information he could use as part of a personal vendetta. He might try to buy his way back into his old job with it, if nothing else.

We were done eating, and I wished him a good day. I took the hat with me for Andre to look at.

I felt a little like a blind woman trying to follow a crooked path. Somehow, I knew that the color and shape of the hat pins meant something. I just couldn't figure out what yet.

It was Sunday, I realized as I saw the carts full of supplies going toward the castle. The King's Feast would be this evening at the close of the day. It was always a spectacle in itself—full of knights and pageantry, fools and beggars. There would be duels and visitors scattering chicken bones from hundreds of tiny chickens. It was one of the biggest events every week. Every resident attended, wearing their finest (as long as they didn't outshine the Royal Court). Maybe there would even be an announcement about the queen's pregnancy. I didn't expect to hear King Harold welcome the child as yet—there hadn't been enough time for a paternity test.

I reached the Hat House to find the rooms dark and silent. There were no laughing, incompetent assistants, no layers of material being made into hats. The door was open to the shop but no one seemed to be there. Where was Andre?

I called his name—upstairs and downstairs. There was no answer. I kept searching until I finally found him in the big chair by the window. He was buried in blankets as I had been while Joe Bradley searched for his hat pin.

"Andre?" I moved a corner of the blanket.

"Go away. I don't want to see anyone today."

"What's wrong?"

"I don't want to talk, Jessie. Please go away. And lock the door on your way out."

Of course, I couldn't let it go. He was too miserable, and the three sisters who were coming to pick up the purple hats we'd made could be there as soon as the Main Gate opened.

"I'll make you some tea. I think there was still some of that jam you like and some brown bread in the kitchen."

"No." He sniffled in a sob. "Tea won't help. Neither will brown bread and *honey*."

"Sorry." It was honey, not jam, that he ate every day. I'd only known him a short time. I couldn't know everything about him. "Let me help you, Andre. You helped me when Chase and I broke up. Think of me like Audrey Hepburn helping George Peppard in *Breakfast at Tiffany's*."

"She didn't help him," he pointedly reminded me. "She ruined his life. Like all women."

"Yes, but in a good way. Come on. You can't stay under there forever. You want to hear how much the three sisters love their new hats, don't you?"

I got him into the little kitchen area. I mean little, too. It was only about the size of a closet. You could tell he rarely ate there.

I made him some tea, and he sat in the rickety wood chair and tried not to cry. His little nose was very red and his eyes were sunken with terrible dark shadows under them. He suddenly looked much older than he had just the day before.

"Is it Eloise?" I guessed. This had to be a matter of the heart for him to look so miserable.

"Yes!" The floodgates opened and it all poured out.

"She dumped me. *Me!* After all I've done—all I've given her."

"I'm sorry." It was inevitable. He was the only one who couldn't see it.

"She still wanted someone else—Bernardo! Can you believe it? Cesar's brother! Apparently they're going into business together. She's abandoning her sisters at the King's Tarts and helping him reopen the chocolate shop. They plan to call it The Lady's Chocolate Shoppe. What kind of name is that?"

Bernardo again. Had this always been the plan? It was seriously beginning to look as though Bernardo had killed his brother because Cesar was overbearing and had the woman he wanted. He got everything—except the chocolate recipe. But I felt sure he could make that up as he went along. I didn't know what his alibi was for the time Cesar was killed, but he had to be lying. No one profited from Cesar's death like Bernardo did.

After coaxing Andre into drinking his tea and eating a little bread and honey, I got him to go upstairs and take a shower. "You should rest for a while. I'll man the shop and let you know when the sisters get here."

He rested his head against my shoulder. "Thank you, Jessie. You're a very good friend."

I didn't tell him how much I could empathize with his problem. I'd been dumped many times before. If things weren't so good right now, I could probably sit down and cry about it with him.

But things were good. Chase loved me and we were happy together. Once I rescued him from the Templars, life would be perfect.

As though thinking of him made him walk through the shop door, Chase appeared. "I thought I'd check in with you while I was down at this end of the Village separating the fortune-teller near the Main Gate from Bawdy Betty. It seems the fortune-teller told Betty that she and her new boyfriend, Phil from the Sword Spotte, are about to break up. I never saw so much scratching and hair pulling."

I ran and threw myself on him, hugging him tightly. I told him about Andre and Eloise. "I know it was bound to happen. I know she didn't love him. But it's still not fair."

"I know. It never is." He hugged me back and we kissed for a few minutes.

"But now we know who killed Cesar." I pulled myself away from him and straightened my gown. "It had to be Bernardo. He's got everything, Chase. The girl, the business. He used the hat pin to throw everything at Andre. I'm telling you, it has to be him."

"And I'm telling you, he has an airtight alibi for the time Cesar was killed."

"What could it possibly be? He probably just had someone lie for him."

Chase smiled. "The reason I haven't told you about his alibi is because he wouldn't want everyone to know. Bernardo isn't a bad guy. Women like him, that's all. Eloise and he have been together for a while—then Andre suddenly decided she was his Aphrodite. It was Andre who was out of place."

"What about Eloise and Cesar?" I demanded. "And what do you mean you didn't tell me because you didn't want everyone to know?"

"Cesar was always the one who used women and dumped them like dirty laundry. He set his sights on Eloise because she was in love with Bernardo. Cesar tried to seduce Belle, too. He had a thing for all the tarts."

"All the more reason for Bernardo to kill him."

"All right. I'll tell you where Bernardo was. But I better not hear it from Daisy and Bart by the time I reach the other end of the Village."

I couldn't believe he was insinuating I couldn't keep a secret. I was keeping *his* secret and the secret about the Templars getting their comeuppance that he didn't even know about. "That's fine. Maybe you shouldn't tell me. After all, I've blabbed to everyone about you leading the Templars."

He gave me his exasperated Chase look, left brow raised. "That's different. I never thought you'd tell anyone about that. But you do love to gossip about other people's problems."

"What are you saying? I never blab anything. I keep secrets from one end of the Village to the other. You just don't appreciate how much I know about what goes on around here."

"Okay. You're right. You never tell anything." He kissed me and smiled. "Even if they tortured you or threatened to give you a costume you didn't want to wear. I know you'd never tell anyone that Bernardo was having hair implants put in the morning Cesar was killed."

I couldn't believe it! *Hair implants.* "Are you kidding me? But he's got all that thick, dark hair."

"It's a wig. He spent the night at a local clinic and only got back after we found Cesar. He woke Marco and the two of them came to the shop."

"That's amazing. Hair implants. No one will believe it!"

"Jessie! You promised not to blab."

"Yeah. I won't tell anyone. I can keep a secret. But that totally ruins my theory about Bernardo. Yet he was the one who got everything he wanted."

"I'll leave you to ponder that issue, my lady." He gave me a gallant bow and kissed me again. "Lunch at Peter's?"

I curtsied a little (he *did* say I had a big mouth) and smiled back. "Yes, Sir Bailiff. But if you ever charge me with telling secrets—"

"I'll take the tomatoes for you in the stocks anytime."

"You really do love me, don't you?"

"With all my heart."

I finally let him go and went around the hat shop straightening up until I thought about the hat pins again. Reluctantly, I returned to ponder them. Even though the answer might be here, I was getting really bored looking at all of them. It might be different if they were all distinctly unique, but sometimes there were three or four that were only separated by one bead or bangle. It seemed hopeless.

I found a set of older-looking hat pins with Hollywood celebrity names on them. There were hat pins from hundreds of actresses whose names I didn't recognize, but there were a few I knew, too—Susan Hayward, Marilyn Monroe, and Bette Davis.

The plastic that held them was cracked and yellowed, but a piece of velvet inside protected each pin. At the bottom of the case was one that said *Kathleen*. I picked it up and looked at the pin. There were several pink stones on it. Neal had pegged it right.

"What are you doing?" Andre asked from close behind me.

Thirty-two

I dropped the hat pin. "Nothing. Sorry. I was admiring all the hat pins. Did you create all of these?" It was the best I could do on the spur of the moment.

The suspicious look on his poor, tortured face immediately changed to pride. "Many of them are my creation. Especially for the actresses. Like Farrah Fawcett—did you see hers? Or Ali McGraw? I created both of those specially for them. They wouldn't take anything less."

I was so close. The pink hat pin was making my fingers itch as I picked it up off the floor—and I don't think it was the dust or the old plastic causing it. "This one says Kathleen. That was your wife, right?"

He took the pin from me. His eyes kind of glazed over as he looked at it. "That's right. I didn't create these hat pins. I found them for her. I only have one left because the police kept the other. They never returned it because the case was never closed."

"It had to be terrible for you." I sympathized because of

his loss—and to keep him talking. I was close to something here. I could feel it.

"I can't tell you how hideous it was, Jessie. The whole thing—finding her dead that way, then being accused of killing her. There was no time to mourn properly. It was all I could do to survive." He looked up at me with tears in his eyes. "I have a scrapbook. I know it seems macabre. I kept it because I couldn't take it all in, you know? And I thought later I might want to remember it, remember her."

"You have a scrapbook?" I hoped I didn't sound too eager. I really wanted to take a look at it without sounding too ghoulish about it. I wasn't sure if the two crimes were linked, but I had to agree with Chase that it was a huge coincidence. Maybe I'd see something with fresh eyes that someone else had missed.

"I do. Would you like to see it?"

I followed him upstairs, and we took out the scrapbook. He wasn't kidding about saving everything. The yellowed newsprint was from several newspapers and magazines. He had every condolence card—there were hundreds of them from famous people he'd worked with to people I'd never heard of.

"Are these crime scene photos?" I asked. They were not the typical pictures you'd see in a magazine.

"Yes. I paid the crime scene photographer—he was a moonlighting publicist's photographer from MGM. He needed the money. I needed to see what happened."

I looked at the terrible pictures of Kathleen floating in the pool in a pretty pink dress. There was another even worse when they brought her out. "But Andre, you were there."

"I know. But you can only take in so much and then your mind shuts down. I think it must be to protect us from going mad. When I look at these pictures, they don't bring back memories. It's like I wasn't there."

I supposed that made sense. We continued to sift through all of the information stuffed into folders and envelopes, scrapbooks and even shoe boxes. It was your typical Hollywood event with plenty of press that followed the case. All of it led to a dead end when Andre's alibi proved to be solid. He was the only suspect even though the papers said his wife was having an affair.

He jumped up from the bed where we sat. "That was never substantiated! They say that every time someone dies out there. If you're famous, your spouse must be having an affair. But I know Kathleen truly loved me, even if she wasn't always faithful."

It was hard to doubt his sincerity—and I didn't question that it was what he truly believed. But I also knew he thought Eloise loved him. He was obviously a little deluded when it came to women who caught his eye.

Wasn't it just like a man to want what he couldn't have when Beth loved him and wanted to be with him? It made no sense.

"I hate to ask you this, Andre, but what about the hat pin they found—er—with her?" There was no delicate way to say it.

"Yes. It was the twin of this one." He held up the pink hat pin. "As I said, I don't ever expect to see it again. And maybe that's a good thing. It might be more than I'd like to collect."

"Funny they don't talk about it in the accounts. They only say an antique hat pin."

"Which was incorrect. There was nothing antique about it. It looked old, but it was just a reproduction. I believe the police withheld the information about exactly what type of hat pin it was. Something about keeping that secret in case I wasn't the killer. It would be privileged knowledge, you see. Only the killer would know."

"But they didn't bother looking for anyone else, did they?"

"No. The investigation started and ended with me. My poor Kathleen goes unavenged but not unmourned."

It was a terrible sad tale, as my grandmother would've said. She hadn't been a well-educated woman but she had a great turn of phrase.

I was glad when our time with Kathleen's murder was broken up by the arrival of the three sisters, who were looking for their hats. I hadn't realized how late it was. I hoped Chase was waiting for me at Peter's and left Andre to know all the pretty words to say to his female customers.

I had to pause before I left and admire the three purple gowns they wore. Each one was slightly different like each hat. They would make a splash as they perambulated through the Village that day. Some people just really had things together.

Peter and Maude told me Chase had been there but was called away when a goat cart flipped over and dumped a dairy maid on the cobblestones. "He said he'd catch up with you later but you shouldn't wait for him," Peter said as he wiped down the dark wood bar.

"That doesn't seem like such a big deal," I whined, feeling guilty because I was late.

"I suppose it is when the back of the goat cart is full of eggs." Peter shrugged. "Can I get you something for lunch, Lady Jessie?"

"No, thanks. I might see if I can find him anyway. He has to eat lunch sometime."

It was then that I remembered I hadn't told Andre about Neal's carriage driver hat. I knew it would take Chase awhile to get people in to clean up the mess—and longer to disperse the interested crowd that would think it was part of the show. I had time to go back to the Hat House and see if something could be done for Neal.

Luckily it was a short trip between the Hat House and Peter's. I waded through the heavy crowds looking at maps of the Village or upending water bottles into their mouths or on their heads.

There was a Scottish group here in full tartan and carrying shields. All of the men had long, braided beards. They all carried peace-tied claymores and axes. They looked fierce enough to scare any poor Renaissance maiden. But their ladies, though dressed in tartan splendor as well, were carrying stuffed animals their mates had won for them at various games. It kind of took away from the tough Scottish gang image.

I got back to the Hat House but no one was there. I searched under the bed and through the material—Andre was really gone this time. Maybe he'd stepped out with the ladies in the purple gowns. He had been known to take lunch or dinner with customers.

Good. That was probably what he needed to get his mind off Eloise and Kathleen. I knew it probably wasn't helpful for me to dredge up the past at this time, but his retelling of the first murder and looking at the scrapbooks might be helpful. I wouldn't know until it was all over.

Since I had a few extra minutes, I went to see Master Archer Simmons, head of the Weapons Guild. We talked about my upcoming prank on the Templars—I knew he could be trusted. He told me I could count on him when the time came.

I knew I couldn't trust Robin Hood even though he was head of the Forest Guild. He couldn't keep his mouth shut. I planned to let him know about the prank at the last minute. And that was only because I knew he'd want in.

Merlin? I wish I could've told him, since he was head of the Magical Creatures Guild, but I knew he'd disapprove and tell Chase. I didn't want either of those things to happen.

I figured I'd waited long enough for Chase to take care of the goat cart situation. I walked down the cobblestones to find him. It wasn't hard. There was a large crowd of visitors still watching as Village maintenance tried to clean up the eggs using Renaissance technology.

"It's gonna be a while," Chase said loudly when he saw me at the edge of the crowd.

Everyone turned to look at me and a few camera flashes followed. I shrugged and blew him a kiss. I was going to have to eat lunch by myself and get back to the Hat House. Maybe Andre would be in a good enough mood now to work on hats again.

I grabbed a pretzel from a traveling pretzel vendor and followed it up with some frozen lemonade as I walked around the Village Green watching people.

There were some acrobats plying their trade, bouncing and jumping around the deep green grass. Some visitors were picnicking while others sat on benches and looked at the Good Luck Fountain spraying water into the air. Ladies curtsied to gentlemen before beginning their stroll that would allow visitors to take more pictures. Knights (not Village residents) horsed around with their shields and recently purchased swords. They obviously didn't know about peace-tying their weapons yet.

I thought about everything Andre had told me and that I'd seen in the accounts of his wife's death. I could see why Detective Almond believed he was guilty of killing Cesar—the two killings were hauntingly similar.

Of course, anyone could go online and look up the information like Chase and I had. But not many people would be that motivated. Andre had been here running Harriet's Hat House for years. Why would this happen now?

And what would they gain from this copycat killing?

All of it whirled around in my head. There were a few people coincidentally (or not) directly involved with the first murder in the Village. The evil twins—Rene and Renee certainly had a score to settle, at least in their minds. Neal was here after working on the first story, and Joe Bradley was involved, too. Any of them could be part of this. I liked the evil twins best for the crime, but they had an alibi for the time Cesar was killed. Neal didn't seem to have a motive and neither did Joe.

That left me with someone in the Village—maybe not Bernardo, Eloise, or Beth. I couldn't imagine who else would want Cesar dead and would be willing to put the blame on Andre. It seemed hopeless. Any of the residents walking by me could be guilty. How would we ever figure out who did it when everyone seemed to have an alibi? I was really beginning to hate the whole alibi situation.

I finished my pretzel and frozen lemonade, then washed the little bit of mustard from my hands in the cool water from the fountain. I thought about my hat pin research again. It appeared that the only way to solve Cesar's death might be to solve Kathleen's death. It made sense with so many people here from Hollywood who could want to lay Cesar's death at Andre's feet.

Something Andre said tickled my thoughts. The police withheld the information about the hat pin that was in Kathleen. Only the police, crime scene photo guy—and Neal Stevenson knew the stones on the hat pin were pink.

If the police had let Neal know about the hat pin, wouldn't he have put it into the paper?

My mind started buzzing with that. I watched one of the carriages drive by—not Neal because the driver was wearing one of the little hats.

Unless Neal made some deal with the police not to use that information. That was possible, I supposed, having heard things like that on TV shows but not really knowing if it was true.

The best way to sort this out might be to get Andre and Neal together so they could compare notes. Maybe three minds might be able to figure it out.

I looked around at the carriage drivers circling the Village Square, but Neal wasn't one of them. Not that D'Amos would look kindly on me snatching one of his drivers away to talk about old times with Andre. I knew Neal would have to be at the King's Feast in a few short hours. Andre would be there, too. Maybe I could get them together then.

With that settled, I went back to the Hat House—Andre was still gone. There was nothing I could do here without him. I remembered to pick up Neal's hat and closed the door to the shop behind me.

I spent the rest of the afternoon lining up help for my prank. Bart and Daisy were definitely in. Several pirates agreed to help—although I thought their motive was probably more seeing Queen Crystal than helping me. But you know pirates. They love a good prank, whatever the reason. Roger Trent was in and so was Hans, the blacksmith. Brother Carl said he'd bring a few monks, and Hephaestus, the owner of the Peasant's Pub, also agreed to be there.

With all those hearty souls behind me, all that remained was deciding on the prank itself. I hoped my visit to the encampment tonight would bring that onboard, too. All that would remain after would be making up with Chase for totally ignoring his judgment on the matter.

The Village was slowly shutting down as all activity moved to the castle for the King's Feast. Most vendors brought a few things to show off and sell to the crowd, except for the food vendors, who just had to stand around and watch. The castle staff who prepared the feast every week got a little cranky about the idea of competing with food vendors on their own home turf. A decree followed quickly, banishing all but castle food during the feasting.

Food vendors, like the rest of us, were still required to attend the festivities. Only death or dismemberment got you out of that. Just the food venders couldn't make any money. We were all ambassadors of good will for the thousands of visitors every year.

Other vendors went cheerfully. It was a big night for those selling artwork, swords, fake fairy wings, shields, and flower garlands. Even clothing was for sale. I waved to

Beth and Portia as they labored toward the castle. Their assistants dragged costumes on racks behind them.

I also saw the evil twins from the gem shop. They weren't carrying any jewelry to sell that I could see—and no serfs behind them. They probably preferred customers to be in their lair. To my horror, they approached me. There was nowhere to run and hide.

Rene bowed his head regally. "Lady Jessie. We wish to apologize again for the misunderstanding between us that led to the unfortunate episode at the stocks."

"Dreadful business," his sister echoed his words. She wore a beautiful black gown that matched his tunic in design.

"What misunderstanding?" I was still raw from the whole thing. They wouldn't get on my good side easily. "You got what you wanted. I heard the police questioned you anyway. I guess you didn't gain as much as you thought."

"Yes." Rene looked down his long nose at me. He was really tall—not many people could do that. "But we were also released. We're not guilty of anything."

"Except, perhaps, wanting justice for our mother," Renee concluded. Her brother glanced at her sharply. "What?" She got defensive. "It's true! That man murdered our mother. Is it wrong to want to see him pay for it?"

Rene put his arm around his sister's shoulders. "Excuse us, Lady Jessie. Renee is overwrought."

They started to walk away from me and toward the castle again, but I stopped them. Maybe they were done but I wasn't. "I can understand wanting justice—even revenge. But what if Andre isn't guilty of killing your mother?"

Rene snarled. "We have lived with this since we were children! Of course he's guilty! Don't you think we've done our research? Everyone else knows he's guilty, too. They just can't prove it."

"You're blind to put your faith in him," Renee said tearfully. "Don't trust him. You see how he turned on his own here, too."

"Seriously—does that make any sense to you? If the crimes were the same, he would've killed Eloise, not Cesar."

They both blinked at me like large, pale owls. Traffic scooted around us with grunts and a few curses.

"I don't know about the murder here, Lady Jessie," Rene finally said. "But we know he killed our mother."

"Why?" I asked. "Why did he kill your mother?"

"The police said she was having an affair with another man." Renee announced it as though she'd rehearsed the words many times.

"How do you know the other man didn't kill her?" I demanded. "Who was the other man?"

"We don't know who the other man was," Rene confessed, "or if there was another man. I don't think Andre knew either. It was enough that he thought she was unfaithful. He flew into a jealous rage and killed her."

"I know. And used a rare hat pin to mark his kill. Andre doesn't strike me as being that stupid."

"Not stupid," Renee corrected. "Arrogant and dramatic."

I had to give them that. I could see where Andre came off that way, although I still didn't think he could kill anyone.

The twins suddenly looked like two kids who wanted their mother back. I could certainly relate to that. And I could imagine Tony and me standing side by side—looking lost and alone after our parents were killed.

"I'm sorry," I blurted. "I know what it's like to lose a parent and feel so alone that you can't even see the world around you. I probably would've done exactly the same thing you guys have to prove it. And you're right. I don't know for sure Andre *didn't* kill your mother. But I really don't think so."

After my admission, the two of them just stared at me. Then the hugging started. Who knew they were huggers? We all cried while we were hugging, then we laughed about the crying and hugging. Lucky thing for us, the visitors went into the castle a different way or we would've ended up on YouTube.

"Thank you," Rene said finally. "We are deeply sorry about everything that happened between us before. Perhaps we can begin again."

"I'd like that," I said, then decided to test a theory. "I hate to ask you this—but do you know the color of the hat pin that was ... *found* ... with your mother when she died?" I just couldn't bring myself to go into the grisly details.

"Why?" Renee jumped at that. "Did you find something?"

"I don't know yet."

They looked at each other again and I could see the psychic mojo all twins possessed passing between them. It happened all the time with Tony and me, too.

"No," Rene answered. "We know there was a hat pin and that Andre had given it to her that morning. But we don't know the color. We never actually saw it."

"It was some deep police secret they felt obliged to keep even from her children." Renee's voice was bitter.

I thought they were better off not knowing. Knowledge can be cruel. "I'm sorry I had to ask," I apologized again.

"Please let us know if you find anything, Jessie," Renee said, her voice pleading. "We are desperate for information."

I nodded. "Sure. Oh, and, you didn't kill Captain Jack and dump him in Mirror Lake, did you?"

"No," Rene assured me without hesitation. "He sold us the shop and moved to Florida to fish. We still have his phone number if you want to contact him."

"No. That's okay. Just checking." I was surprised how calm they were about me asking them about another murder. "I have to run. Sorry. See you later." I waved, lifted my skirt a little, and rushed the last few hundred yards to the castle gate.

I was beginning to have a very bad feeling about that pink hat pin.

Thirty-three

"Nice ankles," Gus muttered as I passed him at the entrance to the castle. "You know, anytime you get tired of Chase—"

"I know. Thanks. Really." I could barely catch my breath. High heat and humidity don't go well with running. "Have you seen him?"

"He's in there somewhere. Have a good one."

I kept my backside turned away from him as I slowed my frantic pace. Even with the petticoat and gown I wore, his pinches could get a little painful. He was an annoying man, sometimes, but he had a lot of redeeming qualities, too. It's probably the only reason he didn't get pranked by the ladies of the Village every day.

The Great Hall was crowded, of course. Nobility was mostly on the dais overlooking the arena where the jousts and entertainment would take place. King Harold and Queen Olivia were both there—looking majestic in their matching red and white costumes, gold crowns on their heads.

They stood apart from one another. Livy looked tearful and pale. Not a good sign. I didn't see Chase up there in his usual midnight blue and silver tunic, so I began searching the rabble.

Visitors were still being seated in the stands on either side of the arena. Kitchen staff were moving around—setting places and pouring drinks. That was normal.

Vendors lined the entrance to the Great Hall, hawking their wares to everyone who passed. I didn't expect to see Andre there and I was right.

I saw him with the three sisters in purple wearing their elegant new hats. He'd changed into a formal green tunic and matching hat with a large peacock plume in it. Very dashing. He looked every inch the master hatmaker he was.

Now I just had to figure out how to reach him.

I clung to Neal's hat as though that would draw his attention, but the three ladies seemed to claim all of that.

I tried throwing my arms up in the air and yelling his name. One of the castle guards told me that madmen belonged in the arena on the ground floor for comic relief during the program.

There was still no sign of Chase. I was tempted to ask the obnoxious castle guard if he'd seen him. But it was so noisy as the cheerleaders (and I use that word loosely) began revving up the crowd by having them shout "Huzzah!" I didn't know if he could hear me and I wasn't sure if he'd pay attention anyway.

There were only two ways to get from one side of the arena to the other. You could go downstairs to the ground floor, where the knights would be readying their horses for the joust, and cross the field. Or you could pretend you were kitchen help and cross the narrow space that separated the royal dais from the barrier that circles the opening above the arena.

Going downstairs would take more time, so even though I wasn't dressed like a scullery maid or kitchen wench, I grabbed a few plates and napkins, then headed across the walkway, hoping no one would notice.

I wasn't halfway across before Rita Martinez saw me. She was the head of the kitchen staff. Her dark curls were damp on her sweaty forehead. Her eyes narrowed. "Jessie! Good to see you. What are you doing in the middle of my dinner?"

Rita was a very nice person, but she was also no-nonsense when it came to serving meals. I worked for her when I first started at the Village. I'd been working for her when I first saw Chase. He was galloping across the arena as the Queen's Champion. Even in a suit of shiny silver armor, he caught my attention. His helm was up and he was getting ready to address the queen and receive her favor before the joust.

I looked up at him and he smiled down at me. It was a moment out of time.

And suddenly, I knew when my magic moment happened. I realized when I looked up at him that night that I loved him—his kind eyes and sweet smile. That was my time out of time that I realized we were meant to be together.

"Jessie? You haven't answered my question." Rita's irritated voice totally interrupted the hearts and flowers circling in my brain.

It was hard coming back from that flashback—like a bad made-for-TV movie—but I had to focus. "Just trying to get across the arena fast." I smiled and waved but didn't wait for her permission. I kept on walking. "Good to see you, Rita. Love what you've done with your hair."

"Jessie!" she yelled back. "You better not try this again unless you want to peel a whole bag of onions by yourself!"

I really didn't want to peel a bag of onions or anything else. My kitchen wench days were over. But I needed to reach Andre faster than I could going downstairs and trying to get through everything happening down there.

When I got across the walkway, Andre was still there, looking for a spot to sit with his ladies. That's what mattered.

"I need to talk to you," I said when I reached him.

"Not now," he refused me. "I'm *very* busy."

"I know. But I need to talk to you *now*. It's about this hat."

He looked at the blue and gold carriage driver's hat in my hand and frowned. "It can wait until tomorrow. Or at least until after the feast."

The ladies giggled at his word play (least and feast—some people are easily amused), and he was still rogue enough to blush.

"No, Andre. It can't wait."

He huffed and shot me terrible glances that could have mortally wounded me if I wasn't supercharged with curious intention. "Fine."

"We'll save you a seat, Andre," one of the purple ladies said. "Right here between us."

His eyes were bright with anticipation of his return—and who knew what else. He was a man on the rebound. Anything was possible.

Reluctantly he let me drag him into a dark corner of the kitchen that was relatively quiet. "This better be good, Jessie."

"I don't know about good, but it's important." I explained about Neal, the pink hat pin, and what I'd learned from the not-so-evil twins.

"And?" he asked, darting impatient glances out at the crowd in the arena.

"And I think something is wrong. How did Neal know about the hat pin?"

"Reporters know things other people don't. Ask him."

"Andre—"

"Jessie—"

"Am I interrupting anything?" Neal's voice came over my shoulder. "Oh. There's my hat. I was hoping I'd find it with you, Andre."

Andre's eyes got wide. He looked like he'd seen a ghost. "Swayne? Is that you?"

Thirty-four

"Of course. Don't be so dramatic. That was always your worst quality."

"What are you doing here?" Andre asked. "Why are you dressed like that?"

"I'm returning the favor, old friend. You had me investigated—I thought I'd come here and see what you were up to."

"Wait a minute. You know each other?" I interrupted the reunion.

"Shut up, Jessie. Anyone ever tell you that you talk too much?" Swayne (Neal) muttered. "Both of you, step into that storage area over there."

Swayne had a gun. I couldn't believe it—and after I got him a job!

Andre held up his hands like they always do in the old movies. "Don't shoot. There's no reason for violence. I just wanted to know where my money had gone. I got a new accountant this year, and he found discrepancies. I wanted

to find out what happened. You were my business manager
for twenty years. Of course he'd start with you."

Swayne closed and locked the storage room door behind
him and stood against it. "I'll tell you what happened, you
self-indulgent moron—I spent all of it. At least all I could get
my hands on. When you started investigating me, I pretended
to be that arrogant reporter, Neal Stevenson from the *Times*. I
didn't want you to know I was here until I was ready."

"I trusted you," Andre charged. "You were sleeping
with Kathleen and I never even told the police. But I *knew*."

Swayne laughed. "And a sweet little morsel she was.
Too good for you. She found out about the money I was
taking and threatened to tell you. But I made a big mistake
that day—I should've killed you instead of her. Kathleen
and I could've run off together with *all* of your money."

"No!" Andre passionately launched himself against
Swayne's large, beefy body. It was like watching a flea
attack an elephant. Andre kind of bounced off him and fell
to the floor.

"You guessed about me, didn't you, Jessie?" Swayne
waved the gun at me—presumably because I was the only
one left standing.

"It was the hat pin," I explained. "No one else knew but
you."

"Too bad, honey. You and I could've had some good
times instead of them finding the two of you here dead in
the morning."

I wanted to say that he couldn't shoot us here without
drawing attention and getting caught. But the crowd was
stomping their feet and yelling *"Huzzah!"* every other minute. There were trumpeters announcing the start of the joust
and galloping horses. He was right. They wouldn't find us
until tomorrow, and by then he'd be long gone.

I looked around—in a stealthy way, I hoped—for something to use as a weapon. I had my tiny pocketknife but I

doubted that would make any difference to him. There were fifty-pound bags of flour that I couldn't lift without a major effort (too slow to avoid a bullet), smaller bags of beans, and a few potatoes. Not much by way of life-saving equipment. Not really even enough to make soup.

Andre got slowly to his feet and wiped some blood from the corner of his mouth. "You bastard," he snarled, hands curled into fists. "You cheating, lying, murdering bastard."

"You're a fool," Swayne said. "It was easy cheating with your wife and stealing your money. Stupid old fool."

Andre was motivated to attack again. This time, I jumped in—what did I have to lose?

I took the pocketknife and opened one of the flour sacks while Andre pummeled Swayne. I managed to cover all of us in flour. Swayne swore and lashed out at me. I hit him in the head with a bag of beans and tried to get close enough to kick him where it would matter.

Lucky for us, Swayne didn't have a chance to recover from our attack. Someone kicked in the pantry door, breaking it off the hinges. Andre and I got out of the way, but Swayne took the full brunt of the door crashing on him.

After the flour had cleared, Joe Bradley stood there. He had a gun, too. It seemed to me that security at the Main Gate was wasting their time making sure swords and arrows were peace-tied. If people were going to wander around the Village with guns, what chance did swords and arrows have?

Chase was right behind Joe with two security guards. But Joe had already taken care of the situation. Swayne lay still on the floor under the heavy door. Andre stood on top of the door for good measure.

"Jessie!" Chase rushed in and put his arms around me. "Are you all right?"

"Fine now." I snuggled in close to him. "At least we solved *one* murder."

"Maybe three," Joe corrected. "I think the police will

find Swayne killed your chocolate friend, too. He wanted to draw attention to Andre's past. I think he was hoping the twins would be blamed for his death."

"That doesn't make much sense to me," I disagreed.

"And he killed my brother, who Andre hired to investigate him," Joe continued. "I followed him here after that. He would've killed the two of you if I hadn't been following him around the Village. He thought I bought his phony Neal Stevenson act. He doesn't look anything like the real Neal Stevenson."

Detective Almond and a few of his officers arrived through a loud chorus of *huzzahs* from the arena—and probably countless little chicken bones raining down on the jousters.

Andre and I were covered with flour as we explained (again) what had happened. I smiled, watching Chase talk to Detective Almond after that. The front side of his tunic was also covered in flour where he had pressed against me, but the back part was clean.

I didn't want to think what all of us must have looked like when the police arrived. The important part was that everyone arrived in time. No permanent damage done— except maybe to Swayne, who was limping when the police led him away.

Chase filled me in on what he knew as we walked back to the Dungeon through the quiet Village, showered, and ate dinner. No castle food for us that night, only the finest microwave cuisine and some warm ale.

"So Bradley wanted to prove Swayne killed his brother for investigating him in Hollywood and followed him here." I was amazed by the whole story.

"Exactly. I'm sure Detective Almond is going to try to charge him with Cesar's murder, too." Chase explained the police theory, which sounded remarkably like Bradley's theory.

"I don't know. It wouldn't make sense for Swayne to draw attention to Andre like that when he was planning to kill him. The whole Village was alerted by Cesar's death—you doubled security at night. Either Swayne had a bad plan or he didn't kill Cesar."

"Let's leave that to the police, at least for now." He took my plate and glass and we lay close to each other for a long time.

"I remember when I first knew I loved you," I whispered, touching his hair and face. "I remember how you looked when you smiled at me that night and I thought my heart would burst out of my chest."

He smiled and kissed me. "That's very romantic—except for the heart-bursting thing."

"You can tell you've never read romance novels. You don't know the language."

"The important thing is that you remembered," he said. "Nothing else matters."

Thirty-five

I don't know what it was that woke me up a few hours later. Chase was gone and someone was throwing pebbles at the window next to the bed. Maybe that was it. I looked at the clock—it was almost midnight. I'd totally forgotten about meeting Lord Robert by the tree swing.

I changed into the black Templar outfit and ran downstairs. Lord Robert met me there, tossing down the rest of the pebbles when he saw me.

"I almost gave up on you." His voice was muffled behind the headgear.

"Thanks for waking me up. I'm sorry I'm late."

"Are you sure you want to go through with this? It's late—everything will be underway before we get there. I don't know how that will help you find Stewart's weakness, if he has one."

"I'm sure. Let's get going." I pulled the headpiece over my face and we followed the trail into the woods. The Knights Templar Encampment sign seemed to be the last outpost as I looked at it. After this, the rules of the Village didn't really apply. I had to remember that while I was there.

I wasn't really worried about surviving the ordeal. No matter what, this wasn't real. The knights might not play by the same rules, but they were still just ordinary people in costumes. How bad could that be?

The encampment was ablaze with torches and campfires lit around the enormous black tents. It looked like hundreds of people were out here, but I knew better. There were some hangers-on who liked being out here with the knights, but it couldn't be more than two dozen or so. Everyone was just so busy that it made it look like more.

"Who goes there?" a knight challenged us before we could enter the protected area.

"It is I, Lord Robert, with a new recruit. Allow us to pass or face the end of my blade."

The other knight nodded and put down his weapon. "Of course, Lord Robert."

He didn't speak to me but that might be because I was new. The monks had a thing like that where new recruits didn't speak and no one spoke to them for a week or so when they first joined the Brotherhood.

I saw several women from the Village—including Crystal the Pirate Queen. They were all doing female things like tending fires and cooking. I never thought of Crystal being the homemaking type, but you never know what people will do in different circumstances. In this case, a knight in shiny black armor stopped to kiss her. Love was the ultimate change in life.

"Assemble knights!" someone yelled, and the knights, most in training gear like me, and Lord Robert, went into the circle inside the area of the tents.

I stood close to Lord Robert without being clingy. That would give us away for sure. Knights probably didn't hold hands or stand up against each other much.

"We have three new recruits this eve," the knight who'd

called them together said. "Let's get started on training so
they may have the experience they will need later."

I wasn't sure that was Chase. He was big but maybe not
that big. He could be Stewart, it was hard to tell if that was
the same person from the Field of Honor.

Another, larger knight joined him—I knew *that* was
Chase. I should've known from the beginning even though
he'd disguised his voice. And maybe I did know and that's
why I was attracted to him. I like to think that it was.

"Recruits assemble here!" That was definitely Chase.

The three of us went to stand with him while the others
began to practice sparring and basic skills around the campfires. Chase laid out all the rules of being a Knight Templar—
not using your real name, meeting here after dark each night,
and other rules, much like normal clubs have.

They talked rough to us but no rougher than the pirates.
Of course, I knew Chase was behind one of the masks, so
that kept me from getting too nervous. If I had to, I could
whip off the hot, itchy mask and yell for him. I hoped it
wouldn't come to that.

When it was time for a break, Robert came to find me.
We partnered up and pretended to spar. "That's his tent
over there," he whispered as I dodged a blow from his
sword and parried with one of my own. "I could create a
distraction so you could get inside for a time. I don't know
if you'll find anything to use against him in there, but it's
all I can come up with."

I was glad that I'd had all that Village training in mock
battle as I dropped down to avoid a mock sword attack.
"Sounds good! What will you do?"

"You'll know when you hear it. Be ready. Don't let your
guard down."

"Don't worry. I'll be fine."

"You're braver than most men I know, my lady. You have
a lion's heart."

I couldn't tell him that some of that courage was derived

because my back was covered if it came right down to it. Chase wouldn't like it if I had to give his identity away, but he wouldn't let anything happen to me either. I was fairly sure most of the Templars didn't know their leader was also the bailiff. That would take away from their bad-boy image.

Lord Robert and I sparred a little longer. My black shirt was drenched with sweat. He was about to thrust his sword my way again when he suddenly yelled out, "Intruders! Knights—be aware. I see flashlights in the forest."

It was a good ruse. All the knights stopped what they were doing and rushed out into the trees to check for intruders. Not that I could see anything so mysterious about what they were doing out here, but it was enough that they wanted to keep themselves secret.

I didn't wait to be given another opportunity. I ran to the large black tent, still clutching my sword, and quickly went inside. I knew I wouldn't have long to snoop around—I was going to have to make my time count.

I felt let down when I got inside. There was nothing here except the barest bones of living—a cot, a crate with shoes in the opening, and a lighted lantern on top of the crate that illuminated the darkness. His suit of armor was carefully hung on a wooden pole structure. There was nothing even interesting about his possessions.

I heard the knights coming back to camp. They were whooping and cheering in triumph because they'd frightened off the imaginary intruders Robert had invented.

I sprinted across to the tent flap to get out—too late. Two knights came through the opening toward me. I fell back and hid behind the large black suit of armor.

"I don't think there was anyone out there at all," one of them said. "The men are getting restless not doing anything."

"You can't raid the Village every night, Stewart." That was Chase! "No matter who you are or how popular the knights are with the visitors, there will be an uprising among the residents. Believe me, they can get nasty."

Stewart laughed. I sneaked a peak at him—tall, broad shouldered, muscular, not so much as Chase, but a healthy male specimen. His dark hair was close cut to his head, and he sported some hair on his cheeks and chin.

"You take things too seriously, Chase! I believe there will come a time when you'll have to choose between being a knight and being the Village bailiff."

"That may be," Chase agreed. "But not tonight. I'm still the leader of the Templars and we aren't raiding anything tonight."

Stewart nodded his head deferentially to Chase. "Of course. You're still our leader—for now. I'll take the men on a ride through the forest."

"No messing with Robin Hood either," Chase warned.

Stewart didn't quite agree or disagree. He nodded again and slipped out through the tent door. A short time later, I heard horses galloping out of camp.

Why didn't Chase go with them? Why was he still here blocking my escape from his tent?

Chase had taken off his headgear and stretched his arms and back. It might be mock battle but it still was rigorous enough to be good exercise. Watching him (with some secret delight), I wondered if Stewart was crazy. I wouldn't challenge someone that much bigger than me. Chase might be ten years older than Stewart, but he was also a lot better trained. I'd put my money on him—in a fair fight.

But from what I'd seen, Stewart didn't fight fair. And that's why I was there. Obviously I was in the wrong tent, but that was only a momentary setback.

I really didn't want Chase to know I was there unless it was a total emergency. I didn't feel this constituted one. I just had to figure a way out without giving myself away.

Chase took off his training outfit, maybe planning on putting on his Village clothes and heading back to the Dungeon. He walked by his suit of armor and I decided this was my best shot. I knocked the lightweight but bulky armor toward him and made a dash for the tent flap. Good plan, right?

But I'd forgotten that for all of his size, Chase was very fast. It was that quickness that had made him so good in the joust. He avoided the falling armor—letting it clank to the ground at his feet. In an instant, he had tackled me and was holding me down on the sandy floor.

I struggled a little but I was too worried about giving myself away to put up much of a fight. I was in a precarious position.

"Who are you?" he demanded. "What are you doing in my tent?"

"I was frightened by the intruders, sir." I lowered my voice, letting it creak like a young teenager. "I rushed into the tent to hide."

He laughed. "You seem to be good at that. And you play me for a fool, wench. I know why you sneaked into my tent." He leaned over me and whispered, "Have at it then, woman. I am at your disposal."

I was immediately too angry to remember to disguise my voice. My temper has always been my weakness. "Have at it? I can't believe you're out here looking for camp followers to warm your cot." I beat my fist against his chest and kicked at him, no longer caring if he knew who I was.

He got up and pulled me up with him. In a single move, he pulled off my headgear. "What a surprise. How did I know you wouldn't pay any attention at all to my asking you not to prank Stewart."

"I suppose you're saying you knew it was me the whole time. Hah! There was no way to know it was me."

"As soon as I knew you were a woman—which was thirty seconds after I tackled you, I knew it couldn't be anyone but you, Jessie. All the other women come out here wearing something sexy. You're the only one who'd come out here dressed like a knight."

I suppose that made sense. I still didn't like it.

"Now get your stuff together and get out of camp before Stewart and the others get back," he said. "I'll be home in a little while."

"I heard you and Stewart talking, Chase. It's not going to be long before what you say isn't going to matter to him. Now's the time to take him out. Let me do it for you."

The last part was probably over the top. Chase kind of drew back, and I realized I'd hurt his manly pride. Of course he could handle Stewart by himself. Blah. Blah. Blah.

"I don't need your help. Go home, Jessie. Don't come out here again."

"Fine." I snatched my mask from him and pulled it over my head.

"I mean it. You could get hurt out here."

"I said fine. What else do you want?"

"Your word that you won't do it again. I can handle Stewart."

I mumbled something that sounded like it could be my word. Of course I wasn't so stupid as to give my word that it wouldn't happen again. I did press my lips through the mask against his before I left the tent. I didn't know if he was watching, but I walked toward the trees and the path back to the Village.

Lord Robert followed and stopped me before I got too far. "Why did you go in *that* tent? You were supposed to go in that tent." He pointed to another large black tent.

"Sorry. They all look the same to me."

He bowed his head. "I am sorry, my lady. I'm glad you're unharmed. I was worried about you."

"Not a problem but thanks for worrying. Now, let's go search the right tent before Stewart and the knights get back."

Thirty-six

Sorry to say, Stewart's tent was as bare as Chase's. There were no easy giveaways about him. If he had a weakness, he kept it hidden. I was beginning to think maybe Chase was right about him being impervious to pranking— a depressing thought.

Lord Robert and I were out of the tent and contemplating our next move when the riders returned. They saw to their horses—except Stewart, who gave his black steed to one of the new recruits.

I noticed he went to find Crystal, the ex-pirate queen next. They kissed passionately for a minute or so, then he went to the makeshift camp shower, which consisted of a bucket of water held aloft and a string that could be used to empty it on the showering knight. The water came from a cistern that collected rain, no doubt. They were a long way from the Village water system. Someone had thoughtfully put up a blanket to shield part of the rough bathing apparatus.

Crystal went with him to the shower and held up an extra blanket for him, carefully shielding him from possible prying eyes that might want to ogle his body. He seemed to be the only one with any qualm about using the shower.

Could it be he had a thing about being seen naked?

Well, not that everyone doesn't have *some* problem with it—but some people are more particular than others.

Crystal carefully folded the blanket around him like a large towel as he got out of the shower. Then she accompanied him to his tent and stood outside (rather than inside, ogling) while he dressed.

"Lord Robert," I addressed my companion, who was aimlessly whittling a tree branch with his sword. (Daisy, the Village sword maker, would have a coronary if she saw it—blasphemy!) "Have you seen Stewart naked?"

"Pardon me?"

I repeated the question, keeping an eye on the tent where Crystal waited.

"What are you implying, my lady?" He stopped whittling. "I assure you I am not of that persuasion. I know Stewart from college, but—"

"Settle down!" I explained the basis of my question. "Does he have a thing about being naked?"

"There was that terrible incident at school, freshman year," he recalled. "It wasn't just him. A fraternity took everyone's clothes on the second floor. We all had to run outside naked."

"How did Stewart handle that?"

"He was—" He glanced at the tent where Stewart was dressing. "He really freaked out about it. His parents had to come and get him. He missed part of the semester. He had therapy. Lady Jessie—you are a genius!"

"Thanks."

"But how do we get him naked and out of the tent?"

"Leave that to me."

Thirty-seven

I went back to the Dungeon to sleep for a few hours before morning. Chase didn't get in until after me. "Where were you?" I wondered.

"I shouldn't bother telling you," he sniped. "After that stunt you pulled at the encampment."

"It's not like I was in any real danger."

"Not that you would've cared."

"And I *did* find something to prank Stewart with."

"Not that you care what I think about that either."

"Chase—this needs to be done. You should be able to see that better than anyone."

"Sometimes, things work out on their own with absolutely no outside interference from you or anyone else. Have you ever noticed that?"

We were nose-to-nose on the bed. But I was too tired to argue with him anymore. "I have to get some sleep." I yawned. "We'll have to talk about this tomorrow."

"Jessie—" He paused, then kissed me. "Good night. I'll see you in the morning."

I sat up. "Don't you even want to know how I'm going to do it?" I was tired, but sleep suddenly seemed impossible with so much on my mind.

"No."

"Aren't you a *little* curious?"

"No."

I sighed—heavily—and stood up. "I can't sleep."

"You're going to be dragging tomorrow—today."

"I know. But I can't sleep."

"Fine." He got up, too. "Let's leave and drive down to the IHOP and eat breakfast out for a change."

"Really?"

"And you can tell me all about your scheme to prank Stewart." I heard him fumble for his street clothes (the kind you wear outside the Village). "Not that I'm going to go along with whatever you have in mind."

"Okay." Lucky for me, I didn't need his approval.

Thirty-eight

We came back a couple of hours later, after we'd stuffed ourselves full of pancakes and maple syrup. We took a nice walk on the beach while the sun was rising and watched Myrtle Beach come to life around us.

Sometimes it's hard to remember that there's a world outside the Village. While I'm here—this is all that matters. I've always known I could get lost in the make-believe. That's why I never decided to stay here full-time. I love this world of fairies, pirates, and nobility—I'm just afraid to let it become my whole life.

Chase and I kissed good-bye at the Main Gate to go our separate ways. He'd had a call from King Harold while we were out, asking him to come to the castle as soon as possible.

I was headed back to the Dungeon after picking up a new gown from the costume shop. It was a little pink for me, but Portia wasn't in an amiable mood so I settled. It did absolutely nothing for my coloring.

I waved to Beth in the back of the shop before I left. Seeing her reminded me that there was something we were all missing about Cesar's death—something important. I didn't believe Swayne had killed him. I doubted I ever would.

I met Robin Hood and Maid Marion (I guess he got her to come home again), who acknowledged me with a head bow (him) and a curtsy (her). I noticed Maid Marion was sporting what looked like an expensive new dress and matching parasol. It might have been a bribe for coming back from the Templars' camp.

They were headed toward the Monastery Bakery, so we walked together for a while down the cobblestones.

"Big doings at the castle last night," Robin said.

"Yes." I didn't go any further. I wanted to hear his version.

"After last night, I would think there will be a spectacular press conference, at the very least." Maid Marion smiled.

"I suppose you're right." I waited to hear them tell me about someone catching Cesar's killer.

"Maybe you didn't hear," Robin suggested, possibly at my lack of enthusiasm for good gossip. "King Harold publicly announced the queen's baby as his."

"Were the tests finished?" I asked in awe, despite myself.

"I haven't heard," Robin continued, "but he said the baby was his. The child will be the new prince or princess of Renaissance Village—to be born around Christmas."

"Really?" I enthused. "That's wonderful news. I hope things work out for them."

"You and Chase were glowing this morning," Maid Marion remarked. "You two seem very much in love. Just like me and Robin."

I said thank you but secretly hoped we had more going on than Robin and his present Marion. My usual mouthful of words wouldn't quite come out though. I kind of felt choked up thinking about it.

I was tired, I considered. I probably needed caffeine to keep me from getting too mushy and teary-eyed about it.

"Did you hear we caught the man who killed Andre's wife at the feast last night?" It was best to change the subject.

Marion glanced at Robin. "No. I didn't realize Andre was married. I thought Cesar died—not Eloise."

"Was he married to Eloise?" Robin was confused. "I thought she was going to marry Bernardo. Or was that Marco with that younger tart—what's her name?"

"Belle?" I suggested. This was news to me.

"That's the one. Not that Cesar wanted them together. Of course, he didn't want Bernardo with Eloise either. That's why he tried to break them up." Robin stroked his beard thoughtfully.

I considered the information and stored it away for the near future. Then I told them my tale of helping catch Swayne. After my glory story, I finally broke down and let Robin in on pranking Stewart—with a reminder to keep his mouth shut.

Coffee was gone and the day was getting later. I took my leave of them, trying to digest what Robin had told me about Cesar dominating his brothers. Cesar had a lot to answer for. I realized he might have answered with his life.

But I'd been all over the thing with Bernardo. He'd gained so much with Cesar's death, but he couldn't have done it. Eloise was out of the picture, too. I couldn't imagine Marco—the quiet, shy brother—having anything to do with it. But maybe that's where I was overlooking something.

"Hey, there!"

I almost walked into Detective Almond. He was looking for Chase. I told him he was at the castle, and he handed me an envelope. "I think this is for you anyway."

"Me?"

"Manhattan said you wanted a picture of the hat pin we found in Cesar Rizzo. I figure we have the killer already after last night—knock yourself out."

"Thanks."

"The castle?" He glanced around like he was lost.

"The big building with the turrets." I pointed toward it. "You can't miss it."

"Thanks. All these places look the same to me. I can't tell the butcher from the candlestick maker." He laughed, his heavy face jiggling a little.

I didn't have the heart to tell him we didn't have either of those places. I smiled and sent him on his way. Then I ran the rest of the way to the Dungeon to see what I'd been waiting for.

I closed and locked the door to the apartment and huddled on the bed. I couldn't even wait to change clothes before I looked in the envelope.

There were three pictures of the hat pin—one from each angle. One of them was in color. I studied them carefully and came up with my deduction—I had never seen this hat pin before.

I was disappointed. I thought this would be the answer to Cesar's death. But maybe the hat pin was still in Andre's collection. Now that I knew what it looked like, I had something to go on.

I changed into my too-pink gown and took off my tennis shoes even though you couldn't really see them under all that skirt. We could wear slippers, boots, or sandals. None of them could have zippers or eyelets to tie shoe laces with. I usually wore a plain pair of sandals even though a lady of my stature wouldn't have worn them during the Renaissance.

The Main Gate was officially open and visitors were pouring in after receiving their Village maps and other free goodies distributed by whoever the hospitality committee could get off the cobblestones. No doubt there would be a large crowd, since Swayne's arrest would've been in the media this morning.

I walked past a group of green fairies who were still getting their act together for the day. I'd noticed the fairies were grouping themselves now—pink, green, blue, and purple. I wasn't sure what that meant and I didn't want to ask. I probably should warn Chase of an impending fairy insurrection. Groups didn't just come together in the Village for no reason.

The acrobats were out showing off on the Green as I got close to the Hat House. Beside them were jugglers, sword swallowers, and fire eaters performing. Little signs said what time their shows were happening during the day and on which of the four stages they were performing.

Someone had definitely pulled out all the stops. There was almost too much going on to take it all in—exactly the way it should be at a Renaissance Fair.

Andre was already busy with several new projects. One of them, no doubt a labor of love, was three new hats for the purple ladies who'd paid him a visit yesterday. Other orders included a new hat for Queen Olivia to match her new maternity wear and a new hat for Mother Goose.

"Jessie! Just in time! I need you to look in the storeroom and find some buckram to stiffen up these hats. I might need to order more. We'll have to see."

"I can tell you had a good night." I smiled as I walked to the storeroom.

"It's not every night a man realizes his mortality and gets over it. Going through that with Swayne made me realize what a fool I've been. I hope I've rectified that situation. I've asked Beth to be my wife."

"Seriously? That's awesome! Tell me you're going to have a big Village wedding."

"I will as soon as I hear from her. She told me she needed time. But I know in my heart we'll be fabulous together. I'm thinking Gable and Lombard, Fairbanks and Pickford, Tarzan and Maureen O'Sullivan."

"You know the last two weren't really married, right?"

He kind of giggled. "Of course not. They lived in the jungle. No reason to worry about legalities there."

He was in such a good mood, I didn't want to spoil it. I got the buckram from the storeroom and returned for red ribbon, pink flowers, and other necessities. Time passed quickly as we worked at the various projects.

When his assistants left for lunch, I asked Andre what made him suspicious of his old manager. "You must've thought something was really wrong to hire a private detective to investigate him."

"I never dreamed that he'd murdered Kathleen," he admitted. "I knew there were serious discrepancies in the money I made during a five-year period in that time frame. I might not look it right now, but I made top money while I worked in Hollywood. Swayne was supposed to be investing that for me. It didn't really show up until recently when I began drawing from that account."

"But you knew he was sleeping with your wife?"

"Yes. I did. It was a terrible discovery." He looked up from what he was doing and smiled at me even though there were tears in his eyes. "I thought it was better that I knew who the person was. I know that doesn't make any sense. It was rather like better the devil you know. I thought at least she was safe with him. When the time was right, she'd come back to me."

His deep sigh was sad to hear. It kind of said it all.

"I was wondering if you could take a look at a picture of a hat pin that might be one of yours and tell me who it belongs to," I said, changing the subject.

"Of course—although truly I'm beginning to consider throwing my hat pin collection away and never making or keeping another hat pin again. These things have almost ruined my life twice now. I hate that Cesar was killed that way. And all to throw off the police and cover his tracks because Swayne planned to kill me. At least that's what they said on TV this morning."

So that was the theory, eh? *Lame!*

I took out the envelope and showed Andre the pictures. He pondered them for several minutes, then said, "It's certainly one of mine. I'm not sure which one. Obviously for a lesser Village character, I think. Maybe that character who used to follow the rhyme—ride a white horse to Banbury Cross. She used to have that sweet little house near Sir Latte's Beanery. I think Will Shakespeare might be there now."

We looked through his collection together, but the hat pin didn't match the one he was thinking about.

"What about Belle? Does she have a hat pin, too?" I asked as he was still going through the hat pins. I knew it was a long shot, but I was curious after talking to Robin that morning.

"You mean Eloise's youngest sister?" He started back through the collection. "I'm sure she does. I created a lovely chipped-straw hat for her. She has a nice little velvet hat, too. I don't recall exactly—here it is!"

I looked at the hat pin in the plastic bag. It looked exactly like the one in the photo Detective Almond gave me. I sat back in the old, broken chair and felt depressed by the discovery.

I'd wanted Eloise to be guilty, even Bernardo. They seemed so greedy and manipulative. Why is it that the bad guys don't seem to be guilty of the things you want them to be guilty of? It was a puzzle for the ages.

In the meantime, I had evidence that had been overlooked because the police didn't realize the individuality of the hat pins in the Village. To them it was just a hat pin. Now I knew it was Belle's hat pin. Did that mean she had killed Cesar? And did she do it alone?

Thirty-nine

I had a choice to make. I could forget about this—Detective Almond was happy believing Swayne had killed Cesar. Or I could keep asking questions until someone realized there was more going on than the police thought.

I considered the answer while walking to Peter's Pub for lunch. Chase had been called away again and left word that I should eat without him. That just depressed me more. This would've been a good time to have someone I could trust to talk to—not that I was sure about telling him. Once he knew about it, he'd feel honor bound to tell the police. What if that wasn't the right thing?

I left the pub without eating and wandered around the Village Square for a while. I sat on the edge of the Good Luck Fountain and contemplated all the problems in the universe while playing in the water. There were no easy answers.

To get my mind off of what happened, I spent the next hour talking to as many trustworthy Village folk as I could. I enlisted them in my prank—now scheduled for tonight so that no one had a chance to give it away. The good thing was that I had someone from each of the guilds.

Hans, the blacksmith, was onboard from the Craft Guild and Sam Da Vinci from the Artist Guild. Master Archer Simmons from the Weapons Guild said he would be there, and Hephaestus, head of the Food Guild, agreed to be there, too.

Fred the Red Dragon would be filling in for Merlin from the Magical Creatures Guild, while Little Bo Peep (who'd have thought) said she would be there from the Entertainers Guild. Susan Halifax from the Musicians Guild offered to help in whatever way possible, since the knights had interrupted so many of their concerts, and Brother Carl promised reinforcements from the Brotherhood of the Sheaf. The pirates were in, of course, and the Knave, Varlet, and Madman Guild said they would come, too, if nothing else, to erase the smear on their reputation when Swayne was arrested after posing as one of them.

That only left me short a member of the nobility. Technically, that could be me, but since I wasn't worried about me not supporting the cause, I was looking for someone else. If I had someone from each of the guilds, no one could complain or tell what happened without implicating themselves as well.

I asked Sir Reginald, who usually carried the queen's favor into battle, but the job was too dirty for him. I knew it was pointless to ask Princess Isabel—she might chip a nail and go home crying. The king and queen were otherwise occupied. It looked like I was going to have to be the representative of the nobility after all.

But as I was leaving Baron's Beer and Brats after speaking with Sir Reginald, I was surprised to find Lord Dunstable coming after me. His basic function at the castle is protocol—he starts the joust at the King's Feast each week. Even though I've been coming here for years, that's all I knew about him.

"Lady Jessie." He approached me. "I could not help but

overhear. My apologies. I would enjoy being part of the event you have planned for those hooligans living in the forest—and I'm not speaking of Robin Hood and his men either!"

I looked at his usually stern features and pointy little beard on his chin. He was a tall man. I'd never really noticed before. "I'd be glad to have you there, Lord Dunstable. Prithee, what motivates you to do this, sir?"

His lips compressed and he shook all over. "It is not something I like to speak of, lady, but suffice to say, the ruffians hunted me down one evening as I took my constitutional around the Village. They rode me to ground like a fox on the hunt. Afterwards, the cowards tossed me headfirst into a large trash receptacle, there to stay until morn when the maintenance workers found me. Revenge would be very sweet."

I shivered at the tone of his voice. This man was serious. "Okay. But no weapons, right? We're pranking their leader—not killing him."

"Of course! And may I say I am proud to be part of one of your famous pranks, Lady Jessie." He bowed his head to me.

"Thanks. We meet midnight at the, uh—tree swing. Good to have you onboard, Lord Dunstable." I almost said privies, but that might be too close to the memory of being upended in a trash can. Who knew Lord Dunstable could be so vicious?

With the whole guild system from the Village in my pocket for the prank tonight, I felt pretty good about everything. It would be nice for Chase to be home at night—barring the occasional Village mishap. And it would be good for him to be away from the Templars, too. Everything was going to work out just fine.

Merlin approached me as I headed back to the Hat House. His usual look of complete happiness was replaced by a dark thundercloud of anger. "Just the mischief maker I wanted to see!"

The jig, as they say, was up. Somehow he'd found out about what I was planning. But I decided to play it cool. "Merlin! Just the wizard I wanted to see."

"I hear there's something going on in the Village and you had a big part in it." He stared at me with his zany brows going up and down on his face. "You've gone too far this time."

"I suppose it all depends on how you look at it." I wasn't offering any information.

"Well then, I suppose it would be how I would look at it."

What was he getting at? If he was looking for a confession, he wasn't getting one.

"Don't you want to say anything in your own behalf?"

"No. Is there something you want to say, Wizard?"

He cleared his throat and straightened his pointed hat. "I know there's something going on. I know you're involved. I just can't figure out exactly what it is. You can tell me now or you can tell me later."

I smiled. He was only fishing. "Later would suit me just fine, thanks."

He ground his teeth a little and balled up his fists. "I guess that's it then. Carry on."

He'd almost tricked me into telling him. No doubt he had heard something—the Village grapevine was a perfect instrument for spreading gossip. But he still didn't know exactly what was going on. He wasn't going to hear it from me.

Forty

Chase and I had managed to miss each other all day. I looked around for him but I was always one step behind. I went back to work at the Hat House again after lunch, and Andre said Chase had been there looking for me. It made for a long, stupid day.

Andre decided to close early. He was too anxious to work, he said. "I thought I'd hear from Beth by now. Maybe she's been busy all day. Or maybe she doesn't want to have anything to do with an old fool like me. I wouldn't blame her. I know what it feels like to be rejected by the person you love."

I consoled him the best I could. Then I tried to talk him out of going to the costume shop and hanging around waiting for her answer. "Go eat dinner. Have a few pints. Don't think about it for a while. Don't, whatever else you do, stalk her. There's nothing worse than knowing someone is waiting for your answer. Especially when you look up every few minutes and there he is."

Andre laughed a little. "I guess I'm that pathetic, eh? You sound like you speak from experience, Jessie. Have dinner with me and you can relate your wisdom to me."

"I'd like to but I've been looking for Chase all day. We usually see each other sometime during the day. It makes me nervous when I don't see him. I start thinking all kinds of crazy things."

"So, despite your lofty wisdom, you have problems of your own."

"Yes. Wisdom comes at a terrible price. See you in the morning, Andre. I hope we both have good news."

I decided to go back to the Dungeon and change clothes, then wait for Chase there. No point in walking the whole Village again. Three times that day was enough.

The sky was clouding up again, lending an air of later evening to the day. Visitors were still straggling to the Main Gate, where residents struggled to amuse them and leave a lasting impression. But it had been a long day. The music sounded a little tired, and the girls throwing flowers weren't quite smiling anymore.

The threat of rain was closing in on everything. Shop-keepers were taking in outdoor furniture, and the goose girls were herding their flock back to the nest on the other side of the Village. Thunder rumbled in the distance, making residents and visitors pick up their paces.

Robin Hood doffed his hat and winked at me as I passed him near the hatchet-throwing game. If anyone gave away what was happening tonight, it would be him. I scowled and shook my head, trying to give him the impression that we shouldn't look so guilty.

It started raining as I passed the Honey and Herb Shoppe. Mrs. Potts, the proprietor, nodded and discreetly smiled to let me know she was onboard. I knew I could trust her to keep quiet.

The whole time, I kept looking for Chase, but there was no sign of him. I was definitely getting worried. What if something had happened to him and no one had told me? I knew the odds of that were a million to one, but that one really bothered me. And there was that vague threat from Stewart that I'd overheard in the tent.

I picked up my own pace as the rain began to fall faster. It felt good hitting my overheated skin, but I knew how Portia felt about damp clothes being returned, too. I breathed in the scent of the rain that smelled like the ocean and heard a sound from behind me. I looked up as the large black horse came steadily closer and I hurriedly stepped out of the way.

But the rider had a long reach. He grabbed me as the horse was going by and pulled me into the saddle in front of him. I struggled, but the horse began to gallop. There's not a lot you can do from there but hold on. I was facedown with the hard saddle bumping into my chest, making it difficult to breathe.

For an instant, I thought it might be Chase. It was definitely one of the Knights Templar. But after that initial thought, I knew Chase wouldn't ride with me this way. Something else was up. Someone had ratted me out, and now Stewart wanted to give me a hard time about it.

I remained calm even though the rain was really pounding by the time the horse left the cobblestones. That meant we were headed into the forest and the encampment. Thunder pounded like the horse's hooves beneath me, and lightning sizzled across the evening sky. I was actually more afraid of getting zapped by lightning than of what Stewart had decided to do with me.

We finally came to a stop, and I looked up through the rain to see the black tents. No one was outside to see us arrive. Stewart hefted me on his shoulder and carried me into his tent, tossing me on his cot like a wet sack of flour.

I got to my feet right away. Being tall all of my life had always been an advantage in physical situations. Short people were nervous when I stood up and looked down at them. Not that I needed an advantage anyway—I knew Stewart's secret.

I watched as he removed his soaking headpiece and tossed it into the corner. "We meet face-to-face at last, Lady Jessie," Stewart said with a smile. "I think you and I are going to have a rather interesting evening."

Forty-one

"I think you're going to have an interesting evening—
without me. Step aside and I'll go quietly without reporting you for this." I tried to look as fierce and tall as I could.

"You think I went to all this trouble to simply release
you? Think again. And while you're at it, fetch me some
ale from that table over there."

Crystal poked her head through the tent flap. "My Lord?
May I assist you?" She saw me standing there and dragged
the rest of her body inside, too. "Jessie? What are you doing
here?"

"This does not concern you," Stewart told her. "Go to
the women's tent and I'll call you when I need you."

"Why is she here, Stewart? If you needed someone, you
should've called me." Her voice was unsteady, filled with
anger that he'd brought someone else here.

"I do not answer to you, woman!" he roared back at her.
"I shall summon you when I desire. Leave us at once."

I really couldn't picture Crystal the Pirate Queen backing

down from him—but it happened. She meekly left the tent after glaring at me like I had something to do with this. What was wrong with her anyway?

"Now," Stewart turned back to me, "fetch me that ale."

"Or what?" I demanded, grabbing an apple that had been left for him on his bedside table. There was also a beautiful red rose. "I'm not fetching anything. I'm not a dog. And you're dangerously close to being charged with kidnapping in the *real* world. Remember that place? No cute little black suits or horses to play with."

He stamped his foot. I'm not kidding—he really stamped his booted foot. Nice boots though.

"You will do as I say or you will pay the consequences."

I took a bite of the apple. "Make me."

He was so angry that it contorted his face. "You think I don't know what you had planned for tonight? You think I'm stupid? I know what's going on. The Templars serve each other. Did you really believe Robert was your friend?"

I was a little concerned about poor Robert at that point. Whether he talked or not, he could be in trouble. Item number one to look into—after I escaped.

"Do you really think I care?" I bluffed. "Robert was a tool to use. I don't care whether he was my friend or not."

"Your plan has failed. Your friends can't help you now. Acknowledge me as your master and I'll be lenient."

I dropped the apple on the floor. "Okay. That's enough playacting. I put up with kids like you all year at school. I'm done here. I'm going home. Stop me if you feel motivated."

He took a knife out of his boot. It didn't have a safety tip on it. I didn't know if it was real or not—I didn't care. I glanced around for a weapon and grabbed his sword from the sheath near his suit of armor. We faced each other across the tent while the lightning flashed around us outside.

"You're a *girl*," he reminded me. "You can't wield that big heavy sword. Give it up."

My sword was not safety tipped either. I moved in quickly and made a few cuts to his black practice outfit. Parts of it fell from him, leaving his side and one shoulder bare. He obviously didn't realize how long my reach was. "What? I couldn't hear you for all of the thunder outside."

That totally enraged him. He came at me with all the skill of a man who's had no formal weapons training. He thrust his knife around like a little kid. I used the sword to cut at him several more times. By then, his chest and one leg were uncovered.

"You fight like a demon," he managed to get out through clenched teeth.

"Thanks. You fight like an idiot. I can't even imagine why I was so worried about Chase. That's probably why he wasn't worried. He'd seen you fight. He knew you were just a bunch of sound and fury signifying nothing."

This wasn't part of my plan to prank him. On the other hand, maybe he'd be so humiliated at being beaten by a girl that it would do the trick. By my estimation, I was hours ahead of the rest of the residents who were coming to join me. Oh well, the best laid plans and all that.

Stewart looked like he wasn't sure what to do. Not surprising. It's different when you only battle people who let you win.

"I'll give you one last opportunity," he snarled. "I've shown you mercy so far. You won't find that the case any longer."

"Have at it, *boy!*" I encouraged him. "In case you haven't noticed, mine is bigger. Not that it would matter, since I know what to do with it and you obviously don't."

That did it for him again. He came at me with his little knife, and I made the most of the opportunity. By the time I got done with him, he was down to his boots and some of his skivvies. I played with him like a cat with a mouse. It was almost too easy.

"That's enough!" He threw his dagger on the floor. "There

are laws that protect people from things like this. My father has a lot of money. You're going to jail."

I laughed at him. "I don't care how much money he has. I might go to jail, but not before you and I take a walk outside in the rain."

"What? Have you lost your mind? You've managed to undress me. At least have the dignity to hand me clean clothes."

I leveled the tip of the sword with his throat. "I lost my mind a long time ago and I have no dignity whatsoever. College professors can't afford dignity on what we make. Outside, *now!*"

I thought a nice walk around the encampment would be good for him—maybe enough to help him see the error of his youthful ways. I held the sword steady and urged him out the door with it. He stepped through the tent flap with me right behind him.

A chorus of huzzahs greeted us, punctuated by several non-Renaissance handheld spotlights. I couldn't see who was there, but I could tell it was quite a crowd.

Stewart started screaming and grabbed his private parts before running into the dark woods that surrounded the encampment. As he ran I heard several slapping noises—I could only guess that some of the residents wanted to get more hands-on in his punishment.

The huzzahs continued, a little party starting up despite the rain. Knights and followers began to peek out of their tents to see what was going on. Someone started playing music from a local radio station, and before I knew it, everyone was dancing.

"Jessie!" Chase grabbed me and swung me around. "Since you were determined to do this, I hope you didn't mind if I gathered your faithful here before midnight."

I kissed him hard on the mouth. "I was never so glad to see everyone!"

"Did you see that little terror take off?" Robin Hood

asked, doing one of his head-back guffaws with his gloved hands on his hips. "Methinks we won't be hearing from him any time soon."

"Don't be so sure," Chase warned. "He might be pranked, but that might only be the beginning."

"You're such a downer," Fred the Red Dragon told him. "Enjoy the moment, man."

"Somebody told Stewart what was going on," I said to Chase. "I think it was Lord Robert. Have you seen him around?"

"Not recently." He grabbed the sword I was still brandishing. "Maybe you should look for him without this. I'll help you."

We found him trussed up and gagged in the back of the camp followers' tent. Chase cut the ropes that held him while I removed the gag.

Robert looked up at us with genuine fear in his eyes. "I didn't want to tell him. Really. He made me tell him. He threatened me."

"It doesn't matter," I said. "It all turned out fine. The prank worked out, thanks to Chase being fast on his feet."

"And Stewart?" Robert asked.

"He ran off," Chase said. "I'm sure he'll be back with a bad case of poison oak. But he'll be fine."

"Well, as good as anyone can be after I prank them." I smiled and enjoyed my success. "I think we should visit the party, don't you, Sir Bailiff?"

"Thank you, Lady Jessie." Robert groveled at my feet again. "I believe there may be a need for a successor to take Stewart's place within the knights. I would be honored to do this."

"That is much appreciated, Lord Robert," Chase told him. "But there was word today that Sir Karl, one of the castle knights, will be the new leader out here. Stewart is welcome back if he can adhere to the new rules being set by the Village guilds for the Templars. You may continue in your present position, if you see fit to do so."

Robert bowed his head. "Thank you, Sir Bailiff. I will do so."

Chase and I left him in the tent to get himself together. "You didn't tell me Karl was taking over," I said. "I didn't even need to prank Stewart to save you."

He laughed and pulled me close. "Just the idea that you wanted to save me is sweet—and frightening. I didn't know about Karl until someone told me about you being picked up by a Templar Knight. Rafe had already told me about your plans for tonight, after you conveniently forgot to. That's why I decided to move the timetable forward."

"Well, at least it will all be cleaned up for Karl to take over," I said, proud of my accomplishment. I saw Merlin gyrating with two of the Stage Caravan belly dancers. "I guess the over-all answer is the guilds rewriting bylaws for the Templars."

"I think so," he agreed. "And I'm free of that, thanks to you."

"Not a problem. I've pranked people for less."

I knew there would still be repercussions—the chances were Stewart's father would want to complain about what happened. But the reign of Templar Terror seemed to be over. We could go back to our semi-normal lives again.

We stayed awhile with the others, dancing and laughing in the warm summer rain. The ground got kind of squishy from so many people dancing on it, and I decided it was time to go home.

Chase and I called good night to everyone and headed down the dark path that led back to the Village. The rain had slacked off enough that the leaves from the trees kept it off us like a big green umbrella.

"Detective Almond told me he gave you the photos of that hat pin you wanted," he said, his arm around my waist. "Did you show them to Andre?"

"Yes. He looked through his collection." I didn't want to lie to Chase—not if I could help it. But I didn't want him to give Detective Almond the information I found about Belle and Marco.

"Did he find anything?"

"We're still trying to decide."

"Is there something wrong?"

"No. Why do you ask?" I hoped he wasn't going to try to get the information out of me. It had been a rough night. Besides, I wasn't very good at keeping things from him.

"You sound kind of funny. Usually that means you're not telling me everything."

"I don't think it happens often enough for you to make generalizations like that," I countered.

Chase stopped walking and turned me to face him. We were close enough to the lights from the Village that I could make out the contours of his face, if not the details. "Jessie, what's going on?"

"If I knew for sure, I'd tell you. I don't, so I can't. I hope that makes sense."

"Does whatever it is have any kind of imminent danger to you involved with it?"

That was easy to answer. "Absolutely not. And really, I'm only thinking about a hot shower and something to eat. Nothing more is on my mind."

It wasn't exactly the truth. But it was enough to get by for now.

Forty-two

The sun was out again the next morning. It was wonderfully cool, though, with strong breezes blowing in from the Atlantic. Some of those strong breezes took Chase out first thing—a few of the tents had blown over and a few more of the awnings and canopies had followed.

It always seemed like a waste of Chase's time and energy to help take care of such small things. But when anything went wrong, they called him. Sometimes it was only to delegate the task of cleanup to the right person. Being the bailiff in the Village meant doing a little bit of everything.

I went to trade my slightly damp gown for a new, hopefully dry one. Portia didn't even yell at me—I was amazed. She handed me a pale green gown and moved on to find costumes for the three fairies behind me in line.

"I hear Portia is going to marry the hatmaker," the slightly disheveled purple fairy said. Her wings must've been caught out in the rain last night. They were drooping badly.

"No wonder she's so happy!" her pal, the pink fairy said. "I love weddings! Portia and the hatmaker were made for each other."

"Which one is the hatmaker?" the blue fairy asked. "I don't think I know him."

All three fairies did a three-hundred-sixty-degree turn, didn't see the Hat House, and started giggling. It was time for me to walk away. Fairies! They never get things right.

After changing clothes at the Dungeon, I ran to see Andre, waving to the Three Little Pigs and Crystal the Pirate Queen. I slowed down to talk to her.

"How are you this morning?" I asked. Crystal and I were never very close. I have nothing against her—it's just one of those things.

"I'm fine. On my way home finally." She didn't sound very fine.

"I'm sure the pirates will be glad to have you back."

She stared at me with her beautiful violet blue eyes. Her face was tan from long hours in the sun, and her long white hair was blowing slightly in the breeze. "No, Jessie. I'm going to my *real* home in Surfside, up the coast. My husband and I are going to give it another try. Maybe we can make it work out if I get out of this crazy place."

"Oh." I didn't know what else to say.

"You know I don't mean it, right?" She looked beyond me at the castle rising above Mirror Lake and the *Queen's Revenge* sailing across with full white sails. She sighed. "I've lived here for so long. I love this place. It's crazy but it's wonderful. I wish I could convince my husband of that, but he doesn't feel the same."

"I'm sorry. I know it must be hard to go. The only way I can stand it at the end of the summer is because I know I'm coming back. I can't imagine leaving for good."

She put her hand on my arm and smiled. "I hope you never have to. You and Chase both love it here. Maybe you can always be here."

"Maybe."

She pulled a necklace over her long hair and handed it to me. "Take this for good luck. Maybe you should take over as the new pirate queen. You were a good pirate, Jessie. After what I saw last night, you wouldn't have any trouble keeping the scallywags in line."

"Did you hear anything from Stewart last night?"

"No. And please, don't say that name again around me. I don't know what was wrong with me, hanging out there with them. You'd think I'd never seen a knight in chain mail or something!"

"Sorry. Maybe it's for the best."

"No doubt. I think you roasted him good, Jessie. Well done! He deserved what he got. I'm sure he ran home to his daddy."

The necklace she handed me was on a silver chain. There was an engraved image of the *Queen's Revenge* on the quartz. I started to give it back. "You should keep this to remember the Village."

"I have to think about the baby and my marriage now. I can't think about the Village without wanting to be here. Take care."

It was really sad watching her walk away. I hoped she could find what she was looking for and that she could sort things out with her family.

But I hoped I wasn't looking at a reflection of myself in years to come. Right now, Chase wanted to be here. What if he decided to move back to Arizona to be with his family? What if we broke up and couldn't be together here anymore?

I stood in the middle of the cobblestones and watched the Green Man practice on his stilts while two knights sparred on the Village Green—sans horses of course. The mermaids were getting into their lagoon, and the goose girl was leading her flock around the Village. Who wouldn't want to be here?

Before I could become completely depressed, I ran on to the Hat House to find Andre packing his bags. "Where are you going? Are you and Beth combining your shops?"

"No, I'm afraid not. Beth turned me down." He drew a deep breath and wiped a tear from one eye. "I don't blame her. I have nothing to recommend me to her. I made a fool of myself with Eloise. What would someone like Beth want with me?"

"So, where are you going?"

"A friend of mine is making a movie in Wilmington. It has a lot of turn-of-the-century costumes, and he needs a hatmaker. I'm leaving to go there tomorrow. Who knows after that? But I won't be coming back here."

I watched him look around the shop as he said it. He was like Crystal—not wanting to leave but feeling compelled to do so. What was wrong with everybody today? Were they all intent on destroying any chance of happiness I had?

Andre had already dismissed his assistants. He planned to finish the projects he'd taken on when he got to Wilmington. It was depressing, but I helped him pack. Funny how I didn't even know who he was until this summer. Now the Village would feel empty without him.

We talked about different things—old movies, hats, life in the Village. He was planning to leave most of his hat-making paraphernalia behind for the next hatmaker. I wasn't sure there would ever be another one, but I didn't say so. I could see he was as sad as Crystal. I didn't need to add anything to that.

At lunch, he went to the castle to say his farewells to Queen Olivia and King Harold. While he ate with them, I went to meet Chase at Peter's Pub. It would be nice to see a smiling face after the morning I'd had.

But it wasn't to be. Chase had been called to duty when two teenagers tried to sneak into the Village through one of the chinks in the wall that surrounded it. Too bad for them that they came out right where Roger Trent was standing, talking to Bawdy Betty. There was no mercy even for youthful offenders, according to him. Chase had to have security throw them out. Once that happened, they were never allowed in again under the threat of going to jail.

I wandered around the Village eating a pretzel for lunch. The perfect weather had brought out a large crowd of visitors who wandered with me, looking for souvenirs, buying scarves, gloves, and headwear they couldn't get in the modern stores. Half of them walked around in something approximating Renaissance wear, munching turkey legs with mustard.

I saw Belle and Marco sitting together on the Green, a blanket and picnic lunch spread out around them. They were picture perfect—he in his Chocolatier cape, hat, and boots (and the rest of the outfit, too) and she in her lovely white gown with the dainty, chipped straw hat on her head.

When I saw them together, I knew. Just by looking at them (as Maid Marion had said about Chase and me), I could see they were in love. The quiet, youngest of the two families, who were ignored, cast into lesser roles by their overwhelming siblings. No one even thought about them.

"Hi. Mind if I sit down?" I invited myself to their intimate picnic.

"Of course not," Belle said. "We have enough food for ten. Please, eat with us. Where's Chase?"

Nothing like someone being friendly and nice to make you feel guilty about questioning them for murder. "He's working. I'm just hanging out, waiting until lunch is over to go back to work."

"You're working with Andre at the Hat House, right?" Marco asked, handing me a glass of lemonade.

"Yep. There's a lot more to making hats than anyone would ever guess."

"Sounds interesting," Belle said, handing me a little pastry filled with vegetables and gravy, kind of like a pot-pie you hold in your hand.

"It is. Thanks. Did you know there is a special, individual hat pin for everyone in the Village? At least everyone Andre has ever made a hat for. No two are quite the same."

The way Belle looked at Marco—the way he looked back at her. It made me want to cry.

"I suppose Andre knows every hat pin." Marco said in a flat, dull voice.

"No. He's been doing this a long time." I took a sip of lemonade. "He has copies of all of them. What he can't identify, he can look up in his collection."

Forty-three

I was so sorry I'd even asked to see a photo of the hat pin. Cesar wasn't really a friend of mine. Why do I get so obsessive about figuring these things out? The police were happy with what they'd found. Belle and Marco could have gone on to live happily ever after.

Marco held Belle's hand as he told me what happened. "Cesar couldn't stand that Bernardo and I wanted to have lives of our own. It was okay for him, just not for us. As soon as he knew Bernardo was seeing Eloise, he went out of his way to make her fall for him. He didn't want her—he just wanted us to know we couldn't do anything without him."

I didn't know what to say. I didn't expect this sadness and Marco wanting to make sense of his brother's murder.

"He found out about me and Belle. He told me he was going after her next." Marco looked up at me with his big, sad brown eyes. "I knew he wouldn't stop until he'd ruined us, like he did Bernardo and Eloise."

"I wouldn't have gone with him," Belle defended herself. "You shouldn't have worried about me."

He kissed her hand and smiled so sweetly. "You're my life. I couldn't bear the thought of losing you. You just didn't know Cesar. He would've found a way."

"So you decided to get rid of him?" I asked.

"It wasn't like that. I knew he'd be at the shop making chocolate like always. I went there to reason with him, but he laughed at me. He said I was a stupid little boy—that Belle would be better off without me. I didn't think about what I was doing. It was like one minute he was standing there laughing and the next I'd hit him in the head and he was in the chocolate."

Well, at least it wasn't premeditated, I thought. Bernardo could testify to that because Marco didn't think to get the chocolate recipe before he killed his brother. Maybe that would help.

"But why try to blame Andre?" I wondered.

"I'm afraid that was my idea." Belle sniffled a little and clutched Marco's hand. "I knew how angry Marco was. I followed him to the chocolate shop. But it all happened so fast. When I found him standing over his brother's body, I just wanted to protect him. I thought about Cesar and Andre fighting over Eloise. I guess I thought if I stuck my hat pin—somewhere—everyone would think Andre did it. I panicked. The hat pin stuck in his eye. It was an accident. I put the hat over him to add more suspicion to Andre."

The real-life account of it made me shiver even though it was a good plan—it almost worked. Not with Andre but with Swayne. "How did you know about Andre's wife dying that way?"

Belle shrugged. "Everybody knows."

I'd thought much the same myself. It didn't really surprise me that most of the Village was aware of what happened in Hollywood. We all enjoyed the Internet after closing time.

"What will happen now?" Marco asked.

"I don't know. I'm not the police," I explained. "I'm not even Chase. I don't know what to tell you. I guess it's totally up to you guys what happens. You'll have to make that decision."

Belle's pretty blue eyes lit up. "You mean you aren't going to tell anyone?"

"I think I've done enough already." I got to my feet. "I'm sorry this happened. Thanks for the pastry and the lemonade."

"Jessie!" Marco stood up, too, and came close to me. "Thank you for telling us. I want to do what's right. As soon as I heard that the other man was going to be blamed for Cesar's death, I knew I had to say something."

"Why?" Belle jumped up and grabbed his arm. "She said she won't say anything. That other man killed at least two other people. What difference does it make if he takes the blame for Cesar's death, too?"

"It makes a difference to me," Marco told her. "Don't worry, Belle. I won't mention you having any part in it. You just keep quiet and let me take care of it."

They kissed—one of those terrible, angsty kisses. The kind that are either saying good-bye or begging for someone to be different. It was awful—especially knowing it was partially my fault. I just wanted to sit down and cry for them.

Instead, I left them alone to sort things out. I really didn't care if Marco turned himself in or not. He wasn't a threat to anyone like Swayne was. He'd just been browbeaten too long by his brother. He couldn't take it anymore and something snapped. It could happen to anyone.

I wanted to go back to the Hat House, but I couldn't face Andre's depression yet. I wanted to find Chase and bury my face in his shoulder, but I couldn't tell him what was wrong. If Marco and Belle decided not to give themselves up, I would have to live with their secret forever. And it wasn't going to be easy.

Forty-four

It was nearly closing time and there was still no word from Marco and Belle. I'd expected to hear about a press conference or something by now. Maybe they'd decided not to turn themselves in. Just because they felt bad about Cesar's death didn't mean they wanted to go to jail. I'd left it up to them. Even if they didn't tell the police what they'd done, I wasn't telling either. I hoped I felt the same way tomorrow—or the next time I saw Chase.

I'd spent most of the day getting all of Andre's gear together. We cleaned up the shop, stacked up the material. I marveled at all the old-time movie posters that had been hidden by hat-making supplies. They looked like originals from 1930s movies like *The Wizard of Oz* and *Gone with the Wind*. We took them down carefully and rolled them up. Andre told me stories about his father and grandfather working on some of the most famous movies in the world.

I put the posters in cardboard tubes for transport, then went to find Andre to ask where he wanted them. He was looking at the scrapbook that he kept after his wife had died. I watched him touch a few photos of Kathleen, lost in his memories. He finally closed the book and put it away to take with him to Wilmington. I asked him about the posters—pretending I hadn't seen him looking through the scrapbook.

By six P.M., the shop was cleaned out, hat frames neatly in place. The shop looked sad and empty. It was strange to see it so organized—Andre was careful with everything else but not when he worked.

It was time to go. I hugged him and said I'd miss him. I dreaded trying to find something else to do the rest of the summer. He hugged me back, then carefully straightened his red tunic.

The door to the shop burst open as we were about to walk out together. There stood Beth—wild eyed and smelling of too many cigarettes.

"What are you doing, Andre?" Her voice was husky and breathless.

"I'm leaving," he answered, chin held high. "I have an opportunity and—"

"You can't leave me now! You said you loved me. You said you want to marry me."

"Well, I did—I do! But I didn't hear from you and I naturally assumed—"

"And you're leaving?"

I echoed Beth's surprised sentiments. I mean, we'd spent the whole day cleaning and packing—me feeling sorry for him because he said *she* rejected him. Now I find out she was just making him wait, no doubt for his past transgressions with Eloise. Served him right, too.

"I think I should go." I tried to slip out the door and leave them alone.

"No!" Andre stopped me. "I need a witness to these proceedings and you're the only person here."

"A witness to what proceedings?" Beth asked, big, fat tears rolling down her face.

Andre took out a beautiful ring (probably meant originally for Eloise, but I wouldn't say so). He got down on one knee, straightened his clothes, and offered it up to her. "Elizabeth Daniels, my lovely lady, will you have me for your husband?"

Beth hugged him to her. "Yes, when you put it that way. I certainly will!"

They kissed, and I realized I was crying, too. Suddenly the sunshine was bright again and the world was a better place.

"We'll have a big, Renaissance wedding, the likes of which no one has seen for these many years," Andre said, smiling through his tears. "There will be unbelievable hats."

"And unforgettable costumes!" Beth added.

They started kissing again and I finally managed to sneak out the door. Maybe Harriet's Hat House wouldn't be closing down after all.

Forty-five

I was actually whistling under my breath after I left the Hat House and the happy couple. I needed to see Chase, cry all over him while I told him about Andre and Beth, then have him hold me close for as long as possible.

I started thinking that not everything had to end like Crystal's experience. There was Roger Trent and Mary Shift, who'd stayed on together in the Village. There was Daisy Reynolds and Bart Van Impe, another couple in love who stayed here. Now there was Andre and Beth. If they could do it, Chase and I could do it, too.

I was so caught up in thinking about those couples—and what I would wear to the wedding—I didn't even notice Bernardo bearing down on me until I almost walked into him.

"What gave you the right to judge?" he screamed at me. "Why didn't you leave well enough alone?"

I wasn't sure what he was talking about at first. Then I understood. "Did they turn themselves in to the police?"

"Yes!" He snatched his showy hat from his head (I thought about his recent hair plugs) and glared at me. "I was trying to protect them. If anyone should have killed Cesar, it was me. Marco shouldn't have had to defend Belle from him."

"Maybe that's true," I agreed. "But they did it—they killed Cesar. They had a choice to make about another man spending time in jail for their crime. I would think you'd be proud of them."

"Proud? I'm infuriated. And I blame *you*. You should've left things as they were. Who cares if that other man didn't kill Cesar? He killed two other people. Marco isn't a murderer. He doesn't deserve to be locked away."

"This isn't the way to help your brother." Chase's voice came from behind me before I felt him standing close. "Get him a good lawyer, Bernardo. Make sure he understands what happened that caused this."

"You don't understand." Bernardo dropped to his knees on the cobblestones. "It should've been me. I should've done it. I was too much of a coward and now Marco might be put in jail for the rest of his life."

Eloise came running across the cobblestones and put her arms around Bernardo. "You can't keep blaming yourself—or Jessie. Marco and Belle were right to tell the truth. We have to take care of them now. Come home with me. Let's decide what we should do next."

I was surprised at the depth of emotion in Eloise's voice. Who knew she felt anything that deeply?

Eloise helped Bernardo to his feet and dusted off his fine hat. "Excuse us, Bailiff, Lady Jessie. Thank you for your help. We must take our leave now."

The pair walked off together toward the other side of the Village. Chase put his arms around me, and we watched them go. We stood that way for a long time until one of the goat girls giggled at us and urged the goat pulling her cart to go around us.

"Are you okay?" Chase asked me.

"I think so." I smiled up at him. "I know so. You won't believe what happened today."

"If it's better drama than a murder, two suspects turning themselves in, and you pranking one of the Knights Templar, I don't want to know."

But he smiled when he said it, and I knew it would be all right. And Bernardo and Eloise were another couple who would be here together. An impressive group that would continue to inspire me.

"Never mind." I took his hand. "Let's go home."

Ye Village Crier

Hear ye! Hear ye! Is there anything better than a day at the Renaissance Faire? The food, the fun, the jousts! Spending a day at Renaissance Faire Village is like stepping back in time to mingle with the lords, ladies, fools, and knaves who inhabit the Village. The marketplace is full of wonderful things from around the world that you might never see again. Shopping is a must!

And as you've just read, hat making is alive and well!

No one knows when the first hat was made—it probably happened when the first cave lady put a piece of saber tooth tiger skin on her head to keep out the rain. Instant fashion!

In the Middle Ages, the church decided that all women should cover their heads at services. Hats became fashionable and expensive as ladies and gentlemen showed off their millinery style.

Felt, straw, and silk were twisted and shaped into works of art. Hennins—the pointed hats with or without scarves—were popular. Women wore muffin caps to cover their hair when they didn't have time to dress their locks properly. Hats said things about the wearer without the wearer saying a word.

Renaissance Recipe

A trip to the Renaissance Faire wouldn't be complete without eating some good food outside as you walk around the shops and watch the events. There is a great deal of debate as to what constitutes Renaissance food. While it's true that funnel cakes probably didn't exist, their ingredients did, and it would be hard to say that no one ever made something like them.

Christopher Columbus changed the way people ate during the Renaissance. Corn, potatoes, tomatoes, chili peppers, and turkey came back with him. It took some time for many of these foods to become popular. Tomatoes had an uphill climb. People didn't trust them. Potatoes (actually from South America) were popular in many parts of Europe. Peasants and highborn folks ate them roasted, boiled, and fried. They put sweet syrup, broth, and herbs on them to give them flavor.

Potato soup was a favorite, and here's a recipe for how people ate it during the Renaissance:

> 5 small white potatoes, diced
> 1 small onion, diced
> 1½ quarts vegetable broth
> cream
> chives to garnish, chopped

Cook the potatoes and onions in the vegetable broth until they are soft. Add cream and chives. Eat with bread, bacon, or cheese.

WILL FEED FOUR